THE COUNTERFEIT
LADY

THE COUNTERFEIT LADY

Daisy Vivian

Walker and Company
New York

First published in the United States of America in 1987 by the Walker
Publishing Company, Inc.

Published simultaneously in Canada by John Wiley & Sons
Canada, Limited, Rexdale, Ontario

Library of Congress Cataloging-in-Publication Data

Vivian, Daisy.
  The counterfeit lady.

  I. Title.
PS3572.I86C68   1987   813'.54   86-23384
ISBN 0-8027-0938-9

Printed in the United States of America

10 9 8 7 6 5 4 3 2 1

for Roberta Faillace,
for a thousand reasons.

THE COUNTERFEIT
LADY

= 1 =

HUMMING LIGHTLY, THE young woman opened the huge armoire and removed a garment from among the many within it. The room in which Susanna Archer stood was one of three which had once been sleeping-chambers but now functioned as storage rooms for the immense personal wardrobe of her employer. The rooms were lined with cupboards, some with shelves, some to hang garments that, in their scope, were a summary of English fashion from the years of her ladyship's girlhood to the present, a very long while indeed. For the most part they were costumes for the evening, scarcely a day dress or a riding habit or a walking costume amongst them. They were all of the finest workmanship and quality—lace, silk, bombasine, painted and embroidered, even occasionally bespangled—but Susanna knew them all very well and paid them little heed today.

The costume chosen for this evening was one of Lady Wycombe's especial favourites, an exquisite black velvet. The companion knew well enough by now what accessories went with it: feathered headdress, black corded-silk slippers. Quite often her ladyship chose to wear her diamond ear-bobs as well and the diamond waterfall across her shrivelled bosom. Although in the daylight hours the old woman was scarcely ever out of deshabille, in the evening she chose to dine in splendour, whether in company or alone. Susanna and the little maid, Tibby, went through this process daily, arraying their mistress with not only splendid garments, but the remembered glory of her past.

When the toilette was completed, the superfluous articles were returned to the wardrobe rooms where they were refolded, hung up, and cleaned with such care that even the older dresses had all the brilliance of the new ones.

In sharp contrast to that of her ladyship and as befitted the garb of a country minister's daughter, Susanna's mode of dress was serviceable and subdued. Her hair, which when unbound in the privacy of her room was glorious, in the day was drawn back tightly across the ears and twisted into a bun at the back of her neck. She wore none of the white lead and gaudy colour with which her employer painted herself, but upon her nose perched a pair of octagonal spectacles. They were there, not because she needed them—her sight was clear and strong—but it was a fancy of Lady Wycombe that her companion should wear them. They were, in fact, of clear glass, but if her ladyship wished to see them, then seen they should be.

But now, from the sharp words drifting through the door, she could hear that the old woman was displeased. Tibby, her maid, was a good girl and well trained, but her ladyship required a great deal of attention paid to her hairdress, which was always an elaborate wig curled in the latest style. Tonight she was annoyed because Tibby, who had only seen the Cretan tuft in illustrations from the ladies' magazines, had not accomplished it to Lady Wycombe's satisfaction.

"Wretched creature! Why I keep you with me, I do not know. I am kindness itself, generous to a fault, and rarely scold or lose my temper. All I ask is a little loyalty in return. Does that make me such a *rara avis?* Eh? Well? Answer me, does it?"

Tibby's voice was thick with tears, for this tirade was a lengthy one. "I don't rightly know, madam."

"What? Don't know if loyalty is deserved, wench?"

"Oh, no, your ladyship! I don't know what 'rareyavis' may be."

Fortunately, this ignorance on the part of her servant put

2

the old woman into an excellent mood. "Rareyavis," she chuckled to herself, preening as she peered into the looking-glass, pulled at a wirey curl, tucked in a stray lock, teased the hair upward with the back of a finger, then, finally, sighed with exasperation.

"Well, I suppose it must do. Take it away for the present!"

Carefully, Tibby lifted the wig from the nearly hairless head and placed it upon the stand. She left behind the appearance of a lavishly decorated skull, the mouth and cheeks garishly painted, the eyesockets outlined with kohl.

"Archer, where are you? Have you not found the velvet yet? What are you doing in there, for pity's sake?"

"Admiring your gowns, my lady," said the companion as she came out of the wardrobe room. She had, of course, been doing no such thing, but she knew how it pleased the old woman to hear it said. "I nearly faint with envy when I am among them."

Lady Wycombe nodded smugly. It was her belief that her collection of gowns was famous, though they were rarely seen by anyone but the servants since she dined every evening in solitary splendour, sitting in great state in her chair at the head of the long table which was always set for a large company. It was never clear to Susanna how much the woman was aware of her own eccentricities. Poor old thing, she undoubtedly deserved whatever foibles she chose to indulge. Let her dress like a queen if she liked, with her diamond ear-bobs and her handsome rings crowding her grimy fingers so that she quite glittered in the light of the huge candelabras which always graced the empty table at dinnertime. Her figure was as slender as Susanna's own, but crabbed and bent, whereas that of her companion was straight-backed and strong. Lady Wycombe was not a cruel woman, merely old, and thoughtlessly unkind when her image of herself was endangered. On good days she was often indulgent.

But this was not to be one of the good days. Tibby

moved carelessly and a flacon of scent teetered upon the edge of the dressing-table, eluded the maid's efforts to recapture it, toppled, and smashed upon the floor, a nauseating odor of patchouli filling the room. A little of the liquid splashed against the hem of the gown Susanna was holding in her hands. It was not much more than a drop or two, but the old mistress noticed it and struck out quickly at Tibby.

"Oh, you stupid, clumsy creature, look what you have done! I shall never be able to wear the dress to dinner now!" Tibby began to cry and her ladyship pushed her roughly away. "Out! Get out of my sight! Archer will finish me . . . I suppose you are able?" she asked her companion sarcastically.

"Yes, madam, of course I am. I am sure Tibby meant no harm."

"Your excuses for her are not wanted. The wretch is forever annoying me! I don't fathom why I put up with her!"

Susanna knew the answer to that, for she had seen a succession of lady's maids come and go from Wycombe Hall. None would put up with the combination of petty tyranny and the isolation of a situation so far out in the country that even on one's days off there was nowhere to go. She herself did not mind the seclusion, having been a country girl all of her life. Reverend Wesley Archer, the Vicar of Bleet, had never quite found his niche, having been in turn a Nonconformist, a Methodist, a Wesleyan and, at last, having taken Anglican orders. The posts had always been insignificant and the livings small, but Susanna had revelled in the country life. She had learned to ride at an early age and bounced about the neighbourhood on the broad old back of Cleopatra until the two became beloved and familiar figures in whatever parish her father pastored. Later, as she grew older, she had helped her father in his duties. Catering to the needs of the ancient parishoners had proved excellent training for the post she held now. Patience was a timely virtue.

It was a matter of great deliberation to choose another

gown. Lady Wycombe had set her mind on the velvet and nothing else was quite right, but she settled at last on a light, summery silk of elegant cut and plunging décolletage. Luckily the wig that had been already prepared would do for this costume, and at last she tottered happily down the stairs to the great dining hall where she would dine in state amongst the furnishings gone victim to rats and mildew. Despite all, Lady Wycombe invariably dined well, for she would not tolerate food of poor quality or badly prepared. She did not mind that the grocer's bills were reflective of waste and overcharging so long as her taste buds were gratified. Rich sauces and desserts were her particular love and she gorged upon them, though they never seemed to add a pound to her scrawny frame.

Left alone, Susanna went to find Tibby and found her huddled on the back stairs, crying as if her heart would break. In the months since Susanna had held her position in the house, she and Tibby had become great friends; it had been at the companion's suggestion that the girl had been elevated to the post of lady's maid, but the child lived in terror of being thrown off.

"I never seem to do anything right, miss. I never know what she wants from me," she sobbed to Susanna. "She tells me this and then tells me that, as if I was supposed to know what's in her mind afore she says it. She quite rattles me, Miss Susanna, really she does."

"There, there," Susanna soothed her. "We shall see what can be done."

And, surprisingly, with a few well placed words she did persuade her ladyship to more indulgence with the girl. From that time forth Tibby was her devoted slave, but there were problems with the other servants as well. Tib had been promoted from housemaid and no one had been hired to replace her in that capacity. Whenever she could, the housekeeper commandeered her for extra tasks. Susanna received permission from Lady Wycombe to speak to the woman on Tibby's behalf.

"It is the amount of work that isn't being done, you see,

Miss Archer," she was informed. "When I had Tibby to help it was bad enough, but since the mistress has taken her away the work never seems to be finished." Susanna, who had a good idea how much time housekeeper spent gossiping with cook in the kitchen, held her tongue to see what else would be said.

"I know I am sometimes sharp with the girl, and I will try to mend my ways with her, but it *is* hard, Miss Archer, very hard. I don't know how much longer I can put up with the amount of work I am expected to do." But since Susanna also suspected that housekeeper and cook were putting away substantial sums by the juggling of household accounts, she did not feel that the implied threat was a serious one.

The next step required permission from Lady Wycombe as well, but Susanna thought there would be no objection raised so long as her scheme did not interfere with Tibby's duties.

"What? You want to give the gel ideas above her station by teaching her to read? I say keep her at her duties. Lord knows I have to correct her a dozen times a day. She is very slow, you know, even when I take the time to explain what it is I want. The only thing she is clever with is the needle and I will forgive her some other fault because of it, but to read? Preposterous! However, I know you will never let me alone until I give in to you. You see, I know you, Archer, I know you! Teach her if you like, but on your own time, mind. I do not pay for charitable work!" But still she managed to give the two ample opportunity for lessons.

Tibby, for her part, was pathetically eager to learn, and when Susanna saw how grateful the girl was for the attention she gave more and more of her time over to it. The parson's daughter had never moved in very exalted society, but she had read a great deal and learned to keep her eyes open. What she had learned she passed on to Tibby. The girl particularly liked the lessons in dressing Susanna's hair, which she loved to do in elaborate fashion.

"Oh, miss, it is so fine and beautiful, I quite love handling it. I don't see why you always wear it in that terrible style you do."

"Her ladyship's instructions, Tib. It hardly matters, you know. There is no one to see it in any case."

The maid continued the brushing she had begun. "I expect she is envious. It must be terrible to have to wear one of them wigs all the time. And when I think how *you* might look in some of them gowns of hers, it quite makes me furious. It idd'n fair, if you ask me. Why, what if someone *did* come here—some nice gentleman with a bit of money. He might take a real fancy to you if he saw you dressed proper, but the way you get yourself up he'd never look twice."

"It makes no difference, my dear little friend, no Prince Charming is going to find his way to Wycombe Hall."

She could not guess how quickly she would be proven wrong.

A little more than a fortnight later Lady Wycombe summoned Susanna to the parlour in mid-afternoon. "You must take a larger responsibility in the house, Archer. I cannot look after everything."

"I will if you so choose, madam, but to what does your ladyship refer?"

The old lady waved her hand, gesturing broadly. "Why, the house. We have guests coming and the place is a shambles! A complete shambles!"

"Guests, your ladyship? This is the first I have heard of it."

"Well, that is as it may be. Luckily the gentlemen will be here only in the evening and a good meal with decent wine will do much. I daresay the shadows will hide a great deal."

"Perhaps, madam. May I inquire what gentlemen are expected?"

"My nevvy for one, Patrick Wycombe, my heir. The other is his dote, his bosom friend since school, only a younger son but nice enough for all that. Clever as a monkey, but a rake if ever there was one, so mind you keep yourself out of his way! Leave him to me, if you please!" And she cackled wildly at her own bawdry. "I shall want to look particularly splendid on this occasion, so see to it that I am dressed well." She seemed to be dwelling on the image of young Patrick's friend, for she tittered again. "I expect I could still teach a young blade a new step or two, eh? Eh?"

Susanna had only once before seen Patrick Wycombe, and that was on the day when he engaged her to act as his aunt's companion. She had been so nervous that day that she now retained very little recollection of him, save as a tall gentleman with an air of extreme seriousness. He had worn a grey worsted coat and a preoccupied expression, she remembered, and had not risen when she was shown into his office in the city. That, in itself, was nothing. He was hiring a servant, after all, not placing himself in a social exchange. But to think of such a man as having as a bosom companion a man who could be described as a rake—even by an eccentric old woman in the country—was most astonishing. The evening, no matter how dull, would at least provide a break in the monotony of their lives. She found herself looking forward to it with almost the eagerness of her mistress.

Pressed to do so, the housekeeper did well by the drawing room. The best pieces were taken from other rooms to refurbish it and the shabbier articles banished to limbo. The brass had been polished so that the firelight glittered upon it, the curtains drawn to induce an atmosphere of intimacy, and, sitting in the shadows, taking no part in the conversation, Susanna was able to consider the two guests with far more candour than she might otherwise have been able. It is scarcely *comme il faut* to stare at a guest rudely when one may be observed, but from the safety of the darkness it is quite another thing.

The pair could hardly have been more of a contrast. Gavin Marshall looked nothing like a rake, for he was quietly and respectably dressed, nearly six feet in height with a square, wide-jawed face and correspondingly wide-set eyes of a dark shade that she could not determine in the candlelight. Patrick Wycombe, on the other hand, was nothing like her recollection, for he was quite startlingly handsome. Taller than his friend and with a sunburst of genuinely golden hair, he had eyes that, even in candle-light, revealed themselves to be a piercing blue. There was a certain atmosphere about him, a splendid sort of gal-lantry, offhand but pleasant and kind. She figured him as well-off but fearfully extravagant, and in her fancy he moved in a world of good-looking, fashionable people and expansive gestures, of charming ways with women.

But it was Marshall who proved most charming to his hostess. He never allowed by word or gesture that he found her in the least bizarre or outré. He listened with interest to her stories of her own past triumphs and then, seeing that she took delight in mild bawdry, recounted similar in-stances—though acknowledging them in no way compara-ble to hers. It was as good as being at a play to see the two of them together, and she felt that she and Mr. Wycombe were merely spectators at a comedy by one of the masters of a past generation—Sheridan or Harley, even harking back to Congreve and Wycherly—in their amusing artifice. By the time the hour of parting had come round—though her ladyship would have sat till morning for the conversa-tion—it was past midnight, and the gentlemen were leaving their inn early upon a journey to the West Country.

Handsome Mr. Wycombe rose from his chair. "Come, Gavin, we must aim for a dawn start if we are to reach Pargate by noon," he warned, standing and stretching. He kissed his aunt upon her rouged and withered cheek and bade good-bye to Susanna with that same blind look one reserves for the invisible in our acquaintance. She had fancied him making a special effort of farewell but saw him go with no special regret, for she was a sensible young woman who realised that there was no reason in the world why a dashing beau should find anything of interest in a drab paid companion.

Even after the man had gone, Lady Wycombe was in a highly excited state. It was evident that she was overtired, but also that the evening had been so pleasurable that she wanted it to go on and on, endeavouring to prolong it by a recital of its incidents.

"And did you hear him tell the story of Lady Eliot and the wedding cake? Most amusing, was it not?"

Susanna, who had heard every word of the tale, agreed, but her ladyship had not done. Instead she began to repeat other of the stories, retelling them as if Susanna had not been in the room.

"And those fascinating revelations about the Prince Regent! Who would believe that he was so little of a gentleman! I quite blushed, you know. It was scarcely a story for ladies!" By which Susanna knew that she had enjoyed it thoroughly.

"Would your ladyship not like Tibby to help you prepare for bed?"

"Bed? It is scarcely past midnight! No, I am too stimulated for bed. When I was a girl I used often to see the dawning. I love that hour of the day, dawn. It is quite the most peaceful time to go to sleep!"

But Susanna persisted in her urging. "You will be more comfortable, madam, if you slip out of your gown and allow Tibby to remove your wig."

The old woman sighed petulantly. "Oh, very well. Let her take me apart. But not at the dressing-table. I need no mirrors before me tonight. Tonight I abominate all looking-glasses. They lie, you know! They show you things that are not really there!

Tibby and Susanna exchanged a superstitious glance. Milady was behaving even more strangely than usual, and even after Tib had removed the rouge and lead, the face remained flushed. Still, Susanna had not, in all the time of her employ, seen her mistress in a happier state.

But gradually the old lady became more docile. "Archer, I want you to sing to me. I have heard you as you went about your duties and you have a pretty voice."

"I did not realise your ladyship had ever noticed."

"Oh, I don't miss much, no matter what some folk think."

"Very well, madam, if you will climb up into bed, I will sing you to sleep."

That was not what Lady Wycombe had in mind. "No, no, not a lullaby! I am not ready for sleep. I want to tap my toes to something lively. I want you to go down to the music room and play upon the spinet in accompaniment. If you leave the doors open I shall hear you well enough. Mind you sing something lively! Sing me 'The Soldier and the Jolly Tar.' "

With an indulgent look, for, after all, she did hold the old woman in considerable affection, Susanna made her way down the stairs and into the music room where she sang as many lively tunes as she could remember: "A Soldier Boy in Buff and Blue," "The Handy Randy Dandy O," and other things that her clergyman father might have been surprised to find she knew. From time to time she interspered them with a sentimental ballad.

She fully expected that when she had sung several of the songs, Tibby would come creeping in to say that her ladyship had gone off to sleep, but after half an hour she began to wonder if the lively old creature meant ever to drift off to dreams. She began a sad melody called "The Curly-Headed Boy," and had almost reached the end when Tibby at last appeared in the door. Her eyes were red and there was evidence of tears upon her cheeks.

"Oh, miss!" she whispered, "Oh, miss, I thought she were only dozing! We was sitting listening to your pretty music and she closed her eyes, you know, as one will. Then she opened them again and smiled at me. Can you imagine, after all the times she has snapped?" Tibby sounded almost indignant at such a change of character. "Then she patted my hand and closed her eyes again, miss, and then I heard the rattle. That terrible sound, that rattle!" She began to cry again.

"Do you mean to say that she has died, Tibby?"

"Yes, miss, that is what I mean to say. Lady Wycombe has died at last. I somehow never thought she would, you know?" Her voice broke. "I allus thought she was going to go on forever."

Susanna drew the sobbing girl's head to her breast. "Perhaps she thought so, too, Tibby. In fact, I imagine that she did."

═ 2 ═

By ALL THE evidence of the neglected house, the skeleton staff of servants, and the wages paid them, Susanna had always assumed that the major part of Lady Wycombe's fortune had been squandered upon her wardrobe, but at the reading of the will she discovered that such was not the case. The proceedings took place in the office of Bainbridge and Son, the solicitors who had handled all the Wycombe Hall affairs. Old Mr. Bainbridge himself took the chair, as befitted the last instructions of a valued client. But if Susanna had hoped to also see Mr. Patrick Wycombe she was disappointed, since his own lawyers would be dealing with the portion left to him.

This section of the will was short and to the point. To cook and housekeeper were each left small bequests, ". . . for in view of the profit they have already made in my employ, it would be folly to give them more." There was rather a larger one to Tibby for the furthering of her education. ("Under the watchful eye of Miss Susanna Archer," the solicitor read.) And "an annuity to the aforesaid Miss Archer, companion and friend to an old woman."

The lawyer leaned forward across the desk as, with a twinkle, he asked, "Can you guess, Miss Archer, how much the annuity amounts to in round figgers?"

Since housekeeper and cook had marched out in disgruntled annoyance, there was no one to overhear but Tibby, and Susanna felt she could answer freely. Judging from the amounts left the others, she calculated quickly and suggested, "I would suspect, sir, about fifteen pounds a year? Or am I aiming too high?"

The good-natured gentleman seemed quite delighted to have caught her out. "Rather say, too low, Miss Archer. You must have been very dear to her ladyship, for she has left you an annunity of no less than fifty-two pounds per annum."

Both of the young woman gasped. "Are you quite sure, sir?" asked Susanna in disbelief. "Fifty-two pounds? Why, that is enough to keep a family."

"Quite sure, miss, and that is not all."

"There is more, sir?"

He nodded benignly. "Substantially more, if you handle it rightly. Her ladyship has, as well, left you her personal belongings to do with as you please. Everything but her jewellery, of course. Although . . ." He opened his desk and fished about in one of the compartments, taking out a small package. "Mr. Patrick Wycombe wished you to have these in memory of his aunt."

Susanna opened the box, and there upon the faded blue velvet lay the diamond ear-bobs Lady Wycombe had so often worn. They were dulled and cloudy from lack of cleaning, but precious nevertheless.

"But the gowns?" asked Tibby. "All them gowns is yours, miss?"

Susanna looked quickly at the solicitor. He nodded. "Yes, all of them." His eyes travelled approvingly over her sedate costume and the octagonal spectacles, which today she wore more out of respect than for any other reason. It had somehow seemed proper that she should attend the reading of Lady Wycombe's will dressed as her ladyship had been accustomed to seeing her in life.

"I expect," Mr. Bainbridge suggested, "that there will be very little of the clothing that you could put to personal use, but, knowing the cost of materials, I daresay you can get a good price for them. I can arrange for a tally-woman to call at Wycombe Hall to look them over, if you like."

"Thank you, but I have no idea how much longer I shall be there."

"Ah, that is the other thing I was instructed to mention. Mr. Patrick Wycombe will take it as a great favor if you can see your way clear to remaining in charge of the house until arrangements for its disposition can be made. Your present salary will continue until that time, of course. Would that be convenient to you?"

Susanna looked doubtful. "I certainly do not expect that cook and housekeeper would remain," she said, recalling the meanness of the bequests made to them.

"You will be authorised to carry on in a normal manner, which would certainly include employing any help you may need. I believe Mr. Wycombe plans to visit the house again sometime in the near future to decide what is to be done."

"Then, of course, I will stay. I should like to retain Tibby, if you please, but no one else of the present staff."

"Tibby? Ah, of course, Miss Weston."

"Miss Weston" was pathetically grateful. Her little face quite lit up. "Oh, I do thank you, miss."

"You will be in charge of the household accounts and so on, Miss Archer—at least for the time being," the solicitor concluded. "You may draw upon them at any time."

When the two young women dazedly descended the stairs from Mr. Bainbridge's office, they paused for a moment, searching for a hackney, and Tibby once more expressed her gratitude. "I don't know what I would have done, miss, on such short notice."

"It will give us both opportunity to find new positions," Susanna said. "With a bit of leisure, I daresay we can find exactly what we want."

Tibby looked at her in amazement. "You don't mean to say that you are going to hire yourself out again, do you?"

That stopped Susanna, for she had, indeed, been thinking along those lines without ever considering that she need no longer pander to the whims of someone else, but, on the annuity left by her employer, could find some small village and live there quite comfortably if she chose. "Well, it remains to be seen," she conceded. "It will take a bit of thought, I expect."

"I shall be sorry to be leaving you, miss," Tibby said, "and that's a fact." She eyed her benefactress's face oddly for a moment, began to make a small, indistinct gesture, then pulled back.

"What is it?" Susanna laughed. "Is my hair out of order?"

"No, not that, miss."

"Then what?"

"If you will excuse me, Miss Archer," and the lady's maid reached boldly up and removed the spectacles from the bridge of Susanna's nose. "I allus hated these on you," she remarked and dropped them in the gutter. "I doubt you'll be needing them again."

But Susanna quickly retrieved them before the arriving hackney could smash them beneath its wheels. One never knew when such things would come in handy.

It proved easy enough to hire local day-help to clean out the house, discard and carry away what was no longer useable, and replace the rest for disposal through Mr. Wycombe's wishes. After an early supper the young women were usually left alone in the house, but they had no fear of being there; it was only that there was little entertainment. Tibby's lessons continued, but even that was not enough to while away the evenings. On one such occasion they decided that they would begin to sort through Lady Wycombe's wardrobe, classifying the gowns and attempting to make an estimate of their value so that Susanna would not be cheated when the promised tally-woman visited. It was only a step or two beyond that for them to arrive at trying on the gowns in front of the tall pier-glass. Tibby, tiny as she was, looked like a child playing at dress-up in her mother's closet, but on Susanna the effect was quite different. One such incident revealed something further about Tibby as well.

The gown was an almost perfect fit, needing only to be taken up slightly at the hem. "Oh, I could fix that quick enough, miss," asserted Tib. "Me mam taught me."

"I had no idea! Why did you never mention it before?"

"No one ever asked," replied the girl with unassailable logic. Then a clever look came into her face, followed by a more calculating one—which was all the stranger because it was so alien to her nature.

"What if . . ."

"Yes, Tibby?" Susanna prompted, her curiosity aroused.

"Well, it is only a thought, you see, but what if I was to alter all of them?"

"I don't understand, Tib. To what end? It would be a great deal of trouble."

"Not so much trouble, I think," answered Tibby rather excitedly. "I'd be ever so careful. It is just such a pity to think of all these lovely things being sold off for a song to some rag-woman. That is really all you would get, you know. She'd pay you a little and resell them to someone else for a fortune!"

"But what would I do with them? Where could *I* possibly wear them?" Susanna asked. "Not as a governess or a companion, surely, if I decide to go back to such a post. I would convince my employers that I needed no money at all if I showed up wearing such things."

But Tibby had her mind on another notion. "D'you know what *I* think, miss?"

"I have a feeling you are going to tell me," said Susanna indulgently.

"I think you should use them to better yourself."

"Better myself? But with the annuity from Lady Wycombe I shall be quite well off, Tib."

"If you forgive me, miss, what you need is a husband. A rich husband."

"Oh, Tibby, really!" Susanna scoffed. "Be serious."

"I am serious, miss. With your looks and manner and these clothes of her ladyship's, you'd make the grandest lady in the world."

"Would I? That is very flattering, my dear little friend, but hardly practical."

"You just think about it. I saw the way you looked at Mr. Patrick the night he was here."

Susanna flushed. "I don't know what you mean."

There was a triumphant gleam in Tibby's eye. "I saw how you felt. He is a grand and splendid gentleman, but *not* too splendid for you! And he never even knew you was alive, did he? He didn't even *see* you, except as a part of the furniture."

With chagrin Susanna had to admit that what the maid was saying was all too true." But it is more than clothes, Tibby. One must know how to act, to move, and what to talk about."

"You could learn all that." She lifted a finger. "Mind you, I am not saying you should set your cap for Mr. Patrick especially, though he is a dream, ain't he? What I mean is that you should find someone *like* him. There must be men out there that are just right for someone like you, a real lady like you are!"

She made it so convincing. Certainly it was the projection of a more interesting life than merely becoming old-maidish in some small village. "But I wouldn't even know how to begin."

Tibby had thought all that out as well. "Have you thought about a vacation, miss? Say, to a spa, where everyone is a stranger to everyone else?"

"That would be very expensive, surely?"

"There is your annuity, you know, which I expect will begin soon. And I could help, you know. The money she left me would pay for my keep, the while you dangle your hook."

"You?"

"You will need a maid, miss. You couldn't go about a place like that without one, you know. And think of being in it together! Oh, miss, haven't you ever wanted a bit more out of life? Haven't you ever longed for a bit of adventure?"

Although she pretended to the maidservant that she would give the scheme consideration. Susanna had no intention of entering into such wildness. It was too much of a gamble and, to say the truth, too demeaning to contemplate wrapping oneself up like fancy goods to go on display.

It was something quite basic, one might almost say primitive, that changed her mind.

=== 3 ===

LADY WYCOMBE HAD been gone for slightly more than two months when Susanna was advised by the solicitor, Mr. Bainbridge, that Patrick Wycombe would be paying a visit to the property on the afternoon of the seventeenth of May, for a brief inspection to determine how the property might best be disposed of. It appeared to be a straightforward enough occasion, but it proved to have far-reaching consequences; for Mr. Wycombe, it seemed, was not arriving alone. He sent ahead to say that his party would not be expecting a luncheon to be laid on, but would picnic from hampers. All they would require would be a modicum of service.

"Those women from the village will never do, miss," Tibby warned. "It will have to be me, I expect."

"But shall you be able to manage all alone?"

"Lord, yes. I may be small, but I am wiry. They shall carry, and I shall serve."

"Perhaps I can help you as well," Susanna suggested. She had never acted in such a capacity, but how difficult, after all, could it be?

Tibby flatly put her foot down. "Oh, no, miss. That wouldn't be right at all. You dress up fine and show yourself the equal of any of them."

"Don't be absurb," said Susanna rather sharply. "I shall wear my brown merino wool and look respectable."

In the end she wore the salvaged octagonal spectacles as well, at which Tibby was outraged. "If you don't mind my

20

saying so, Miss Susanna, I wonder about you, really I do. Why, this is your chance to make Mr. Patrick sit up and take notice of you!"

Susanna smiled tolerantly. It would certainly be a good joke to dazzle Mr. Wycombe in his late aunt's finery, but equally profitless. A man like that would not be interested in a mere hired chatelaine, no matter how gaudily garbed.

The party was to have arrived at about one o'clock, but it was nearly two before the wheels of a landau were heard upon the drive. Three riders cantered along behind it, two of whom—Mr. Wycombe and his friend Mr. Marshall—were known to Susanna. But the third was a lady on a jet-black horse, which she handled with every evidence of superior skill, despite the fact that the beast was skittering at the moving shadows of the overhanging trees and dancing nervously about. She was fashionably beautiful and dressed superbly. Her pearl grey riding habit was possessed of the latest mode—sloping shoulders and full, long skirts that almost swept the ground. A smart top hat sported white cock feathers and a long, flowing veil through which gleamed flaxen ringlets so pale as to be almost colourless. She would have been a formidable opponent for any woman. Susanna was glad that she herself had chosen to remain unobtrusive.

"Archer!" Patrick Wycombe called out as they approached the house. "How good of you to allow our feast here." Then, when he saw the trestle table laid out with snowy linen and sparkling china, he looked even more gratified. "I fear you have gone to a great deal of trouble."

She curtsied slightly. "No trouble at all, sir. I hope everything will prove to be to your satisfaction. Tibby, here, will serve you, if that is convenient, and I shall be within call if anything further is required. You have but to send one of the other women for me."

"Oh, but I hope you will join us? I am sure there is enough food for a regiment."

But she demurred. "If you will excuse me, sir? I have

already had my own luncheon. Perhaps you will summon me when you are ready to go over the house? There are several things I should like to call to your attention, repairs which have been long neglected."

"Of course, Archer, of course." She had the impression that he was looking at her in a particularly odd way, slightly furrowing his brows. It made her face feel quite naked. Then she realised why: unconsciously she had removed the spectacles when she was talking to him. Quickly she put them on again, as if they were a barrier behind which she could take refuge. Immediately his face cleared.

"Ah," he chuckled, "so that is what was missing. I knew you were different in some small way." He turned back to his arriving guests and to the disposal of the hampers, but Tibby quickly took over the chore of opening them and setting out the food. "Let me introduce you to my guests, Archer. Mr. Marshall you already know. And this is Mrs. Fairfax and her friend, Lady Morphy, Mr. Marshall's aunt.

"And this," he continued with a certain amount of diffident pride, "is Miss Cecily Fairfax." Miss Cecily was, of course, the flaxen-haired equestrienne.

Susanna played the devoted servant for all she was worth. "I hope you will tell me if there is anything I can do to make your visit more comfortable. Perhaps the ladies would care to refresh themselves after the ride?"

The women followed her gratefully inside the house, exclaiming as they went how quaint and old-fashioned was the Elizabethan interior. "Quite rackety, though," commented Mrs. Fairfax, giving Susanna a sidelong glance. "There are some who would call it poor management."

"There are many, many things which were left undone while her ladyship was alive," Susanna answered straightforwardly, "but it is to be hoped that Mr. Wycombe will see to setting things to rights. It would be a pity if such a fine old house were allowed to fall to ruin, don't you think?"

"Oh, I believe Patrick is going to sell the place as soon as he can," Miss Cecily advised them all. "I cannot imagine anyone of fashion wishing to live here, can you? Quite impossible."

The third of the women, Lady Morphy, had kept silent until this point, but now she entered the discussion by disagreeing with Cecily. "Not at all," she said. "I can remember visiting here when I was a child, and it was a very pleasant place, indeed. It may need repair, but a loving hand could return the gloss it once had, I do assure you."

Then, as if remembering something of which she had only heard, she asked Susanna, "Whatever became of Lady Wycombe's famous wardrobe? I expect the gowns were all dispersed in a sale?"

"As a matter of fact, madam," said Susanna smoothly, "it was left to me in her ladyship's will as a special bequest. I expect some of the items will be sold eventually."

"Really, Clementina," laughed Mrs. Fairfax, "I never thought to hear you hankering over some poor old woman's clothes. Next you'll be setting up as a 'rag-and-bone' and crying them up for the highest bidder."

"The bids certainly would be high," said Lady Morphy. "I am surprised that such a fabled attraction has never come to your attention, Irene. I believe that some of them are quite wonderful."

"Nevertheless," sniffed Cecily, "the idea of slipping into a dead woman's clothes! Ugh!"

"Some of them were never worn, Miss Fairfax," Susanna observed. "Quite a number were made after I came into her ladyship's employ and she never even tried them on."

"How peculiar," Lady Morphy observed. "One would think she could hardly wait."

"How amusing if we could see some of them," giggled Mrs. Fairfax. "But I expect they are all packed away?"

"Not at all," answered Susanna. "It would be no trouble if you would care to look at some of them while your picnic is being set up."

"I suppose you will be wanting to try them on as well, Mama," scoffed Cecily, but Susanna, observing Mrs. Fairfax's partridge-plump figure, knew that such would not be possible.

However impertinent Cecily might have been to her mother, there was no doubt that all three women were very much impressed by the gowns Susanna laid out on Lady Wycombe's bed. "Edad," marvelled Mrs. Fairfax, "I cannot think when I have seen such things. Look at the workmanship! These stitches are all but invisible." She puckered her brow. "But . . . well, my dears, these are all the gowns of a young woman, and Lady Wycombe was . . ."

"Yes," Susanna agreed, "there is no doubt that her ladyship had a very youthful outlook upon life. I believe they made her very happy."

"And now," said Cecily a little spitefully, "I suppose they will do the same for you." Then her eyes fell upon a gown of silver-gauze. "Oh, Mama, will you look at this!"

Mrs. Fairfax waxed as ecstatic as her daughter. "Oh, quite lovely! What an angel you would look in it." She turned to Susanna as if to a shopkeeper. "How much will you ask for this? Something low, I imagine, since these are all second-hand goods?"

But Susanna, though she was a parson's daughter—or perhaps because of it, and knowing what it was to want for a shilling—was not fooled by this obvious tactic of bargaining. "That is one of the dresses I spoke of which has never been worn. You can see that it still has the dressmaker's tissue."

"Oh, I dare say," sniffed the matron. Then she took another tack. "It does seem a bit out of the mode even now. I am sure it would not do for Cecily in any case." The gown was cut with an almost timeless simplicity.

"I rather like it myself," said Lady Morphy, "and if you find you cannot afford it, Irene, I believe I have a sufficient sum at my disposal."

"Mama!" Cecily wailed and Mrs. Fairfax capitulated.

Reluctantly she opened her reticule. "Oh, very well. How much do you want for it, Archer? Mind you do not push up the price. I know the cost of such things."

Lady Morphy and Susanna blinked at each other in amusement, and her ladyship said with amusement, "You shall pay twenty-five pounds and not a shilling less. It is well worth thirty. Just look at this workmanship!"

"But, twenty-five pounds!" cried Mrs. Fairfax in horror.

Miss Cecily stamped her dainty foot and pouted. Mrs. Fairfax sighed. "Twenty guineas, then."

Since this was almost twice what she had hoped to realise, Susanna took her cue from Lady's Morphy's slight nod, but spoke without undue haste, as if considering. "Very well," she said slowly, "because you are Mr. Wycombe's guests. Another time, you understand . . ."

"Another time?" cried Mrs. Fairfax. "You have beggared me for a fortnight!"

"But think how happy you have made Cecily," said Lady Morphy soothingly.

And, indeed, Miss Fairfax seemed quite minded to change into it immediately and wear it down to luncheon.

"I rather think that would be a mistake, Miss Fairfax," said Susanna. "Of course, it is yours now, to do with as you like."

The pretty eyebrows were raised in disdain. "What could you possibly know of such things?"

"Very little, I am sure, but it seems to me you will waste its effect twice over, if you do."

"Twice over? What do you mean?"

Susanna smiled as a schoolmistress might smile at a fairly dim pupil. "I rather believe this particular gown was meant to be viewed by candlelight or even . . . moonlight. The glare of the sun will certainly reduce it to mere glitter instead of enchantment, do you not think?"

Miss Fairfax pouted. "Well, I *know* it is not a day dress," she conceded, "but what is your other reason?"

Susanna spread her hands. "Why waste the effect of it on

only two men . . . when you could bring a ballroom full of them to your feet?"

It was exactly the right thing to say. Both mother and daughter beamed at the implied compliment. "Oh, Mama, did you hear?"

Mama smiled indulgently. "I heard, my sweet, and I must confess, I think Archer is right. You are a clever woman, Archer. Have you yet found a new post?"

The thought of being at the beck and call of this preposterous woman turned Susanna's blood chill. "Why, not quite yet, Mrs. Fairfax. I am still contemplating one or two offers."

"One or two? Fancy!" she sniffed. "My, how we apples swim!"

But, as the Fairfaxes left the room and Susanna began to put the other gowns away, Lady Morphy paused beside her. "If nothing comes of your other offers, my dear, please consider coming to me. Any woman who can outface Irene Fairfax is the sort I should like to have about me."

A little smile played about her mouth and Susanna responded to it gratefully. "Thank you, madam, I will bear it in mind."

The luncheon went off with great *panache*. Susanna, standing just inside the door, made it her business to oversee all the arrangements, making sure the guests were content. The gentlemen, in truth, paid little attention to the food or the service, and it was easy to see that Miss Fairfax was well versed in the art of charming the opposite sex, for both Wycombe and Marshall paid court to her with great animation.

"Quite got them wrapped about her finger, don't she, miss?" murmured Tibby on the way to the pantry for a condiment. On her return she added, "Just you be paying attention to how she does it. It is never too late to learn, you know."

Susanna grimaced in distaste, but, mostly out of curiosity, she did watch to see exactly how Miss Fairfax went about being a fascinator. As she watched, it seemed to her that the woman was so patently artificial in her airs and graces, so transparent in her acquisitiveness, that it was difficult to believe that any man in his right mind would be taken in by her. But it was evident that they were, for the men seemed to hang on her every word, though there was a quizzical expression on the face of Mr. Marshall. Susanna saw, too, how avidly Mrs. Fairfax watched her daughter as if she were reliving her own triumphs of the past.

When the luncheon was done the ladies again retired; this time to a pair of the more presentable guest chambers to rest, while Patrick Wycombe went about the house with Susanna.

"I feel I must rely strongly on your advice, Archer. Do you think the old place can be brought back, or is it wiser to simply put it on the market and 'let the buyer beware'?"

"If you intend only to divest yourself of the house, sir, it would seem hardly to matter which you do, but I am bound to say it does not seem fair."

"Fair?" He asked it in surprise. "Fair to whom?"

Susanna did not really know. "To the house itself, perhaps. You can see that it was once a beautiful old place and, according to Lady Morphy, not too long ago. I fancy one can discern that, even behind the neglect."

He looked at her curiously. "So you are saying it should be put to rights, are you?"

She knew he was still not *seeing* her, but the more she talked to this man, the more she found she liked him—even though, for him, she was scarcely more than a part of the furnishings. She nonetheless felt she could speak frankly and be heard out.

"No, sir, I am not saying that. It would hardly be my place to do so. I only hope it will not be pulled down to make room for some silly country villa. That would be a great pity."

Wycombe shrugged. "That may be, but sentimentality is

poor business. If it is to be restored, it will be to earn a greater profit in the end. So far as that goes, I think you are very probably correct, Archer."

Even though she had said nothing of the kind, Susanna did not disagree with him. And even though she knew better than to indulge herself in such a manner, she was annoyed that to him she was still invisible.

When the party of picnickers had gone and the day-women sent home, Susanna asked Tibby into the music room, which she found less oppressive than the parlour. The little maid came reluctantly.

"I still remember that night as if it were yesterday, miss. Funny how I don't mind going into my lady's old room. But coming in here, I remember how you was singing 'The Handy Randy Dandy O,' and her ladyship loving every bar of it. Fancy lying on your deathbed and listening to a naughty song!"

To steer the conversation away from such a sad topic, Susanna began to speak of Miss Fairfax. "Honestly, Tibby, I don't know what it is you think I should ape her in. I took your advice and tried to see what it is she does, but, you know, I don't believe I could copy her. She seems to have had years of training."

She began to satirise Cecily. "Why, Mr. Wycombe, how could a helpless woman like myself *dare* go riding alone? *Every* woman needs a *man* by her side."

Tibby frowned at the broad burlesque. "You are laughing at her, Miss Susanna, but you must admit that what she does works very well."

"I should be ashamed to be so deceitful," said Susanna indignantly. Then added, more sadly, "Women should not be reduced to such subterfuge, Tib."

"Needs must," replied the girl, and Susanna reflected how the saying went directly to the point. Idly she reflected upon Lady Morphy's kind offer of employment, which would provide a certain cushion of security in case she did decide to . . . She stopped suddenly in mid-thought. If she did not believe in Miss Fairfax's methods, she must devise ones of her own.

"Tibby," she said, "Tomorrow morning I think we should begin sorting out the gowns to decide which should be offered for sale and which retained."

With a look of excitement and rising comprehension the little maid asked, "Retained, Miss Susanna?"

"Yes," Miss Archer replied. "We must be very careful not to seem ostentatious when we take our holiday at Cheyne Spa."

=== 4 ===

As it fell out, Tibby's fears concerning the disposal of the clothing were all too justified. Several offers were made and reviewed, but none they felt was advantageous. In the end they allowed only the least useable costumes to pass out of their hands. From some of the plainer materials a few day costumes were contrived by Tibby's quick needle, and Susanna's present wardrobe was turned into uniforms for the little maidservant.

"Oh, miss, if only I had a complexion like yours!" she sometimes sighed.

"But Tibby, you are already such a pretty girl. I can't think why you want to change," Susanna protested. "I am sure there are many young men whose eye you catch."

Tibby tossed her head. "I don't say I do not have my points and I rather like my eyes, but men don't care much for little dun fillies, you see."

"You amaze me. I had no idea you were a woman of such experience."

"Oh, you well may laugh, miss, but I know whereof I speak. *You* are the sort they admire."

"Cecily Fairfax is the sort they admire, as we have seen."

Tibby was full of scorn. "Yes, we have seen it, but even men are not such fools as to be taken in by the likes of her forever. Not the sort you want, at any rate."

"I am not sure I *know* the kind I want."

"You'll soon learn," Tibby promised. "It won't be the likes of that Mr. Marshall, of that I am sure. He's a dark 'un, miss, and you'll do yourself a mort of good by staying away."

Susanna had had no particular designs upon Mr. Marshall, but she could not help wondering why she should avoid him. "I am not sure, altogether," Tibby answered, "but there is more to him than meets the eye. Sharp as needles, he is, but he hides it. All congenial he was that night he buttered up her ladyship, but there is a cool spot in him somewheres, you know. I've felt it."

"A cool spot? Oh, Tibby!"

"Really, miss, if we are going to Cheyne Spa you will have to learn that I am never wrong about certain things. You may scoff, but I know what I know. Wasn't my mam one of *them?*"

"One of whom, the gypsies? Are you telling me that is why you are such a 'little dun filly?' "

Tibby dropped her voice confidentially, although the servants had long since gone home to their cottages. "One of the old religion, miss. They knows things the rest of the world hasn't a glimmer of. I have it a bit, but not like my mam."

Susanna knit her brows, unable to believe what she was hearing. "Do you mean to say that your mother is a witch, Tibby? Isn't that rather a dangerous thing to talk about if it is true?"

Tibby bridled. "Well, I hope you don't think I talks about it on the streets, miss, nor takes the preacher into my confidence. I am only telling *you*, privately, to prove a point, like. They all comes to my mam, though they have enough sense not to say witch, which is rather rude. What they calls her is a wisewoman. They only dare to be rude to the poor old women who live alone and talk to their cats. They daren't speak to mam that way. I don't know *what* she'd do, but it wouldn't be pleasant." She shuddered deliciously. "It wouldn't be pleasant for them at all."

"I suppose you mean she would lay a curse on them, or something of that nature?"

But Tib was not to be further drawn out. "Oh, she is a terror, my mam is, when she is aroused." Abruptly she changed the direction of the conversation. "Since the workmen are to begin the repairs on the house next fortnight, why shouldn't we nip off to Cheyne Spa then, miss? A sort of trial run, as the racing blokes have it. We could just look about a bit, you know, and spy out the lay of the land."

And, once Susanna thought about it, the timing seemed as feasible as any other. "We can come and go very quietly. At least no one will know us."

Tibby giggled. "They will by the time we leaves, miss. You wait and see."

Cheyne Spa, in the valley of the Rouse, has been so brilliantly described by so many authors that it seems rather to be gilding the lily to speak of it in any great detail. It is neither so large nor so staid as Bath, yet not so frivolous as Cheltenham. It is built of a similar golden-hued stone as the larger city, so that even when the skies are overcast (as on the day that Susanna and Tibby—perhaps one should say Lady Kinsale and her maid, for such were the identities they had assumed—arrived), the town seems to bask in a sunny glow. It is, in short, an altogether pleasant place to while away one's time if one is in need either of its acrid waters or, indeed, even if one is not. Cheyne Spa: its handsome crescents laid out by Landsdowne and Hurd, its Upper and Lower Assembly Rooms where one may dance or gamble respectively, and, above all, the handsome and justly celebrated Cheyne Abbey with its magnificent perpendicular windows and cloistered walks about the square which, though it no longer belongs to the Abbey and harbours shops instead of monkish offices, retains still the flavour of past centuries.

In the matter of their first emergence upon the scene, the young women had taken considerable thought. Rooms had been engaged at the White Hart in Stall Street for the first few days and dress-filled trunks and boxes sent ahead. The question of first appearance had been looked into and the proper costumes chosen. There had also been that question of identity, but Tibby had been the decider about that.

"Well, miss, I think you should set yourself up as a widow. It is more respectable than a young woman living alone, somehow, and there is always the suspicion that a deceased husband has left a tidy sum behind if the widow is gadding about. Your costumes can be a bit sedate right at first. I think we should be there a bit before the really grand clothes are taken out, don't you?"

Susanna considered all of it carefully. She agreed about the clothing, but she was not sure about the identity. She had meant all along merely to let her appearance and quality speak for themselves, without committing herself to any sort of background. Now she saw that Tibby was undoubtedly right; but was such an imposture really going to be practical? How much could be invented in advance and how much must be left to the imagination upon the spur of the moment? How much there would be to remember.

She suspected that the most workable fabrications were those that most closely resembled truth. Well, yes, she could attach a "Mrs." to her name, or even, considering the lavishness of the wardrobe, a noncommittal "lady," but she would not indulge in useless and unnecessary embroideries which would only render the task more difficult.

In the end her travelling dress was quite severe but comfortable, with a plain, easy sleeve, a high waistline and a hem trimmed only with a lowset horizontal braid. Because of Tib's sense of cut, the costume had an innate elegance and an understated effect much in keeping with the idea of present-but-passing bereavement. Not wishing to tempt fate too far, she amended her name only to Lady Kinsale, after her mother's easily remembered birthplace, in the hope that the Irish flavour it implied would account for any unfamiliarity with presently fashionable customs.

On the day they arrived Susanna almost thought she had

made a grave error, for the pealing of the bells as the coach came into town, the dash of the other carriages, the continual bawling and brawling and hustle of the street hawkers were things she found immensely disagreeable. Despite the lowering skies, the crowds had turned out to promenade, to visit the shops, or to take tea in St. Gerrans's Gardens just as they always did. Only an actual thunderstorm could keep them indoors.

Luckily the sedate quality of the White Hart did much to calm her fears for, despite its nearness to the Pump Room and the baths, it had an old-fashioned stoutness which greatly pleased her. When the inn-keeper approached, she stood back and let Tibby take the lead, this appearance of reticence having been decided upon in advance.

"You see, miss, if I am delegated to tend to the business for you, it makes you out to be rather more special, don't it?"

"Does it?" Susanna had asked in surprise.

"Oh, yes, miss, you know it does!" Tibby's assertiveness had grown in direct proportion to her importance to their enterprise. "When *you* speak, you see, it must be with a kind of ladylike forcefulness, if you take my meaning. Rather as if you generally needn't take notice of such things. That is rather like you already, you know—quiet but firm. I've seen you take that exact line with Lady Wycombe. Now, never you mind about the strangeness of it all, you'll float along with the best of them. You'll see."

Luckily their chambers did not front upon the busy pavement, but were at the rear and upon a quiet square of trees and solitude. "They've given you the best chamber, I believe, miss," Tibby commented. "Shows what they think of you already."

"It will certainly do for a few days," Susanna answered, "but it will be ruinously expensive to remain here long. I think we must seek out lodgings in some genteel and quiet street. Perhaps if we walk about a little we shall come across a suitable place."

And ambulating about the Upper Town the next afternoon, they felt they had found the exact spot.

Hanover Crescent is the architectural showplace of Cheyne; but just beyond it, upon the actual crown of the hill, is Upper Orson Street, pretty and secluded, an Eden of already maturing trees and pleasant buildings of the honey-coloured stone which Susanna so loved. In several of the front windows were discreet placards, indicating that chambers were to be hired within.

The first house at which they stopped had only a cramped and inconvenient bedroom on the second floor, according to the landlady. "I would be more than happy to accommodate your ladyship if I had anything at all suitable."

She seemed to be utterly sincere, for she not only suggested the house of a friend, but offered to guide the women there so that they should not lose their way. The dangers of going astray proved minimal, since this second house was only across the street and a little further along; but it was gratifying that the woman took such pleasure to lead them there, chattering all the way about the excellence of Cheyne Spa, and Upper Orson Street in particular.

"For you know it is scarcely a step to anywhere. Why, a walk to the baths is five minutes only! You will find the house of my friend quite convenient, I do assure you."

"Well, Miranda," she announced to this new proprietress when the door was opened to them, "I have brought you some custom. I hope you will not disappoint me, for I have told her ladyship, here, that, barring my own, yours is quite the most comfortable house in Upper Orson Street."

Susanna had already been impressed by the entrance. The front steps were scrubbed and whitened though it was only mid-morning, and the areaway, which she had easily seen by peering over the edge of the entrance steps, was well-swept and neat. The interior followed out this impression, for Mrs. Maundy was a small, well-proportioned woman in mourning purple, her house neat as a pin and smelling pleasantly of soap and beeswax. A small black kitten played about the stairway.

"I hope you do not mind cats, your ladyship?" Luckily, Susanna held them in great dote.

The apartment off the drawing room was pleasant enough, but it had only a dressing-room and no place to put a bed for Tibby; but on the first floor was the ideal situation. There they were shown not only a handsome sitting room overlooking the view toward the Lower Town, but there was, as well as the bedroom, a chamber for Tibby and a substantial room for dressing with plenteous space to house their main stock in trade, the gowns of Lady Wycombe.

"Oh, we have such a select clientele," Mrs. Maundy enthused to them. "There is another lady of title staying here even now, a sister of the old Duke of Quince. Very refined, you know, but quite condescending in the kindest way imaginable."

It was upon the stairs that a shocking confrontation took place. Susanna had already agreed to take the rooms and breakfast for, by signs and expressions, she and Tibby had agreed that this was very nearly ideal for their purposes. It was near enough for peace and quiet. Not so expensive as to be ruinous, but with an address which was respectable enough for Lady Kinsale of Ireland to reside there. Congratulating themselves as they descended the stairs, they saw the front door opened by the housemaid and another lady's figure outlined against the rays of sunlight streaming in.

"Ah, your ladyship," cried Mrs. Maundy with delight, "I was even now speaking of you! What a fortuitous encounter. May I present another of our guests? Lady Kinsale has just taken the chambers on the first floor."

The woman moved inside and for the first time her face could be seen. The features were known to both Susanna and her friend, for they belonged to a woman they had seen scarcely a month before. The woman on the landing, smiling up at them, was none other than Lady Clementina Morphy.

She looked straight into Susanna's face with no sign of recognition. "Lady Kinsale, is it? How happy I am to meet you. I dare say we have a great deal in common and shall find much to talk about."

A thousand thoughts flew through Susanna's head: that she had been discovered, that they must take immediate flight, that she might be put in gaol for impersonation! Behind her she heard Tibby's pronounced intake of breath, but there was in Lady Morphy's face nothing more than genuine pleasure in their meeting. There was, after all, no help for it. Instead of fleeing, she gave a pleasant nod of her head.

"Lady . . . Morphy, is it? How very charming to make your acquaintance."

=5=

"ARE YOU ABSOLUTELY sure it is the same person?" asked Gavin Marshall of his aunt. "I believe I spent a full evening with Lady Wycombe's companion, and all I recall is a plain face, pulled-back hair and spectacles. I am certain I would not know the woman if I found her in my bed."

"And I am completely sure," Lady Morphy replied, "that such an occurrence has more than once taken place. Nevertheless, I would stake my life that this so-called Lady Kinsale is Lady Wycombe's Miss Archer."

"How amusing," laughed Gavin. "It opens up limitless possibilities for diversion. Do you suppose Patrick and the Fairfax ladies will know her?"

"I doubt it," said Lady Morphy. "No one recognises servants. Can you tell me what the waiter looked like who served you dinner, or the shopwoman who sold you ribbons, or the flower-girl who actually put your bouton-niere in your lapel? And it was well over two months ago that Irene and Cecily saw her. As for Patrick . . ." She grimaced.

"I know your feeling that he is dull, but he is most charming and a good friend to me. Let me point out as well that *you* recognised the woman."

"Oh," said his aunt, "but I am *I*."

"Remind me what she is like," demanded Gavin. "Is she pretty or plain?"

"Neither, I should say, as the world judges beauty.

Rather handsome in her own way, and with real possibilities if she were taught to capitalise upon them."

Gavin shot her a quick glance. "I say, are you reading my mind again?"

"Our minds always work alike, my boy. It is an unlikely scheme, but it might be implemented if the young woman were to be convinced that we are friends."

It is pertinent that, although Lady Morphy and her nephew were not as poor as they might have been, there was a certain rankling in the breast of each, and a certain annoyance, at the way in which fate had dealt out their hands. Both were excellently connected—Lady Morphy being the daughter of the fourth Duke of Quince, and Gavin the nephew of the fifth Duke. The mischance for him was the fact that two elder cousins stood directly in the line of succession before him—youngish and exceptionally healthy chaps, both of them, and likely to sire hordes of children, any one of whom would thrust Gavin even further down the line. The lady had a settlement from her brother's interpretation of their father's will, but she loved to gamble. Gavin had a passion for the tables as well, but rarely had anything to gamble *with*. It was a vexing and perplexing situation, but one for which a solution might just possibly present itself.

In tune, as they often were, Gavin and his aunt had seen the same possibility in this piquant situation, an amusing way of increasing their incomes. A long shot, perhaps; only a possibility, most certainly; but if "Lady Kinsale" did not stick at living in the same lodgings, she would have no opportunity of evading their company, for both Gavin and Clementina Morphy knew how to make friends and then cleave closer than a limpet. Their very lives had often, of late, depended on this ability when the wagers were not running in their favour.

"But what if she bolts?" he asked. "Do you think I should investigate her situation? Is this merely a lark for her, or does she have the same sort of thing in mind that we do?"

His aunt had already considered the question. "Perhaps you could find out something from Patrick Wycombe?" she suggested.

Gavin considered. "I think we must be very careful not to bring anyone further into this," he warned. "Besides Patrick is as honest as the day—he'd tip the game at once." He shook a finger playfully to illustrate a point. "And all this is merely a notion, you know. She may not be at all suitable. His lordship's tastes, after all, are fairly well defined. She may not even be the person you believe her to be!"

"Ah, I am convinced of that," said Lady Morphy confidently. "I would stake my reputation on it."

Her nephew smirked. "Well, considering . . ." And she tapped him playfully with her fan.

"Mind you find out what you can about her, and do not flush the quail from the thicket until we have decided how best to snare her."

"Or until we have decided how best to use her."

"What if she prefers to go on with her own scheme and abjures ours?" her ladyship mused.

Gavin's sly smile increased its guile and he delicately flicked an imaginary fleck of dust from the sleeve of his coat. "Why then," he said suavely, "we have our duty to society, do we not?"

"Do you mean, to expose her? Surely that is rather extreme and unfair?"

Gavin's look was all innocence of heart. "But we must protect our friends from people such as that, do you not agree? We have a duty to our class."

"Well, miss, you must admit, you look a very different person, come to that."

The two were in a quandary, not knowing if they had been unmasked. Had Lady Morphy penetrated their masquerade? "What do you think we should do, miss?"

"I think we should run away as fast as our legs can carry

us," answered Susanna. "It was a mad idea, and now we know the danger of it."

But Tibby was undaunted. "You disappoint me, really you do. Why, you are ready to cry off afore we've even fairly begun. If you remember, this Lady Morphy scarcely saw you for half an hour at Wycombe Hall. You showed the gowns, but *I* did all the serving . . . while you stood inside the house goggling over Mr. Patrick, but were too afraid to let it be seen."

For the moment Susanna had forgotten about Patrick Wycombe, but the danger now appeared even greater than she had seen. If Lady Morphy was at Cheyne Spa, it seemed probable that her friend Mrs. Fairfax might be here as well; and if Mrs. Fairfax, Cecily; and where Cecily was to be found, there was a very good chance of finding Patrick Wycombe. Her heart gave a little flutter. What would his reaction be if he met "Lady Kinsale?" Would he recognize her for the impostor she was?

And if he did not?

"After all, Miss Susanna, what is there to lose? If we run away now, we shall never know what we might have accomplished. What can they do if they should know us? We can always go to another town. We could go to Dublin, if you like, and pretend to be an *English* peeress, or to the continent, or to America, even! Think of that, miss, the Countess of Kinsale at large in Boston!"

"You fly too high," Susanna warned. "If we stick to a mere 'Lady,' we shall have less risk of someone examining our credentials."

There was a knock on the door of the chamber. "A gentleman asking for you in the parlour, my lady."
"A gentleman? Who is it?"

"Didn't give 'is name, madam."

The two young women exchanged startled looks. Were they already unmasked? Susanna touched her hair nervously; Tibby straightened her mistress's gown then pulled at her own apron.

"Shall I come with you, miss? I hate to see you face it out alone."

"Oh, yes, please do," Susanna said gratefully. She paused, "Oh, and another thing, I think you must get into the habit of saying 'your ladyship' or 'madam.' Calling me 'miss' certainly will not do in public."

"And when we are alone, miss?"

Susanna pressed her partner's hand. "When we are alone it is simply Susanna and Tibby."

Hearts in their mouths, they descended the stairs to the common room. Tibby nudged her friend and pointed across the room. "Look over there, miss . . . I mean, your ladyship. Isn't that Mr. Patrick's friend?"

Susanna's eyes followed Tibby's. "Yes, you are right, that is Mr. Marshall, but we must pretend not to know him. Lady Kinsale would not have his acquaintance."

When Marshall saw the two women making inquiries of the innkeeper, then saw the man pointing toward him, he rose gracefully from his chair and came toward them. He could hardly believe that his aunt's supposition was correct. Surely, if he had seen this handsome creature ever before in his life, he would have remembered her. The little maidservant, though, looked decidedly familiar.

"Lady Kinsale?" Trembling, Susanna assented. "My aunt, Lady Morphy, has commissioned me to ask if I may be of any assistance in your removal to Upper Orson Street."

"How very kind," Susanna murmured faintly. Since she was supposed to hail from Ireland, should she supply an accent? She decided against it. "We shall be remaining here for the night."

And fly away in the morning? Gavin wondered. "Then perhaps you will allow me to show you about the town?" he suggested. "It is very easy for a newcomer to get lost in the confusion of streets hereabouts."

It was on the tip of Susanna's tongue to remind him that

she and her maid had already done a bit of exploring and had found the lodgings in Upper Orson Street with no great trouble, but she felt it wiser to refrain. "That would be very pleasant," she agreed. "Tibitha, you will attend me, if you please."

"Oh, will that be necessary?" Gavin's eyebrows rose. "I had hoped that we might become better acquainted."

"I am sure we can do so with my maid in attendance, sir. I am sure that your guidance will benefit her as much as myself." She looked him directly in the eye. "You must remember that you are a complete stranger to me."

"Am I, Lady Kinsale? I have the most dashedly nagging feeling that we have met before. Some past lifetime, perhaps?"

"Along the Nile, I daresay," said Susanna, curling up the corners of her mouth just slightly. "I expect you were the Pharaoh and I was . . . the Priestess of the Temple?"

"Something like that," he agreed genially. They strolled out along the High Street with all its smart shops, and Susanna watched avidly to see what other women were wearing and how they comported themselves. There appeared to be a great deal of social freedom here. A great many women seemed to be walking alone with gentlemen, some even altogether alone, as if no chaperones were tolerated in such a cosmopolitan *milieu*—though Susanna thought the silly, capricious way they had of greeting their friends and acquaintances with exaggerated little pecks upon the cheeks and cries like land-trapped seabirds was quite indefensible. She knew she would never allow herself to be so insincere as all that, no matter what seemed to be required in her new role.

They walked for a bit, along the River Walk with its lovely, overshading linden trees, which gave an illusion of the tranquility the busier areas of the spa lacked. She wondered how those people fared who had been prescribed here for peace and quiet. Not that she was allowed much quiet either, for Mr. Marshall kept up a running barrage of charmingly inconsequential conversation that, nevertheless, was larded with questions about herself and her situation. Some were pointed and specific, others vague and full of implied innuendo. Since she knew nothing of Letterkenny or Coleraine when he mentioned them, and less than nothing of the semi-tropical Kenmare or even Kinsale itself, she took refuge in . . . a husband who had never taken his bride to his own homeland, . . . and had thoughtlessly passed away before acquainting her with more than the faintest picture of it.

By the time they reached St. Gerrans's Gardens she was becoming very flustered and confused, trying desperately to remember what she had said and what she had not, and seriously considering a hasty retreat from Cheyne Spa by the afternoon coach. Scarcely had they been seated at a table under the trees when her eyes opened wide in a horrified expression which, luckily, only Tibby noticed. The maidservant turned in the direction toward which Susanna's eyes were directed, and her heart sank. Coming toward them with every mark of geniality were Mrs. Fairfax and her daughter, and with them was Mr. Patrick Wycombe.

He was every bit as handsome as they remembered, tall and golden as a god. Susanna's heart turned over and she forced herself to take a deep breath to calm her nerves. Mrs. Fairfax looked the same, too; and when she saw them, she began to wave animatedly.

"Mr. Marshall, what a surprise!" As she approached them, her sharp little eyes swept over Susanna with a puzzled little frown; but she turned her attention back to where it belonged, to the man of the party. "I had not heard, sir, that you were in Cheyne. Is your dear aunt in residence as well?"

Gavin, who had risen with her approach, nodded assent. "We have taken rooms in Upper Orson Street. May I present Lady Kinsale, who will soon be joining us as one of our neighbours. Your ladyship, Mrs. Fairfax." The two smiled vaguely at each other, Susanna trembling within. "And her daughter, Miss Cecily Fairfax, with my friend Mr. Wycombe," he added as the others joined them.

"I hope you will not charge me with familiarity, Lady Kinsale," Mrs. Fairfax pleaded, "but I could not help wondering . . . *(Ah, here it is, we are undone*, thought Susanna despairingly)" . . . if all Irish ladies have your divine complexion? I declare I am quite ravished by it, especially with your glorious hair!"

Before Susanna could answer, Cecily spoke up as well. Perhaps she was not so enchanted with what she considered undue competition for attention, for she said with a harsh little laugh, "I expect all that boggy air is marvelous for the skin, but I expect it is heavy with ague, is it not? They say that Irish women grow ancient before their time, which is such a pity!"

Now Susanna took the plunge and cut off her retreat by returning to the tale she had spun for Gavin Marshall, hoping that she had all the details right. "My husband always promised to take me on a visit to his birthplace, but for most of my married life we lived quietly near Bleet."

There was a surprised silence, and Patrick Wycombe leapt gallantly in to fill the gap. "I am certain that wherever Lady Kinsale has lived, she has been considered the crowning glory of it."

His words took Susanna slightly aback, but it seemed evident that his ardent glances were completely sincere. It was also evident that her secret was safe from Patrick, and that he in no degree remembered having seen her before. Idly, she wondered what he might do if she were to whip out the octagonal spectacles and clap them on her nose.

And why was Mr. Marshall favouring her with that sly and almost catty grin? Really, if these people had no use for the eyes in their heads, they *deserved* to be hoodwinked to a fare-thee-well. And there was Tibby standing straight in front of them, too, looking no different than she ever had.

In that moment she resolved to go on with the impersonation no matter what might befall. She felt a surge of confidence and, rather grandly, she said, "I hope you will join us? There is so much I want to learn about Cheyne Spa!"

= 6 =

"I MUST SAY that I believe you are quite right in believing our 'Lady Kinsale' to be an impostor," Gavin Marshall reported to his aunt, "though I confess I would never recognize her as Lady Wycombe's Archer. If it is she, the transformation is quite astonishing."

"Fiddle! You men are so thick. The girl has removed a pair of dreadfully disfiguring spectacles, put on a little rouge and rearranged her hair. There is no need to make it out to be the transmigration of a soul! The question is whether she is clever enough for our purposes. What do you think?"

Far cleverer than you suggested. When I first interviewed her she was rather unprepared. I believe she had not completely thought out her story and it did not hang together at all well. But, let me tell you, when she was faced with the challenge of routing Mrs. Fairfax and dear Cecily, she quite rose to the occasion. I was prepared to help her out by backing her story if the necessity arose— and draw her into our scheme through gratitude—but it never did. She handled everything like a winner. You would truly believe she had been to the manner born."

"So the Fairfax women were satisfied, were they?"

"More than satisfied. Cecily quite bristled when Patrick Wycombe paid the wench a smidgen too much attention." He puffed carelessly at his thin cheroot while his relative grimaced and fanned the air. "No, no, I think that once enlisted in our cause, she will prove an asset."

"I really wish you would not indulge yourself in those dreadful things while you are in my sitting room, Gavin. The smell lingers for hours. As for the girl, I caution you against overconfidence. On close examination she may not do at all. We know nothing of her background other than that Lady Wycombe thought highly of her. But, seeing that the old dear was more than a little mad, that may or may not be a recommendation. In addition, we know nothing of her intentions, which may be quite unscrupulous."

He could not help laughing aloud at this. "Horrors!"

But his aunt looked not in the least chagrined. "Well, my dear, I hope you do not put us in a class with highwaymen and murderers. We are only trying to pry a little of what is rightfully ours from my dear brother. If he were not so tight-fisted . . . " She sighed. "I do not like having to do this, you know. William John is a perfectly charming man. If only he were a little more generous!"

Gavin patted her hand as he prepared to take his leave. "I expect he did not take into consideration that a lifelong infatuation with the tables must necessarily be an expensive affair. As for the girl, I never anticipated that we should throw her at him unripe and untrained, Aunt. That will certainly depend much on you."

"Upon both of us, dear boy. Do not think that you will escape your fair share of training her as easily as all that."

Gavin winked roguishly as he shrugged into his coat. "From what I saw of her yesterday, that should be no hardship whatsoever."

Her ladyship did not smile so broadly as he had expected, though a small indication of appreciation lurked about the corners of her mouth. "I hope you are not taking this simply as a lark, Gavin. I agree that there is a great deal of amusement to be had from it, but we must bear in mind that at bottom it is a serious business, not to say a great gamble."

He nodded. "I agree, though I think it deserves a deal more lightness than you seem willing to afford it. The young woman, at any rate, will profit from the association whether our objective is reached or not."

"But, you see," said Susanna to Tibby over their morning chocolate, "I had the distinct feeling that he had already tumbled to the truth about us when Mrs. Fairfax arrived. Did you not think it?"

Tibby seemed unsure. "But why would he say nothing then, miss?"

"Susanna, if you please."

"Yes, Miss Susanna. Why would he not simply warn them off us?" She sipped appreciatively, but looked rather mournful. "Unless he told them something later when we had gone."

The carter arrived to take their boxes up the hill to Upper Orson Street. He was a rather strapping and not unhandsome young man whom Tibby eyed with appreciation. It pleased her, though, to put on a great show of indifference." I expect you know that these things you are tossing about are all quite valuable?"

He gave her a slow grin. "Perhaps, then, you should ride along with me to be sure they reach their destination without harm. What d'you say, are you game for a bit of a joggle up the hill?"

Tibby drew herself up to her full height. "If I was to do such a silly thing as that, I should never hold my head up in Cheyne Spa again, my good man. I will have you know that I am companion to Lady Kinsale. I'll thank you to remember that and not take liberties."

He hoisted another box upon his shoulder and she took pleased notice of the way his upper arm rippled as he did so. Her look was not lost on him. "Will you be staying at this place on Upper Orson, then?" he asked with elaborate casualness.

"I expect we will, if it proves suitable."

He stowed the boxes in the cart, then returned for a second load. "And if I was to call at the back door of this place some evening, and if I was to ask for you?"

Tibby held her breath in expectation. "Yes? If you were to ask for me?" But he waited until his final trip to finish his question.

"If I was to ask for you, do you think you might care to walk out a bit?"

She pretended to consider. "I might. It all depends."

He gave her the sort of look usually given by young men who are aware of their own susceptibility and embrace it gladly. "Does it, then? On what?"

Tibby tossed her pretty head and bridled charmingly, succeeding in coquetry without the least intention of it. "I should have to discuss it with my mistress, you know," she said in a straightforward manner. The carter nodded. He understood from experience in dealing with them that the ways of the gentry were sometimes unfathomable and that they often took baseless notions about chaps. Sometimes they were advantageous notions, he admitted, and good for a generous tip; but other times they were senseless and without point, not at all a good thing for a working man.

"And anyway, if you were to ask for me, how would I know who was calling? We don't even know each other's names yet."

"Tibby!" called Susanna from inside the sleeping chamber. "Will you help me with this fastening?"

The man quickly doffed his hat in a very gentlemanly fashion. "The name is Fred, Miss Tibby, Fred the carter. I look forward to seeing you. Shall we say . . . tonight?"

Susanna's voice caroled from the sitting room. "Tibby? Are you there?"

"Coming, miss . . . your ladyship!" Then, to the carter, "I'll have to ask, won't I? She may not want me walking out with anyone just yet."

Fred turned his cap in his hands almost nervously in his eagerness. "I shall be there in any case. I shall ask for you and if you are not free . . ."

"If I am not free this evening, I shall walk with you

50

another time, Fred," said Tibby impulsively. "And that is a promise."

The removal was carried through without difficulty, for nothing of consequence had been unpacked yet, and the two young women strolled leisurely toward their new lodgings, Tibby carrying only Susanna's dressing case. Mrs. Maundy met them at the door.

The boxes have all come, your ladyship—or rather I suppose them to be all, for the carter said nothing of more. My, you brought a mort of gowns, I expect, from the look of it. I had the man carry them to your dressing room, which I hope was correct?"

"Quite correct, Mrs. Maundy. Thank you."

"There is further storage space if your ladyship should require it."

"We shall see, but I expect we shall not trouble you."

Mrs. Maundy wrapped her hands in her apron in consternation. "Oh, madam, it is no trouble! That is what I am here for, is it not? To be of service? May I make your ladyship a pot of tea?"

"Perhaps her ladyship would care to share her tea with me?" asked Lady Morphy, entering at that junction. "We cannot confine our acquaintance to the stairway, do you think, Lady Kinsale?" Her eyes seemed to twinkle with good will, but Susanna was not certain how far appearances should be trusted.

Lady Morphy went on to say, "My dear nephew has spoken of you in such glowing terms . . . there are a thousand questions that I wish to ask you about Ireland."

"I fear your nephew should have explained to your ladyship that I have never set foot in Ireland," answered Susanna coolly, and with just a hint of implication that she found the notion of catechism unappealing. She tried to project the thought in a way she believed a real "Lady Kinsale" would do.

As Mrs. Maundy led the way up the stairs, Tibby following with the dressing case, Susanna trailed behind with an air of self-possession. "Oh, very good, *Archer*," said Lady Morphy, as Susanna passed her. "Spoken out quite like a lady."

Susanna hesitated only slightly, then said loudly enough for the others to hear, "Will you not join us, your ladyship? I am sure you are very welcome." She saw that Tibby was looking worriedly over her shoulder, but Mrs. Maundy was beaming on them with great good will as though she were a professional matchmaker and this bringing-together was her triumph.

Perhaps it was to impress her new guest or perhaps it was the opportunity of serving two peeresses at once—perhaps it was only as expression of an impulsive nature—but the tea she laid on was lavish, with extra water in a jug, fresh butter and hot scones, and tidy little seed-cakes.

"I brought these up specially," she said in reference to the latter, "for I remember how you like them, Lady Morphy. This is the third season her ladyship has honoured my little establishment," she explained to Susanna. "I think of her as an almost permanent guest." She managed to look both quite smug and friendly at the same time. "I hope you will like it here so well, your ladyship."

"I am sure I shall," Susanna replied. But, frankly, she was not at all sure how long she would be able to remain, now that her impersonation had been penetrated. She lifted the tea cloth.

"Oh, but you have brought only two cups."

Mrs. Maundy verged on confusion, then grasped the source of the complaint. "I thought perhaps Miss Tibby would grace my kitchen and share a pot there with me."

Susanna thought quickly. "I am sure she would be delighted to do so. Why don't you run along, Tibby. Lady Morphy and I can see to ourselves."

Tib's expression showed apprehensive concern. "If you are certain, madam?" Her voice went up at the end, turning a reply into a question concerning the wisdom of such a decision.

"Oh, come along, girl," Mrs. Maundy said, laughing. "Can you not see that the ladies are ready to settle in for a good gossip? Begging your ladyships' pardon for the familiarity."

"Go along, go along," Lady Morphy said, laughing as well. "We shall suit ourselves admirably."

When the two had gone, there was a constrained silence, which Susanna broke by taking up the teapot. "May I serve your ladyship?" she asked guardedly.

Lady Morphy favoured her with a kindly smile that crinkled the corners of her eyes in an engaging way. "There is no need to be nervous, girl. I am on your side, you see." She waited half a beat to see the effect of her words, then amended, "Or rather, I believe we may well be together on the same side."

Susanna eyed her guest coolly. Though she might only be a country vicar's daughter, she was not without experience of people. Looking into this woman's face, she tried to decipher what she saw there, but Lady Morphy wore such an expression of benignity that it was difficult to tell whether it was real or merely a clever calculation. The girl decided to take a chance.

"Tell me something, if you will, your ladyship."

"Certainly . . . milk, no sugar, if you please . . . I hope we shall come to be quite frank with each other."

Susanna nodded meditatively, then after a moment asked, "If you had not seen me previously at Wycombe Hall . . ."

"Would I have accepted you as Lady Kinsale? Probably, although there are certain small signs which would have made me wonder."

Susanna flushed, sensing a veiled slur, but her ladyship hastened to place her at ease. "They were nothing glaring, you understand—only, perhaps, attitudes or stances or even things which might be perfectly acceptable, but that no lady of the higher quality would allow in herself. The ease with which a woman moves in society, you know, is as important as the gown she wears or the way she dresses her hair. Yours is beautifully coiffed, by the way. Does that little maidservant do it? Perhaps she could show me how to dress my own."

"I expect the things you speak of come from familiarity," Susanna shrewdly observed, "but I daresay there are niceties that take years to absorb."

Her ladyship smiled encouragingly. "Such things can be taught and easily mastered if you have the ability, my dear. I think you have." The implied invitation lay there before them as palpable as the tea-table. Susanna dropped her eyes and pretended calm as her mind raced through its long corridors searching for a calm which eluded her. She picked up a small fan and lightly waved it before her face.

"Do I understand you, Lady Morphy? Are you hinting that you might undertake to supply a teacher?"

"There is an old saying, 'When the pupil is ready, the teacher will come,' " said her ladyship enigmatically. "Perhaps the best lessons are those which are not so much taught as absorbed, though there are specific languages which have accepted interpretations and must be learned by rote."

Susanna was puzzled. "I fear your ladyship has me at a disadvantage."

"Only temporarily, I am sure. I speak not of words, but of a more subtle level of communication." She indicated the little fan with which Susanna was lightly moving the air. "The fan has a language, for instance; flowers have a language, the movements of the dance are certainly a mode of intimate communication. Do you do the *valse à la francaise*, Miss Archer?"

"I fear I know only the country dances."

"My nevvy shall teach you. It is all the rage since Madame Lieven introduced it at Almack's last year. Naturally, there were some staid old mamas who declared it immoral, but I am sure that only contributed to its popularity. I am sure the anti-waltzing faction will exist only until they themselves have mastered the intricacies of it. Even here in Cheyne Spa the musicians in the Assembly Rooms have become accomplished in the rhythms. You look as if you have a natural sense of grace. Do you ride?"

She admitted that she did, though as a young girl she had only been allowed to ride astride and had never become quite comfortable with the sidesaddle.

"It is certainly more comfortable astride," agreed her ladyship, "but it will never do to be seen that way in public. What is good for a young hoyden,"—and she smiled to show she had perhaps been a young hoyden herself— "will not do for a lady of the ton. Mr. Marshall shall be your riding master as well as your dancing master for a time. It is only a matter of time."

"I beg your pardon for asking such a blunt question, Lady Morphy, but what is your purpose in all of this? I apprehend that it goes well beyond mere pleasantness. Too much trouble is being taken for that, I fear."

With a shrug of her shoulder, her ladyship effectively cast the question aside. "Call it a caprice—an amusement, if you like. I was pleased at the way you faced down Mrs. Fairfax and the fair Cecily that afternoon at Wycombe Hall and, from what Gavin has told me, you repeated the maneuver yesterday in St. Gerrans Gardens. Now, I must say that, though Irene Fairfax is a silly old thing a great deal of the time, she has decidedly sharp eyes for a weakness. If you passed muster with her, you are, for the most part, on very firm ground."

"You have twice volunteered your nephew's tuition, madam; are you so certain he will agree?"

The older woman chuckled. "How much time did he spend with you yesterday, my dear? An hour?"

Susanna calculated the time in her head. "Rather more than two, I believe."

"Then," said Lady Morphy, "I think we need not fret about his willingness to undertake the tasks."

7

WILLIAM JOHN DALTON MOBRAY-MARSHALL—5th Duke of Quince, Hereditary High Steward of the Liberty of St. Selevan, patron of thirty livings and Lord of the Manor of Seldesbury—looked older, if not measurably wiser, than his fifty-five years, for he still affected the accoutrements of the bygone age when he was in his youth. He wore a powdered wig, a silk coat, knee-breeches, and one boot. His left leg was pegged, having been lost in an engagement of the Third Mysore War. The disability did not hinder him in the slightest, but endowed him with the rather fanciful aspect of an old privateer, beached by the storms of the Carib and living on the spoils of his endeavours. It must remain an amusing trifle, for the Dukes of Quince are of that ancient line which sprang up in the wake of Simon de Montfort and have interfered, more or less effectively, with the politics and the governing of the kingdom ever since.

But it was true that he had the soul of an adventurer, for he had served flamboyantly with his regiment until he was invalided out in 1792; he had survived three wives and dared to dangle for still a fourth, since his only offspring had been of the female sort, one who had died after six weeks of the endless ignominy of being unable to inherit. William John wanted a son, bedad, because he wanted his line to persevere. There were nephews, of course—three of them, and as sorry a lot as could be imagined: two psalm-singers and a rake. But he believed his own blood, though thinning, could still sire a son. He had already sired two outside the blanket, had he not? What he needed was a fresh start, a young country wench with a strong constitution and wide hips. God knows, there were enough women eager to marry him and become the 5th Duchess of Quince; but he wanted something better than the squint-eyed older daughters. He wanted his son in the worst way, but he also wanted a wife who would make the getting of the heir not a duty but a delight.

There were, it is true, other specifications. Since he expected to live a good long time, perhaps forever, he desired a helpmeet pleasant both in looks and temperament. He wanted not a society woman, nor a bluestocking, but something of each. He wanted a woman who could ride to hounds and who was accomplished in all the old, slow dances which his wooden appliance allowed him to tread. Edad, it was not easy finding a wife!

One of his favorite spots in the manor house was the library in the left wing which looked out over the garden toward the west. There on summer evenings he would often sit before the open window, pining for something but not knowing exactly what. It was not only the body urge which calls for a woman, nor even the desire for continuance which calls for a son, but something he could not put a name to.

Crosbie brought him his long-stemmed pipe and a glass of Madeira, setting the glass on a napkin on the table beside his master and holding the already-lighted pipe to his master's lips with an almost effortless instinct to please. He might have gone away then, but he lingered, became so obtrusive that the duke finally paid him the due of noticing him.

"Well, dammee, what are you hanging about for? Have you got nothing better to do?"

Crosbie was used to this sort of thing and paid it very little mind. He was not subservient by nature, but he had a great tolerance and affection for the duke. "If it please Your Grace, the woman is here."

"The woman? What woman? Don't act like a fool, Crosbie, Who is it?"

"The . . . ah . . . marriage broker, sir."

"Well? Well? You needn't shally about it like an old woman. A marriage broker is a good and useful creature at times. Perfectly honourable and useful!"

"Yes, m'lud, I will remember it."

"I daresay you will not. Where is she?"

Crosbie eyed the master warily. One never knew what his temper would be in the evening of a long day, and His Grace had been out on Shylock riding about the neighbourhood all afternoon. Crosbie had the feeling that His Grace had been looking over the crop of healthy farm girls. He shuddered at the thought of one of the locals becoming the Duchess of Quince.

"I have kept her in the anteroom, sir, until I discovered your wishes in the matter."

The duke's already prominent nostrils flared wider. "Then . . . bring . . . her . . . in," he said slowly and distinctly, as if he were speaking to an idiot.

The manservant was unperturbed. He had ascertained the duke's mood. It was only another normal evening. No better, no worse. "Very good, m'lud."

Mrs. Nightshade was a small, pretty woman of early middle years and trim, compact figure. The duke thought it a pity she was past the age of easy child-bearing, for he much liked her brisk and optimistic nature. In her profession she had every intention of pleasing, which she usually ended by doing, though she prided herself on speaking her mind exactly as things came into her head and without regard for position or authority. She was, therefore, undaunted by the duke's facade of cynical tolerance. For one thing, she didn't believe in it for a moment. His brusqueness flowed past her as easily as water and made as little impression. In her business she could not afford to be easily intimidated.

"I think I have found you just the right young woman,

sir," she told him. "Pretty as a sunbeam, rides like a young centauress, good family, pretty face, and mightily anxious to be the means of continuing a dynasty."

"Humph," said His Grace, "mightily interested in becoming a duchess is more like it. How are her hips?"

"Wide and strong, m'lud. To judge by her mother, she will fill out to be a handsome woman in middle age, but just for now she is as trim as you could ask. Name of Fairfax from over Biddecoombe way."

"The father?" the duke enquired.

"Deceased, sir, and that is the only drawback, for the mother is anxious to keep as much of the estate as possible for her own use."

He waved his pipe airly. "Wide and strong hips, you say? Well, the dowry is no great matter. An heiress would not come amiss, but it is no boot. I expect I will ride over Biddecoombe way in a day or two."

But Mrs. Nightshade shook her head. "They've gone off, sir, to take the waters."

"Ah, yes, the waters. Husband hunting, eh? Bath, I suppose. Or Cheltenham?"

"Cheyne Spa, sir."

He seemed almost pleased at this. "Ah, Cheyne. I have not visited there since old Beau Carlisle had the running of it and absconded with the funds he made by gambling. Two or three years, now."

"Five, Your Grace."

"What, eh?"

"It has been five years, sir, since the Beau was at Cheyne. And, if Your Grace will forgive me, it was not a matter of *absconding* with the money . . . He won it at the tables after his duties as Master of Ceremonies were done."

"Is that so?" asked His Grace roughly. "Well, dammee, woman, he absconded with a good deal of my silver, I can tell you that!"

"You will find it much changed," said she, quite unruffled. "They have some silly fop as Master of Ceremonies

59

now, and it is all masquerade balls, early rising and morning chocolate, the while they float about in that odiferous
water. For my part, I can't think how they can drink
anything with such a stink in their noses. The gambling has
quite declined, they say, and you know that it was quite
rampant when the Beau was there."

"Declined, has it? I don't know that that is not a rather
good thing."

"My lord, sir, you have gone mightily moral since we
spoke together last!"

"Not at all, madam, not at all. It is still a pretty town to
visit? Still a pleasure to walk about in? Gambling can be
revived, you know, if there are folk there with the where-
withal to indulge in it, laws or no laws!"

Mrs. Nightshade smiled slyly. "Your Grace is right as
ever. I expect it can, for it often has."

He almost smiled at this, but instead harrumphed and
looked thoughtful. "Well, then, when do you want to go?"

"At Your Grace's pleasure. I am at your disposal in this
matter."

Instead of ringing for him, the duke shouted out Crosbie's name at the top of his voice. Luckily, the manservant
was only a room or two away and came running.

"Yes, m'lud?"

"Thursday a week, Crosbie, we shall be leaving for
Cheyne Spa."

"I expect you mean yourself, sir, and the valet and,
perhaps, the coachman?"

"No, Crosbie, I do not. Do you never listen? I said 'we,'
man. I meant you and I." Then, as an afterthought, "but I
expect we had better have the coachman as well, though I
want no livery. Let him wear plain clothes. We are going
incognito."

"*Are* we, sir? May I ask, for what reason?"

"Because for just a little while I don't want to be a duke,
you demmed wax-nose! What difference does it make to
you, eh?"

Crosbie raised his eyebrows and rolled his eyes toward heaven. "I only asked, sir."

"Well, then, I will tell you more," thundered His Grace. "It is for your benefit as well that we are going. You look as if you would vastly benefit from the waters!"

Crosbie's aplomb was for once badly shaken. "Take the waters, sir? Me? Heaven forbid!"

Mrs. Nightshade's laugh followed him out of the room.

"No, no, Lady Kinsale, the rhythm is *one* two three, *one* two three, if you please. Try, if you can, to follow instead of leading."

"Oh, was I leading again, Mr. Marshall? I *am* sorry. I know that gentlemen prefer to give the direction. Have I mentioned, sir, that you have a very resonant voice? You do the orchestra very well indeed. Excepting the violins. I think you do not quite catch the violins."

Gavin, laughing, promptly lost the tune he was humming as they danced about Mrs. Maundy's drawing room. "It is the upper register, I expect," he said. "I was never comfortable up there with the sopranos and counter-tenors." He drew a deep breath. "Shall we sit down? I feel that we have been waltzing for hours."

"Oh, must we?" mourned Susanna. "I felt as if I were just about to catch the trick of it."

"Relaxation is the key, Lady Kinsale," he assured her as he led her toward the settee. She sank down upon it with a sigh of relief and looked at him with affection.

"I want to tell you how much I appreciate all you and your aunt have done for me, Mr. Marshall," she said. "I expect I am still very rough along the edges, but even *I* feel I have made some improvement."

He looked at her guardedly. The seeming withdrawal disconcerted her.

"Oh, what is it? Have I said something I ought not?"

He laughed. "It is sheer exhaustion, I expect. No, my dear lady, you have done nothing wrong. You are near perfect, as you always are." And, as if bestowing some sort of accolade, Gavin Marshall leaned quickly forward and kissed her lightly upon the mouth.

Susanna's eyes blazed. "That, I think, is not part of the tuition, sir!"

"Quite right, madam," he laughed. "That is what the Creoles call a *lagniappe*, a little something extra."

Her look would have frozen another man. "Extras, sir, are not required."

Lady Morphy entered with a tray upon which three wine glasses reposed beside a napkin-wrapped bottle. "It seemed to me that a bit of refreshment was in order," she announced. "I have been watching the two of you and you look quite beautiful together. You have quite mastered the *valse*, I think, Susanna."

"Mr. Marshall says that I tend toward leading."

Her ladyship smiled at this. "I should not be surprised. You are a very forceful young lady, my dear."

Gavin popped the cork and poured the pale wine into the glasses, then raised his own in a toast. "To the brightest and loveliest dancing pupil I have ever had," he said.

Why, Gavin, how appropriate," said his aunt. "I am sure it is true." She sipped slowly. "Susanna, you will be ready for your first ball on Thursday. Have you decided which of those lovely gowns you are going to wear?"

Susanna's hand flew to her lips. "Not only do I not know, but it has never even crossed my mind. You and Mr. Marshall have kept me so busy with lessons that I quite forgot about it."

"Calm, be calm," soothed Lady Morphy. "There is plenty of time, and Tibby is such a genius with your hair that I am sure you will look ravishing."

"You have done so well at your lessons, in fact," said Gavin, "that I am thinking of giving you a reward."

"A reward, Mr. Marshall? I have no need of that. I should be happy if only I could repay some of your kindness and give some recompense to you and your aunt."

"Perhaps you can some day," said her ladyship with a small, secret smile. "But what is the reward you promise to Lady Kinsale, Gavin?"

He grinned boyishly at the two of them. "What has Lady Kinsale been begging me to do all this while?" he asked.

Lady Morphy raised a delicate eyebrow. "I am sure *I* don't know, my dears. Susanna, what have you been begging of him?"

"I know, I know!" the girl cried with excitement. "It is the gambling rooms, isn't it? I do so much want to go there, and he kept saying it must wait until I have made a debut in the Upper Rooms."

"Are you a great gambler, then?" asked her ladyship. "I would never have suspected it."

"Oh, no," the pupil laughed. "I have never gambled in my life save for playing Fish-in-a-bowl at a church bazaar. It would not have done for the vicar's daughter."

Lady Morphy patted her hand in a motherly and encouraging fashion. "I am sure there were compensations, my sweet. No life is without its own charm, I always think."

But, energised by the wine, Susanna did not care to think of the dreariness of her past life. She held out her hand to Gavin. "Come along, Mr. Marshall, lesson time is not yet over . . . but mind you get the violins this time."

=8=

"BUT, MAMA, HE is old enough to be my grandfather!"

Mrs. Fairfax quickly clapped a warning hand over her daughter's lips. "I hope you will *never* say such a thing to an elderly gentleman's face! If a man is *that* old, you may allow him capable of being your father, and it will probably flatter him that he is still attractive to a young girl. But never say more than that. No handsome man was ever, in his own eyes, old enough to be a grandfather, even if he already was one. Give a man a chance at youth and he will *be* young—or at least he will not be entirely old."

"But if he is really a duke, why is he afraid to say so?" Cecily did not exactly whine, but it was close enough not to matter. "Surely he cannot be ashamed of it?"

Mrs. Fairfax shook her head slowly at the lack of subtlety in her offspring. "No, my sweet, he would not be ashamed of it, but I expect he wants to be certain he is loved for himself alone, and not for his title."

"But are they not the same thing in the long run of it? Especially in a man who is so old?"

Mrs. Fairfax almost ground her teeth, but she strove to be calm, for much rode upon this meeting. Dear Mrs. Nightshade had made such plans that it would be a pity to put them into disarray. "That may be, my darling. But if he chooses not to believe it, then you must allow that you do not believe it either. Men rather like being admired for the power they have attained, but not often for those advantages with which they were endowed at birth. They love their lineage, but believe they themselves have transcended it."

She eyed her daughter shrewdly. "Would you not like to be a duchess, Cecily?"

"Of course I would, Mama, how silly a dear you are!"

"Then you must pretend to the duke that it does not matter in the least that he is a duke, but only that he is the most fascinating man you have ever met. You must not lay all your cards out at once, of course. If you let him pursue you, you will have a stronger hand in the end."

"But what should I say to him?"

"You must pretend, dear, that the title does not really matter. You must pretend—Cecily, are you listening to me?"

The girl, startled, blinked her large blue eyes. "Listening, Mama? What else can I be doing?" Behind her mother's back she rolled her eyes heavenward. Mrs. Fairfax continued to pace about their chamber. "You must convince him that, while you honour his title, it is really nothing compared to your feeling for the man who bears it. Do you follow me?"

"Certainly I do, Mama, but he is still very old."

"He is also very rich," said Mrs. Fairfax firmly.

"Well, yes. That is a point, Mama."

The Pump Room at Cheyne Spa always had a convivial atmosphere. From the time of the Romans, I expect, the baths have led to a certain social intimacy. It could scarcely be avoided. One can hardly avoid chatting with someone to whom one has already been introduced while one is soaking up the medicinal effects of the waters and floating only five feet away. But it was with the invention of the Pump Room that the social aspect of the spa became paramount, and the thrice daily glass of mineral water was only an excuse for wandering about the room while one sipped. The Pump Room became the ideal rendezvous for both the sick and the well. In its humid atmosphere, people of *ton* and the least significant tradesmen could rub shoulders and think nothing of it. The brackish beverage was a mighty leveler.

The first meeting had been auspiciously arranged by Mrs. Nightshade after a considerable study of omens and signs. The participants, all well-briefed as to their actions, were intended to meet in a casual way and pretend that they had never before set eyes on each other, though His Grace had insisted on ogling Miss Fairfax from across St. Gerrans Gardens and Mrs. Fairfax had made sure her daughter could fairly well identify the duke with a blindfold over her eyes.

Nothing was left to chance, though it is certain that chance, or something very like it, saw fit to intervene.

The duke came there a trifle earlier than the appointed time and looked at the crush with horror. "No, Crosbie, you will not get *me* into the center of that melee! There is time enough to quaff that wretched stuff after the ladies have arrived!"

"What do you plan to do to pass the time, Your Grace? Mayn't I go back to the lodging-house?"

"The lodginghouse? Edad, no! Enjoy yourself, Crosbie. We are at Cheyne Spa!" He considered. "I tell you what, man, you hie yourself over to the White Hart there and bring us back two tankards of foaming ale. That should lighten your heart, eh?"

He positioned himself carefully upon a bench with a good view of the square, where he could amuse himself by watching the parade of strolling dandies and their lady-friends who passed by. It always gave him a chuckle that the bucks of this benighted age struck such excesses in the matter of their dress: coats cut to such an extreme that the wearers could scarcely raise their arms without ripping a seam, pantaloons so narrow and so fitted as to be untenably comfortless, collar so high that the points actually dug into the dandy's cheeks. Far better, he believed, were the good old English fashions of his own generation instead of this silly, Frenchified style. The old costumes were still comfortable and elegant so far as he was concerned, and still the only possible garb for a gentleman. The women, on the other hand, were something to watch. He quite approved of this new neo-classical mode, especially the habit of damping the muslin so that it more closely followed the line of the figure. Gave the gels a certain piquant charm, what? And gave an old dog the longing for new tricks.

But what the devil was this? Did he see his nevvy, that rake Gavin, coming along toward him, promenading along with two women on his arms? The sly dog! But when the trio came closer he saw that the female on the right, who was taking refuge under a huge brimmed hat to escape the sun, was none other than his own sister, Clementina, Lady Morphy!

But who was that devilishly handsome creature with them, who moved like a classical goddess?

He raised his hand and waved jovially. "Hello, Clemmie, old thing. How have you been keeping?" He rose and kissed her hand.

Lady Morphy surveyed him dispassionately through a quizzing-glass. "Old thing, yourself," she said. "What on earth has dragged you out of the fastness of the country and into the whirl? I had it in my mind to come down for a visit, but I see that my plans have been superseded."

"Just here to take the waters," the duke said evasively. "Doctor thinks I need a constitutional, you know." He could hardly take his eyes off the handsome creature on Gavin's other arm.

"Hullo, Gavin, my boy," he said heartily, and waited to be introduced to the charmer; but no such introduction seemed immediately forthcoming, for here was Crosbie with the two foaming tankards.

"Sorry to be so long, my lord."

"Taking the waters, are you?" asked Lady Morphy. "What an old fraud you are, William John."

"Not so old as all that, I hope," he answered with a faint warning note in his voice, which suggested that this was not to him a pleasing topic, especially in the presence of an unknown beauty. He turned to Susanna with a determined twinkle in his eye.

"Since neither of my relatives seems eager to introduce us, madam, let me present myself . . ."

"This is Lady Kinsale, William John, a recently bereaved lady from Bleet who has come here for her health and for no other reason. I do not believe she is quite ready for your rather hurly-burly way of doing things. Ladt Kinsale, may I present my brother, the . . ."

"Mr. Mobray-Marshall, your ladyship, at your service," the duke interposed quickly. "Just a plain man from a small and plain town."

"And what town would that be, sir?" asked Susanna cordially. She knew perfectly well who he was, of course, for he was quite a public figure. But she rather liked what she had heard of the old rascal; certainly she meant to cause him no embarrassment.

All the same it was rather amazing to the three, and to Crosbie as well, to hear him floundering about for the name of a town, any town but his own, where he might make his home if he were not the Duke of Quince. "Why, ah . . . Burriton . . . yes, I am from the town of Burriton," he extemporised, though he had never been there and had no idea how the name had popped into his head. "In the West Country, you know."

Susanna's throaty chuckle entranced him even while her words proved vastly disconcerting. "Why, yes, I do know," she said. "I have an aunt at Burriton, a Mrs. Jowan Smith. Perhaps you know her?"

The duke scowled and pretended to cogitate, plucking at his lip. "Perhaps I do. A small, pert woman . . . like a pretty partridge?"

Susanna, who had no aunt in Burriton or anywhere else, but believed that his fabrication might well be met by one of her own, clapped her hands together joyously. "What a small world it is, after all! I believe I remember my aunt mentioning your name, sir. You are an apothecary, are you not?"

"Oh, just a farmer, your ladyship. A gentleman farmer."

The girl nodded affably and tried to keep a straight face, but it proved beyond her powers and she began to laugh out loud. "It is of no earthly use, Your Grace, I know perfectly well who you are as, I am sure, do half the people here. But I shall keep your secret if you wish me to."

"Oh, pshaw! Do you really think they all know me?" He sighed. "What a bore, to be sure. I suppose I shall never have a moment's peace, then, as long as I stay."

"That depends upon you," said his sister. "I believe most people are willing to respect an incognito, if only to demonstrate how much within the inner circle they are." Lady Morphy suddenly looked past her brother. "Oh, there is Mrs. Fairfax. I wonder why she keeps looking this way and grimacing in that absurb fashion?" She waved at the Fairfaxes and motioned them toward her. "Irene, dear, come!"

"Oh, I say," said His Grace, "I wish you had not."

"Why ever? Irene is my dearest friend, as well you know!" And as the mother and daughter approached, she ran forward and embraced them, kissing cheeks. "Irene, my dear, do you know who this is? Do you see who is here? This is my brother, William John." She gurgled a little laugh. "Sometimes known as the Duke of Quince! William John, this is Mrs. Fairfax and her lovely daughter, Miss Cecily Fairfax, of whom you have so often heard me speak."

The duke bowed gracefully, though he had a rather hunted look. "I am truly delighted to make the acquaintance of such lovely ladies." His eyes quickly raked over Cecily, then flew back to Susanna. Reaching out, he took Susanna's hand in his, tucking it firmly under his arm. "May I offer you a glass of the Cheyne water, Lady Kinsale?" he asked. "I understand it is said to be a sovereign remedy for any ill, in any portion of the body. I daresay, though, that you have little need for such things." Beaming, he led her away without so much as a backward glance.

"Well!" said Mrs. Fairfax, "really! Who in the world *is* that hussy, Clementina? I have never seen such a brazen creature in my life!"

Lady Morphy turned to her slowly and shivered her with a look. "Lady Kinsale," she said coldly, "is the widow of a very dear friend of mine as well as being the daughter of the Lieutenant-General of Ireland, an hereditary position. I can assure you, Irene, that she is no hussy!" And with that, she turned upon her heel and walked away, leaving the Fairfaxes open-mouthed.

"Who in the world is the Lieutenant-General of Ireland?" asked Gavin as he escorted her toward the pump and waited while their glasses were slowly filled. "Is there such a position?"

"I have no idea," said her ladyship, "but if there is not, there should be."

"What did you think of Susanna? I thought she did rather well, considering that it was all on the spur of the moment."

His aunt favoured him with a pitying look. "My dear, what ever are you babbling about? Do you think I would risk our most valuable asset on a mere chance encounter?"

Gavin looked perplexed. "Do you mean to say that you knew Uncle William John was going to be here today? How could you possibly?"

"Do you see that small, dark woman speaking to the Fairfaxes?"

He nodded. "But what have . . . "

His aunt shushed him with a upraised finger. "Her name is Mrs. Nightshade and she has a deserved reputation as the foremost marriage broker in Somerset."

He began to understand. "And she brought them together?"

"That is what a marriage broker does, my dear, brings

people together." But her cat-in-the-cream expression gave her away.

"So instead of the Fairfax family, her first duty is toward you?" he asked.

"I suppose you might say that. She promises satisfaction to the highest bidder."

"Guarantees it, do you mean?"

His aunt looked at him again. "Pray do not be frivolous. Who but a mad person would make an absolute guarantee in matters such as this? For that matter, who would extract it? My only protection is that we have paid her much more than Irene Fairfax has done."

Gavin raised an inquisitive eyebrow. " 'We,' aunt?"

She patted his arm. "I knew you would want to share the cost."

"But what about Miss Archer . . . " He paused and amended his question as she gave a discreet shake of her head from side to side. "What about Lady Kinsale? When are we going to bring her further into the plan?"

"Very soon, my dear."

Gavin glanced back at the Fairfaxes, who were deep in acrimonious conversation with the marriage broker. "I feel rather sorry for Cecily. It must have been a major set-down to be so definitely snubbed."

"I cannot think you should waste too much sympathy on little Cecily," counselled his aunt. "There is always Patrick Wycombe, and I am sure she would prefer him, even if her mother would not."

The idea made Gavin's sympathies shift. "Then poor Patrick, I say. He is so sunny-tempered and good-hearted that I doubt he could withstand such a combined onslaught. Mrs. Nightshade has a deucedly efficient look about her."

"I believed it is a deserved reputation," Lady Morphy agreed. "One of these days I shall turn her loose upon you! It should be an amusing chase. Quite as good as the Norfolk hunt!"

=== 9 ===

THE THREE NEIGHBOURS were gathered together in Susanna's sitting room to discuss the aftermath of the day's outing. "How did you feel, Susanna?" Lady Morphy asked. "No butterflies in your stomach, I hope?"

The girl shook her head. "It was all rather like play-acting. I know I should have taken it more seriously, but somehow I could not. It was neither like real life nor so solemn as I expect it is in more stringent surroundings."

"You felt secure, then?"

"Secure, madam? I do not follow you."

Lady Morphy tried not to seem impatient. "I mean to say that you were not unduly nervous nor afraid to let yourself flow with the play of the hand?" She couched her thought in gambling terms, knowing that Susanna was likely to understand the sense if not the literal meaning, and wishing, as well, to let the cant of the card rooms become a part of the girl's common vocabulary as it was with most of polite society.

"Oh, it all seemed very easy to me. The worst was being faced with Mrs. Fairfax and Miss Cecily again, but I do not believe they thought anything amiss, do you, Mr. Marshall?"

Gavin, who had only been half listening, turned when he heard his name. "Will you look at that, now," he said, looking down into the street.

"What is it?" Lady Morphy asked. "I do wish you would

come and sit down. It is very difficult carrying on a conversation with one who is not attending."

"I think you will be rather interested in this," he answered. "Just come and see if you identify this crest."

The two women crossed to the window and, pulling back the curtain, Lady Morphy peered out into the late afternoon sunshine. "Good Lord," she said, "I could not be more surprised."

"I suppose we can guess to whom a call is about to be paid?" asked Gavin. "What are we to do?"

Lady Morphy turned to Susanna. "Forgive us, my dear. A little family business has arisen." To Gavin she instructed, "Go at once to Mrs. Maundy and say that she is to tell the person at the door that neither of the persons asked for are at home to visitors at present." He nodded. "You understand me?"

Gavin grinned. "Oh, yes, there is no doubt in my mind. You will proceed here?"

"Of course." And after this mysterious colloquy she returned to her teacup and the conversation with Susanna.

"You will find," she said, "that the Dress Ball, handsome and impressive as it is likely to be, is nevertheless immensely crowded until quite late in the evening. You cannot see the company for the crowds. Early on, it is quite different, for the number of card parties quite spoil it. One is expected to attend four or five before one goes to the ballroom. I suppose it is reckoned quite vulgar to come early. People are such fools. The rooms are not half so agreeable as they were a few years ago when the late London hours were not thought of."

"It does sound rather daunting," Susanna agreed. "Is there another night which is more suitable?"

"Decidedly so," said her ladyship. "It is best, in my opinion, to begin your introduction at the Thursday Cotillion Ball. It is more select, for one thing, and only country dances are allowed for another. It will allow you to be more comfortable in company before you must venture the *valse* in public."

"Oh, I think she has become quite proficient at waltzing," protested Gavin who had heard this as he came back through the door. "I have undoubtedly given her my best tuition."

"I am certain of it," said his aunt, "but the deciding factor is that today is Wednesday and the Cotillion Ball is tomorrow evening, while the Dress Ball is not until Monday next. Do you propose that we wait until then?"

"Well, no," he admitted. "The quarry may be gone away again by then, if one considers his erratic habits."

His aunt frowned and shook her head warningly, but the damage had already been done. "Quarry?" asked Susanna.

"See what you have done!" said Lady Morphy sharply to Gavin. "Kindly allow this to remain in my hands." Then to Susanna she said, "It seems the cat is about to leap out of the bag, my dear. Gavin was referring, in a rather disrespectful way, to my brother."

"The duke? What a nice man he is!" the girl said enthusiastically. Then she knit her brow. "But why do you call him the quarry?"

Lady Morphy ignored this last question, preferring to respond to the enthusiasm. "So you like William John, do you? I myself have always thought him my favourite brother, though I am, of course, sorry the others have died."

She seemed suddenly a little tense, almost as though she were approaching a difficult subject. "Since we have all become friends, Susanna, may I ask a rather personal question?"

Susanna looked a little surprised. "Why, I suppose so, Your Grace. You have both been so kind to me that I could hardly refuse."

Gavin and Lady Morphy exchanged questioning glances. He nodded slightly and she went on diffidently. "My dear, since we all know you have come here to . . . well, shall we say . . ."

"I have come here, your ladyship, in search of a husband," Susanna said calmly. "I think we all know that. There is no mystery about it, is there?"

Lady Morphy nodded, happy to have got over *that* difficulty, and moved on to the next. "I think you know me well enough to know that I have no dire motive in mind," she went on, "but have you considered the *sort* of man you ought to be looking for?"

"What my aunt means," Gavin interposed, "is that surely it is as easy to love a rich man as a poor one—perhaps even easier, all things considered."

Susanna took this bold sortie in good spirit. "So that is it? You hope to ride on my coattails? I wondered why you were taking such great pains with me. I believe in disinterestedness in friendship, but yours went just a bit too far. I was beginning to believe you just the slightest bit of a saint, your ladyship, and I had a bit of difficulty in accepting it altogether."

Gavin broke in again. "There is no lack of friendship here, Susanna. Please believe that my aunt and I are quite willing to give up our project or, at least, postpone it to another season if you choose not to join us."

"Your plan being, I suspect, that I allow myself to succumb to the duke?"

He flushed. "She is quick, is she not, aunt?"

Her ladyship was marginally more diplomatic. "We are not in the position of auctioning you off to the highest bidder, my dear, but the fact remains that my brother has a great deal of money and two heirs in line for it before Gavin. With even a substantial settlement upon a new duchess, they would lose comparatively little. And if that settlement were to be divided into three, there would still be a handsome amount for each of us and more when he passes on his way."

"To heaven, do you mean?" Susanna asked drily.

"Wherever," said Gavin. "The fact remains that you would be a rich woman."

"And supposing I produced a son? Would that not put you out?"

He laughed. "Oh, not at all. You would undoubtedly be the guardian."

"And we would divide the profits among us?"

"Just the three of us," said Lady Morphy.

"Four," said Susanna. "Tibby is in this as much as I am."

"Tibby?" asked her ladyship. "What a droll idea."

"Tibby," said Susanna, "and there is one further stipulation."

"Indeed?" asked Gavin. "What might that be?"

"If there should be a child, all promises are void."

Lady Morphy gasped. "What on earth do you mean . . . void?"

"I would not raid my own child's inheritance for you or for anyone else," said Susanna. "If it were to be a girl, of course, and there were no question of inheritance, the money we gained would be portioned into five, is that agreed?"

"Not entirely," said Gavin, "but it is certainly open to negotiation." He poured himself a glass of cordial from the sideboard and raised it in a mock toast. "To the success of our enterprise."

"I mean it, Mr. Marshall," Susanna warned.

"Well," he said, "we shall see how it all falls out. For our part I think we should ask for certain guarantees. The foremost of which is that if we should run into difficulties—and we might, you know; Cecily Fairfax is a force to be reckoned with—this will remain a secret between the three of us."

"Four," said Susanna. "Tibby will be as silent as I am. But," she added, "we can stop at this point, if you like, with the understanding that I will say nothing and leave you where you were before I came. There are other wealthy men and, though the duke is pleasant enough, I have no *overwhelming* desire to be a duchess."

Both conspirators looked at her with surprise. "But," Susanna suggested, "why do we not wait a few days and see how it all falls out? The fancy His Grace seems to have taken to me may well only be a momentary infatuation to which, I have heard it said, all men are subject."

There was nothing to do but to agree among themselves upon that point; but, as the others were leaving the sitting room, Susanna asked one final question. "It was the duke's coach you saw in the street?"

"Yes," said Gavin. "I thought it best to let him . . ."

"I know what you thought," Susanna said, "and I daresay you were quite right."

Later, with Tibby, Susanna was in a state of near exhaustion. Tibby, who had heard it all from the sleeping chamber, was loud in her praise.

"I don't know how you did it so cool, miss, really I don't. I was all in a state just listening to you."

"I don't know exactly how I did it myself, Tib. And, to tell you the truth, I don't know what I think of myself for having said it. It was not altogether pleasant finding out I was no better than I should be. Hardly the kind of behaviour expected of a vicar's daughter. Perhaps we should never have come here, after all."

Tibby, who had begun to remove the pins from her mistress's hair, considered this for a moment. "Well, one thing was said, miss . . . I mean, your ladyship . . . that cannot be disagreed with."

"Really, and what was that?"

Tibby took up the hairbrush and began to stroke the long, lustrous hair as she repeated Gavin Marshall's words. "It is as easy to love a rich man as a poor one, miss. I heard my own mam say that many a time, and I believe it. My mam always felt she married down in the world, you see."

"I thought your mother was a witch, Tibby?"

"So she was, miss, but my father was only a farmer withouten no family to speak of and my mam could trace back through ten generations—through the mothers, of course, as the Wicca count. There is no lineage through the fathers there."

"Through the mothers? How very odd."

"Yes, miss, perhaps it is and perhaps it isn't. I mean, one always knows the mother, doesn't one?"

Quite unassailable logic.

"So you think I should consider the duke if he asks me? Not that he has done more than pat my hand so far, you know."

Tibby caught up the hair and began to plait it becomingly. "I should think, miss . . . your ladyship . . . the duke is not the only man in Cheyne Spa, let alone the world, is he? I expect there will be more than one chap who will think you are pretty tippy, and why limit the field to just one? Allowing a few gentlemen to call might even encourage the old duke, might it not?"

Susanna unaccountably thought of Patrick Wycombe's sunny charm and good looks. "Yes, Tib, that is certainly true. There may be many gentlemen out there. And the bargain I struck did concern only the duke, didn't it? There is nothing binding about anyone else."

"Not even anything binding about the duke, miss. All you did was agree to wait and see."

Susanna smiled in sudden relief. "Then that is just what we shall do, Tibby. We shall wait and see."

= 10 =

UTILISING HER NEW subscription, which allowed her the run of the reading and card rooms during the day, Susanna wandered about the Assembly Rooms with Tibby in attendance until she was familiar with their configurations and felt she need not be nervous in unfamiliar surroundings. Unlike that of the famous Almack's Club in London, the ballroom in Cheyne Spa was quite undistinguished in its decoration. Though architecturally handsome, it depended upon the costumes of the guests to lend colour and piquancy to the scene during the evenings. But the rules of dress and conduct were equally as strict as those of Almack's; for Beau Carlisle, who had quite revitalised the town while he was Master of Ceremonies, had been adamant about certain things:

> Neither boots nor half boots are to be worn at the balls, and trowsers or coloured pantaloons are not permitted on any account.

Or, again, for the distaff side:

> Ladies who do not dance minuets are requested not to take up the front seats at the balls.

It was a well regulated society, Susanna decided, as she read through the list of do's and don'ts, and it would do her well to rely upon the greater knowledge of Lady Morphy and her nephew rather than attempt the social swim all alone. Turning away from the board upon which the list was posted, she found herself staring into a handsome, smiling face.

"Good afternoon, your ladyship," the gentleman said genially, doffing his hat. "My name is Patrick Wycombe. I hope that you remember we were introduced in the Gardens a day or two ago."

Instinctively her hand flew up as if to adjust the octagonal spectacles which had adorned her nose for so long, but she compromised by brushing in a coquettish way at the wisps of hair at her temple. From somewhere behind her she could hear Tibby clearing her throat lightly, and she took courage in the realisation that she was not alone in this.

"Why, yes, Mr. Wycombe, I believe I do remember you. You were squiring that pretty Miss Fairfax, were you not?"

It was amusing to find that a gentleman could blush as easily as a lady, she decided, when his courtly manner turned into a stammer. "Why . . . you see . . . the fact is that Miss Fairfax and I are merely friends, you know."

"*Good* friends, I believe," Susanna said mischievously and watched his confusion mount even higher, his deeply tanned good looks turning almost a pale terra cotta with embarrassment.

"I assure your ladyship that I . . ."

Susanna almost giggled, aware of a sudden surge of power. So this was what the tyranny of an attractive woman could reduce a man to. She began to sense something of that which drove creatures such as Cecily Fairfax to their ridiculous antics, but, scorning to intimidate him further, she extended her hand for him to kiss.

"Perhaps your ladyship would care to stroll along the river? Or tea, perhaps? Would your ladyship care to visit St. Gerrans's Gardens for tea?"

"No, I do not think it would be proper, Mr. Wycombe.

Why, I scarcely know you," she managed to say without laughing.

But he was not deterred. "I do not know what they do in . . . in Bleet, was it, your ladyship? . . . But in places like Cheyne Spa it is considered quite acceptable for a lady to walk about the town with a gentleman, particularly if they have already been properly introduced, and particularly . . ."

"And particularly if the lady has brought her maid along to act as duenna," continued Susanna, "and Tibby is very proper. Very well, Mr. Wycombe, let us walk along the river and then you may offer me tea at St. Gerrans's Gardens."

"Capital!" said Patrick. Then turning back to the little maidservant, he said, "Come along, Tibby, you shall have tea as well if you want it," and he laughed almost triumphantly.

There was an answering triumph inside Susan Archer, for in all her years she had never heard a man sound that particular way because of her. For a little while they walked along the river while he asked her all the usual questions about her childhood, her husband, her impressions of Cheyne Spa, and she answered in the way she had been coached by her tutors: evasively in the first instance, embroidering in the second, and enthusiastically in the third. For his part, Patrick Wycombe told her how much she had impressed him from the very first instant he laid eyes on her. She did not dare meet Tibby's look.

On Lower Valentine Street one of the shopfronts had been turned into a tiny theatre entrance which advertised magic lantern shows within. They paused outside to look at the painted representations of the wonders to be found inside, and Susanna was entranced. "I haven't seen one of these since I was a child."

"Is that an invitation?" asked Patrick. "Can I lure you into being a child again?"

He paid the three admissions, but Tibby hung back nervously. "Oh, I don't know, mi . . . milady. I've never been in one of these places before. It looks all dark in there."

"Your eyes will grow accustomed to it very quickly," Susanna promised. Following Patrick's lead, they stepped into the dim interior, Tibby trailing nervously behind. Settling into their seats, they watched in turn painted representations of the Alps, the palace of Versailles and the Piazza San Marco in Venice, all presented in some ingenious way which rendered them three-dimensional and so immediate that one could almost reach out to touch them. These were followed by a shadow play of that pretty tale, *Rose White and Rose Red*, and finally a varied and exciting Chinese Show of Fireworks which were safely produced by the manipulation of a series of paper circles with pinpoints, slits and diamond-shaped holes cut into them. With the paraffin lamp behind them, they presented an exciting illusion of dazzling fire in stars, pinwheels and showers.

When the program came to an end, Susanna and Patrick rose to leave the theatre, but Tibby remained rooted in her seat. "Oh, I don't want to go! Oh, please, miss, I don't want to go!"

"But, Tib, we must. They need to empty the theatre so that a new audience can come in."

"Oh, no, your ladyship. Please, sir, couldn't I see it again?"

"I think that can be arranged," said Patrick, looking to Susanna for permission to do so.

She agreed. "But mind you go directly back to Upper Orson Street when it is done," she warned.

Thus it fell out that Susanna and Patrick continued their walk alone, and went to sit in St. Gerrans's Gardens alone and drank tea and ate cakes alone; and Susanna was scarcely certain when they had done, what they had said, or where they had been, or how much time had passed, except that the summer afternoon was over and she was still alone with this gentleman.

"Shall you be at the Cotillion Ball this evening?" he asked, "Or is it still too soon after . . ."

"After what?" Susanna asked, perplexed by his air of concern.

He flushed again in that engaging way. "You know, your ladyship . . . I mean since your husband's passing."

To tell the truth, Susanna had quite neglected her fictional husband. For most of the afternoon she had scarcely given him a thought. It was difficult to assume a sad face after so much jollity as they had had, but the very shadow of confusion which crossed her face must have seemed to Patrick Wycombe to be the shading of grief, for he at once apologised.

"My dear Lady Kinsale, do forgive my clumsiness. Of course you will not be at the ball. What could I have been thinking of?"

Susanna guessed that if she once allowed Lady Kinsale to sink into the morass of bereavement, she would never dare emerge again while at Cheyne Spa. Looking as courageous as she could, raising her chin just a trifle as if to face the world, she said, "We must all learn to put sadness behind us, must we not, Mr. Wycombe? Of course I shall be at the Cotillion Ball."

"What a stout-hearted little thing you are," he said admiringly. "I shall look forward to keeping you company as you watch the dancers. They have special seating there for those who do not wish to actually participate."

"Oh, but I do intend to participate. I feel I must!"

He reached out and squeezed her shoulder firmly. "What a plucky little soldier."

Like the Dress Balls, the Cotillion was not expected to move into full swing until all the card parties had been visited and the new gossip exchanged. Which was lucky, for when Susanna hurried up the stairs, almost tripping over Mrs. Maundy's black kitten, there was very little time in which to prepare for the evening's festivities. Lady Morphy in deshabille was, half angrily, pacing about Susanna's sitting room and when the girl entered she almost flew at her.

"Here you are at last! Are you all right? I was so afraid something had happened since Tibby came home two hours ago."

"Yes, I am all right. I suppose it was indiscreet of me, but I have had a very pleasant afternoon."

"With Patrick Wycombe," said her ladyship. "Yes, I heard."

"I daresay I should have kept Tibby with me."

"It was not from Tibby that I heard it. Dear Irene Fairfax felt it her duty to call my attention to the fact that you were taking tea alone with Mr. Wycombe."

"Ah, and I suppose I am ruined? I saw many ladies there with gentlemen."

Lady Morphy snorted. "Don't be absurd. Of course you did. Just as I told Irene, it is perfectly acceptable for a lady to be with a gentleman in the afternoon, particularly in a public place. It is when one is alone with a gentleman after dark that the gossip begins. I hope you will not set our chances spinning for a whim?"

"Of course I would not," Susanna answered.

"Oh, there you are, miss," said Tibby coming into the room. "I fancied I heard your voice. Your hot water cans are all ready to be poured and you have only to decide which of the gowns you will be wearing tonight."

"I will decide that," said Lady Morphy. "You slip into your bath."

As Tibby poured the water, scrubbed and sluiced her mistress, Susanna thought back across the afternoon. Had she imagined it, or had it been quite the most enchanting afternoon she had ever spent? Patrick was virile and handsome, an utterly delightful gentleman, just as she had always thought he would be. She was glad she had reserved the time to consider before entering into an involvement with the Duke of Quince. Patrick Wycombe's wealth might not be so astronomically vast as that of His Grace, but she imagined that it must be considerable. And he had made it quite obvious that he was taken with her.

And, she could now afford to admit to herself, she had always been taken with him.

But then she had been Miss Archer, and now she was Lady Kinsale. Patrick Wycombe had never known that Miss Archer was even alive. It was Lady Kinsale to whom he was attracted.

The gown her ladyship had selected was an evening dress in half-mourning. It would remind whomsoever would require it that Lady Kinsale was a respectable widow and not to be taken liberties with. The gown was a white crape round dress over a white sarsenet slip. The reminder of mourning came from the jet trim and the slight embroidery in black all around the hem. There was a necklace and earrings of jet and armlets to correspond. The headdress, *la toque de Ninon*, was ornamented with white ostrich feathers and a jet butterfly. Susanna would rather have been in some simple classical gown, but that sort of thing was reserved for the Dress Ball on Mondays.

"Oh, you do look tippy," sighed Tibby. "Ain't she a picture, your ladyship."

"She is indeed. Quite fashionable. How lucky we are that Lady Wycombe was possessed of such exquisite taste. One would think that she had the forethought to look ahead and see this very evening. Luckily, this is not one shown the Fairfax ladies at Wycombe Hall. We do not wish to tempt fate."

Lady Morphy was herself rather splendid in a deep wine-coloured *gros de Naples* with a matching wrap of lace, and when Gavin appeared, in his knee breeches and satin coat, they made an impressive trio.

As predicted, the Assembly Rooms were already beginning to be filled when they arrived. But Lady Morphy had chosen the time well, for there were neither too few nor too many who saw Susanna's arrival into the mélange of polite society. The men in the room, of course, were under her spell from the beginning; but within only a little while, prompted by the whispering campaign initiated by Lady Morphy, the ladies as well were singing her praises.

"Widow of the Lieutenant-General of Ireland, you know," and no one seemed to question the fact that she made no pretense of ever having been in Ireland in her life. Nor did they even put two and two together to see where the seams were not quite smooth. It appeared to be enough that she was new to them—a novelty, and fashionable, and quite, quite beautiful in a faintly unconventional way that made her all the more attractive to them.

"She has so few friends here, I believe, since dear Edmund passed away."

"Edmund?" murmured Susanna to herself. "What name *did* I give my husband when I was talking to Mr. Wycombe?"

It was Gavin Marshall who undertook to run her through her initial paces. He danced with her a bit, took her through a minuet and the first figure of a counter-dance; but he could, of course, dance only twice with her without exciting comment or lending the belief that they were engaged to one another. It was no matter; others were eager enough to partner her. Later Gavin undertook to escort her through the rooms until she should feel at ease among them. This was, it became apparent, not merely a charitable impulse upon his part.

"I believe I have heard," he mentioned as they left the card-room, "that you spent a considerable time this afternoon with my friend, Mr. Wycombe."

"Yes," she answered brightly. "He gave me tea and proved himself to be quite a charming gentleman."

He fell silent for a moment, then said a little diffidently,

"I hope you will understand when I say that I believe it to be a poor association."

"Do you, indeed?" She was rather taken aback by his temerity which verged upon impertinence. "I hardly consider that that is something for you to decide, Mr. Marshall. You, your aunt and I have not yet settled any sort of arrangement between us. I have explained to you that I will consider your proposition, but I have agreed to nothing."

He led her out upon the terrace where, along with other couples, they gazed down upon the lovely tints of the setting sun reflected in the waters of the river. "I think you mistake my meaning," he said, and explained. "I do not make reference to our 'arrangement' one way or the other, but to Mr. Wycombe, who is my friend."

"Whatever can you mean? If he is your friend, I hope you do not mean to slander him to me, for that would certainly prejudice me against any purpose you may have in mind concerning . . . concerning another person." She dropped her voice upon these last words and looked about, but no one was near enough to have heard her.

"Your forthrightness does you credit, Miss Archer," he answered in the same low tone, "but I was not thinking of the effect of my words upon the other matter, fulfilled or unfulfilled, but of yours upon Mr. Wycombe."

She stared at him, aghast. "What a terrible thing to suggest. Do you think I mean him harm?"

"Come, come, my dear, honour among thieves and all that. Mr. Wycombe is a gentleman of some substance, and so open-hearted that he is something of an easy target. He is also one of my few remaining friends and I do not wish to see him hurt."

"Then you think me injurious to him."

He paused, considered, then said in reply, "Like myself, Miss Archer, you have a keen eye for the future. You take my meaning?"

"All too well, sir. You think me as scheming as yourself," she answered hotly.

"Let us say, my dear colleague, that we are at bottom well matched, being two of a kind." Glancing back toward the doors to the ball room, his tone changed sharply. "Ah," he said, "see who is coming our way. Be on your best behaviour, partner."

The Duke of Quince, Susanna thought as he approached them, was certainly a distinguished looking man. It was true that his handsome face was somewhat lined with the marks of experience, but his disability spoke of valour. There was in his nature none of the extreme pride which marked the dispositions of many men of his rank and lineage; no arrogance arose from his vast wealth and power.

"Well, my boy," he called out to Gavin, "I see you have swept away the very centerpiece of the assembly. Do you not think it only fair play to allow the rest of us a chance to win the lady's smile?"

"I bow to your request, Uncle," Gavin responded graciously. "I expect the lady longs for the thrill of the crowd rather than the importunities of a lone suitor."

"Then she must, by all means, come back inside. Will you, my dear? What say you honour me with a minuet, which I believe is next on the list and which I still dance superlatively, despite all."

She gave him her hand. "With pleasure, sir."

She did not look back, but as he led her away the duke stole a look at her pensive face. "It seems to me that when I found you, there was some difficulty with young Gavin, was there? Has the young dog been abusing you in some way?"

She almost stumbled over the words to bring out the denial. "Oh, la, no, sir! No one could have been kinder to me than your sister and Mr. Marshall. He was merely concerned that I understand the conventions of Cheyne Spa society, so that I might not put my foot wrong so early in my visit."

The older man snorted. "Very kind of him, I am sure!"

"I think it is," she said.

"I don't know that I'd put too much stock in that young puppy if I were you, dear girl. His record with the ladies is not altogether spotless."

Knowing something of the duke's own matrimonial adventures, and guessing something of his past romances from the very dash with which he carried himself, Susanna held her tongue.

As they entered the room again, a thread of vagrant conversation floated toward them—"Good Lord, what is he *doing* here?"—and was as quickly gone. The odd thing was the way in which the verbal emphasis fell. Not "*What* is he . . ?" nor even ". . . doing *here?*" No, the very intonation of the phrase was imbued with a kind of fearful intensity. She looked about, interested to see who it was that inspired such a reaction.

But the response was entirely conversational. From the vicinity of the entrance door there was a small commotion and a deep, carrying voice said forcefully, "Get out of my way, you toad, or I shall *put* you out of the way!" The crowd fell back and Susanna was staring at a tall, hawk-nosed man who would have been startlingly handsome except that the left side of his face was terrible scarred, with angry red welts puckering it out of shape.

"Edad," said the Duke of Quince, half under his breath, "it is Cumberland. What the devil is *he* doing here?"

=== 11 ===

IT IS LIKELY that if a poll were taken as to the most publicly abhorred man in England, then Ernest Augustus, Duke of Cumberland, would have won hands down. This was not altogether a just situation, for there is no doubt that the fifth of George III's sons was the consistent target of political attack. But it was also true that, as the Prince Regent himself was once heard to remark, "In reference to anything in which a female is concerned, there is no believing anything he says." Little boys were still being threatened that "Old Boney" would get them if they did not behave, but little girls might well be frightened into virtue by the name of Cumberland and his badly scarred face.

The minuet which Susanna danced with the older duke was to that lovely tune of Fielding's, "Hark, Ye Shepherds, Dance," and Quince had spoken no boast when he vaunted his dancing prowess. The loss of his leg seemed not to bother him at all, so secure was he upon its wooden replacement. Susanna, who had been unworthily afraid that they might provide a spectacle for the onlookers, soon discovered that no one paid heed to that at all; though she soon became supremely aware that they were being closely regarded by many eyes for quite a different reason, one over which she could exercise little control.

She had become acutely aware of the attention being paid her by the aquiline-nosed gentleman who had created the disturbance. It made her rather uncomfortable to be so regarded, and imparted a distinct chill to her spine. There seemed to emanate from him a certain power, a highly charged energy which others about him sadly lacked. She thought of old legends which featured sorcerers or magicians and, though she chided herself for silliness, he did have the distinct aspect of evil genius. It dismayed her that his attention was riveted upon herself.

When the minuet was finished and Quince began to lead her from the floor, something sparked in Cumberland's eyes. Against all rules of polite conduct, he strode across the room, directly in their path.

"One moment, Quince, if you please. Will you not introduce me to this lady who dances so superlatively?"

The old duke's eyes blazed and it seemed, for a moment, as if he were going to make some terrible reply; but he remembered himself (the sequence could be seen in his face) and held his tongue except to say grudgingly, "Your Grace, may I present Lady Kinsale? My lady, His Grace, the Duke of Cumberland and Earl of Armagh."

"A very great boon, Quince," said the Regent's brother patronisingly, as if dismissing the older man. "Madame, may I claim the honour of this dance?"

Susanna had had the rules of polite society drilled into her by her mentor, Lady Morphy, and she knew that, much as she would have preferred to refuse, she had little option but to dance with this notorious man. A refusal would not only have offended him, but it would have put her in the position of dancing no more this evening with anyone at all. Her eyes searched frantically for Lady Morphy, looking, if not for rescue, then for some sort of advice. But there was no hope in view. Curtseying gracefully, she allowed the peer to lead her back upon the floor.

Luckily, he did not press her to conversation, rather seeming to let her become accustomed to his presence. At last he spoke in a dry, sardonic fashion. "I am not good at the demmed chit-chat, I admit, your ladyship, but I wish you could at least try to look less like a page from *The Book of Martyrs*. I am not at all a bad chap when you get to know me, and I can be particularly charming to pretty women like yourself."

Susanna willed herself to go through the motions of the dance as mechanically as possible, trying to close herself off from the odious man. They were involved in the intricate patterns of a Roger de Bevis and, when the dance was drawing to a close, she congratulated herself on having endured it. At the final bow and curtsey she prepared to flee from the floor; but before she could do so, he grasped her arm. "Ah, wait, I claim the next dance as well!"

Turning his head upward toward the musician's gallery he shouted, "Enough of these patch and powder tunes. Give us a waltz!"

The leader of the ensemble looked quite stricken, and the Master of Ceremonies, who should have taken the matter in hand, was conspicuously absent from the room. It would take a brave man to defy the Duke of Cumberland; but one, at least, was prepared to do so.

Susanna, who was standing with downcast eyes, heard a familiar voice at her shoulder. "Begging Your Grace's pardon, but waltzes are not danced at the Cotillion Balls. Only minuets and country dances."

The royal duke's face contorted in outrage. "They will play what I command them to play, sir! Do you know who I am?"

"Yes," the other man answered, "I am well aware of Your Grace's identity. But here in Cheyne Spa you are a guest of the Assembly Committee, and we do not waltz on Thursdays."

The royal eyes blazed. "By God, sir, we shall dance what I say we shall dance! Who the devil are you, you arrogant puppy?"

"My name is Patrick Wycombe, sir, and I think we will not be dancing waltzes." He gestured to the gallery and Cumberland looked furiously upward. It was empty. The musicians had prudently elected to take this time for their rest period. The remainder of the guests had drawn back to the edges of the long room and all eyes were trained on the three in the center.

"By God," the duke cursed, "I should call you out for your impertinence!"

Patrick flinched not at all, but offered a perfectly serious half-bow. "I am at your service, sir."

The duke merely stared at him furiously, face contorted even further with impotent rage. He was well aware that another public incident at this time would bring the Whigs down on him in full cry, and he was not prepared to risk such a thing for an incident as trifling as this. But he had no taste for public humiliation. He could threaten and he did.

"I shall remember this, sir! Both you and this 'piece' of yours will rue this evening's work, I assure you!"

And, so saying, he spun upon his heel and stalked out of the hall. When he had gone there was a short moment of shocked silence; but then, beginning as softly as the patter of falling rain, the applause began, swelled and crested upon the music as the musicians took up their instruments and began to play the sprightly "King's Brigade."

Patrick Wycombe extended his arm to Susanna. "May I have this dance, your ladyship?"

They swept through the patterns with great verve, and after the final promenade there was again a round of applause, and the roomful of dancers and spectators crowded about them with congratulations.

"It is our Cotillion Ball, after all, and we shall dance what we choose, shall we not?" asked old Lady Beddle, who could not any longer dance a step, but kept her fingers in the management of the assemblies.

It was all a series of gratifying moments for Patrick Wycombe, for the way he had stood up against the Royal Duke's roughshod tactics in what he saw—probably correctly—as a potential difficulty for Susanna. As for Susanna herself, cast in the role of the beleagured princess, it was a triumph in terms of establishing herself in Cheyne Spa.

She danced continuously with one gentleman or another for the rest of the evening, never able to repeat a dance with any of them if she had chosen. And when the last dance, the traditional Roger de Coverly, was struck up, Gavin Marshall forced himself through the crowd to her side. Noticing her look of elated exhaustion, he led her at once from the floor as Lady Morphy converged upon them from another direction.

"Well, my dear, I would say from the look about your eyes," she proclaimed, "that you are ready for bed and a late sleep in the morning."

"Ah, now," Gavin protested, "I thought we were off to the tables in the Lower Rooms as a reward for good behaviour."

Susanna recalled with amusement how eager she had been to try her hand at the tables, but she knew she could not do them justice tonight. She also knew, exhaustion aside, that she could not go directly to bed; for she would never sleep if she did, and dawn light would find her still tossing about if she did not somehow ground this energy before they went back to Upper Orson Street.

They were just emerging from the building, and it was gratifying to see that the night had remained so fine. The nearly full moon was riding high, bathing their pathway with silver light and obviating the need for link-boys. Only the edges of the square before them were dark. Susanna turned to Lady Morphy. "Are *you* very tired, your ladyship?"

"I? Nonsense. I never felt better. It did me a world of good to see that meddlesome oaf put in his place!"

"Not merely meddlesome, aunt. Cumberland may be unpopular, but he has a certain following," Gavin warned morosely. "I agreed with what Patrick took upon himself, but I fear it was a bad business to so openly cross one of the reigning house. The duke is close to the heart of the Prince

Regent, even though they are on opposite sides of the political fence." He shrugged. "But be that as it may. What did you have in mind, Lady Kinsale? A visit to some questionable wineshop, a late supper at the White Hart? Your wish is my command."

"Could we walk along the river? I feel as if I shall not sleep a wink if I do not work off some of the excitement."

"Why not? What a capital idea, eh, aunt? Just what we need?"

Her ladyship looked doubtful, then relented. "Indeed, it will clear our heads after the fugginess of the ball room. We shall gamble another time."

This was the first that Susanna had an inkling of Lady Morphy's deep devotion to the play at the tables. Now she took the older woman's hand into her own and tucked it under her arm, squeezing as she did so. "Thank you," she whispered. "I am rather too scattered. Dancing tonight, dicing tomorrow?"

But the excitement of the evening was not yet done. Hardly had they taken more than a few steps when, from the shadows on the far side of the square, they heard the sounds of a scuffle and a random curse as another voice cried out.

"What the devil is going on?" Gavin fairly leapt forward, displeased with the odds of what appeared to be two men beating a third. The two women followed hurriedly, crying for help to other persons leaving the hall.

"Fetch the watch!" cried Lady Morphy as she sped across the square.

Seeing the crowd descending upon them, the two thugs abandoned the attack and took flight; but a third man—who had evidently been standing by, watching with pleasure the sight of a fellow human being subjected to such brutality— paused for a moment, sneering insolently at the fallen victim before turning on his heel and striding off into the night. As he passed through the edge of a patch of moon- light, Susanna saw the livid scar on the side of his face and the eagle-beaked nose. Then with a little cry she threw herself to the ground beside the victim. Her fears were correct. This was no mere attack by footpads, but an act of vengeance. The fallen man was her champion, the hero of the evening, Patrick Wycombe.

Susanna lifted Patrick's head from the cobbles and laid it in her lap, noticing as she did so that he was slightly bleeding from a scalp wound either from the attack or from striking the stones when he fell. It leaked onto her white skirt, but she hardly paid attention. Lady Morphy knelt beside her and examined Patrick with an expert eye. "There is a doctor in Beacon Street, just down the way, Gavin. Fetch him at once—in his nightclothes if necessary! Patrick may be badly hurt, I cannot tell."

Without questioning her, Gavin hurried off into the darkness. In the meantime the night watch arrived and, hearing the particulars, began asking pertinent questions.

Did anyone see them?" he asked. "Can anyone give a description?"

"I saw them," Susanna volunteered.

But, to her surprise, Lady Morphy interrupted her sharply. "No one could have seen them properly by this light. They were footpads, I expect, who became frightened by my nephew's intervention and the prospect of facing the crowd coming from the Assembly Rooms. I daresay they ran off when they saw they would be detected."

Stealthily her fingers closed about Susanna's wrist as if warning her not to contradict what she had heard. Susanna said nothing further, certain that a reasonable explanation would be forthcoming in due time.

Gavin returned with the surgeon, a stout man dressed only in his small clothes. "How is the patient?" he asked rather officiously, as if he quite resented being dragged out of his house at this time of evening.

Patrick opened his eyes and stared at them groggily. "I can move," he said. "Help me up."

The surgeon quickly held his hand before Patrick's face.

"How many fingers?" he enquired, but Patrick merely thrust the hand away. He began to struggle to his feet.

"Help me up, Gavin, old man. There's a good chap."

The other duke, Lady Morphy's brother, came to them across the patch of moonlight, skittering a bit as his leg found little purchase on the cobbles.

"What the devil is going on here?" he demanded.

"Bit of a mishap, Your Grace," the constable answered touching his hat respectfully. "Seems this gentleman was attacked by assailant or assailants unknown."

"And you're standing about, of course!" said His Grace furiously. "Why the devil ain't you after them, man?"

"Begging your pardon, Your Grace, but no one could give me a description, you see. It would be terrible difficult to catch the right man if you don't even know what a one of them looks like."

"I shall be quite all right, Your Grace," said Patrick, struggling to his feet and still clinging to Gavin's arm for support.

"Edad, that may be," said Quince, "but you'd better be off to be looked at. Better safe than half-safe, is what I say!" He peered into the face of the surgeon. "Here, don't I know you?"

The medical man bowed obsequiously. "Dr. Franklin Jerrad, Your Grace. I had the honour of attending your late wife in her illness."

The duke regarded him sourly. "Ah, yes." He turned away toward Patrick, then back to the doctor with a final bit of news. "She died, you know."

The man looked acutely uncomfortable. "I know, sir. I was with her, if you recall."

"Ah, yes." Quince clapped him on the shoulder. "Not your fault, you know. They all died, all three of 'em. Hadn't given me a son among 'em! Well, come along, Mr. Wycombe. You just go along with the doctor here. He'll fix you up right as rain. Nothing much wrong, I expect. Shook up a bit, is all, I daresay?"

"Yes," said Patrick wearily. "Just shaken up a bit, Your

Grace." He sagged slightly and Gavin put his arm about him.

"Just lean on me, old chap. We'll have you fixed up in no time. I saw you there, you know. Three men, and you fought like a demmed tiger."

"Did I?" asked Patrick. "I don't remember that."

Gavin helped him off in the direction of the doctor's surgery for examination, while the Duke of Quince volunteered to walk his sister and Lady Kinsale back to Upper Orson Street. He was all in a fret of indignation.

"I don't know what the place has come to," he fumed. "Imagine such a thing happening in Cheyne Spa, of all places! In London, I am sure, it is no unusual thing. But in Cheyne? I can't think what the place is coming to."

"It was Cumberland, Quince," said Lady Morphy. "We saw his face as he walked off in the moonlight, cool as you please."

The old duke's eyebrows shot heavenward. "Cumberland, eh? Be demmed!" He sighed. "Well, I expect you did the right thing by not telling the watch, my dear. It rather surprises me that you have such a head on your shoulders, but if the newspapers got hold of this, there would be the very devil to pay! Pity that poor boy had to take the brunt of it, though."

"Do you mean to say," asked Susanna indignantly, "that you mean to do nothing about this?"

The older man eyed her shrewdly. "A fine and brave sentiment, my dear, to be concerned over the man who took your honour as his own this evening, but this affair must be handled delicately. If it should get out of hand and a question should be raised in Parliament, the ministry might fall overnight. Bad enough that it should be Cumberland, but that it should come at just this time is disastrous." He looked at Susanna with almost pleading eyes. "Lady Kinsale, may I beg your indulgence in this?"

"Very well, sir," she agreed, "unless Mr. Wycombe is more seriously injured than you think. Otherwise, I shall hold my tongue."

"Agreed," he said. "If Mr. Wycombe should prove to be more than superficially injured, I shall join you in your condemnation of the blackguard, Prince Regent's brother or no. But let us first see what greater harm it may do than keeping silence."

═ 12 ═

TIBBY SEEMED VERY nearly to be floating about their rooms
when Susanna awoke the next morning. Questioned, it
appeared that while her mistress had been disporting herself at the Assembly Rooms, Tibby had been walking out
with her carter. Susanna treated this news with appropriate
gravity.

"I hope he is a proper person, Tib?"

Tibby sighed deeply. "Oh, I do hope he is, too, miss. He
appears to be well raised up, I'll say that. He didn't take
liberties, you know, nor make remarks. And he is that
handsome!"

"I am sure you are a good enough judge of character not
to be taken in by a handsome face."

Tibby sighed once more. "I hope I am." But she seemed
quite relieved at the evidence that her mistress was prepared to be understanding about the association. "Then
you ain't against my seeing him?"

Susanna reached out and lightly patted the maidservant's
cheek. "Not at all. I can think of no reason why you should
not enjoy your stay in Cheyne Spa as much as I. We are
partners in this, after all, are we not?"

Tibby agreed, but then fell silent for a moment or two,
brushing her mistress's hair with long, sure strokes. "Begging your pardon, miss, but have you answered Lady
Morphy and Mr. Marshall yet about their proposition?"

"No, I have said nothing yet. One reason is that they

have never yet been specific about their plans, and another is that I hesitate to enter into an agreement I may later find cause to regret."

"But they has it in mind that you shall marry the old duke, is that it?"

"I believe so, and he is a charming gentleman—and not so old as all that, you know."

Tibby nodded agreement. "No, I expect I misspoke. Mature is what I meant to say."

Susanna caught the long hair out of Tibby's grasp and deftly twisted it into a French knot at the nape of her neck. "Yes, my dear, mature and very well off. I expect he has enough to support us all in high style for the rest of our lives."

"It sounds quite nice to me, miss."

Susanna smilingly agreed, but there was a modicum of doubt in her mind. Certainly she had previously had no prospects, but was it enough that a husband be charming and rich? She chided herself tolerantly for such a thought. When one was offered so much, was one entitled to request romance as well? It seemed likely that certain concessions must be made. There was a soft knocking on the door and she pulled her wrapper more closely about her to answer it.

"You should let Tibby do this, my dear," said Lady Morphy as she came in. "It creates a poor impression when you answer the door yourself."

Since her ladyship had no maid at all and must answer her own door, Susanna took this lightly. "Tibby is otherwise occupied, madam. I imagine the world could survive the shock of seeing me in my morning clothes. Will Mr. Marshall be joining us?"

Lady Morphy eyed her sharply. "Yes, he has just gone down to inform Mrs. Maundy that we shall all be taking breakfast in your parlour. You needn't pull your nose at that, girl; there are things which must be discussed among us."

"Ah?" Susanna exchanged a glance with Tibby who

came out of the dressing room at that moment. "What things?"

But her ladyship was not to be drawn out. "Gavin will be along presently, I think it should wait until he arrives."

Which he did, just at that moment—Tibby answering the door. He came in with a slight frown upon his face and a nosegay in his hand. "These were delivered for you, Miss Archer."

"Gavin," his aunt reprimanded on a rising tone. "If you do not become used to saying 'Lady Kinsale' . . ."

"Yes, I know, aunt, if I do not say it regularly, I will say the wrong thing in public at some most inconvenient time, eh?"

"Quite," she agreed.

"Oh, I believe Mr. Marshall is quite aware of what he is doing, your ladyship," Susanna said. "I expect he does it to remind me that my role is only a masquerade." Gavin made no move to deny it.

"From whom do the flowers come?" asked the older woman. The question was addressed to Susanna, who had received them, but it was Gavin who truculently answered.

"They come from Patrick Wycombe."

"From Patrick? How unfortunate. Was there a message with them?"

Susanna broke the seal and opened the folded scrap of paper. Her eyes danced as she read the words, then refolded it and laid it down on the table. "Tibby, would you be good enough to put these in water?"

"Well?" asked Lady Morphy impatiently. "What does he say?"

She reached for the paper to see for herself, but Susanna deftly slid it out of her reach.

"I beg your indulgence, madam, but the message is rather personal."

Lady Morphy's eyebrows shot upward, her look one of almost comic inquiry. "Personal? I fail to understand. How can anything between us be personal? We are all partners here, I believe?" Her glance included the maidservant, though with reluctance. "All four of us, since you insist. At any rate, there is no room for secrets."

"None, your ladyship?" asked Susanna smoothly. "Then perhaps it *is* time we settled down to a very frank conversation."

"I expect you are correct, miss." Her ladyship's usually tolerant tone was sharper than Susanna had yet heard it, though she fancied it could become knifelike if necessary. She found that the imperious note irritated her immensely.

"Perhaps you and Mr. Marshall should explain to us now exactly what arrangements you have in mind concerning myself and His Grace, your brother?"

This seemed to drive her ladyship to even further sharpness. "You approach this with a good deal of impertinence, young woman. I think it best that you stop to recollect who it is you really are."

The escalation of the spat seemed beyond recall. Susanna's long experience with demanding employers had most certainly worn her reserves of patience down to an alarming degree. Now that she was beyond the need for absolute prudence, she found it difficult not to rise to the challenge. "I expect you mean to say, madam, that I should remember who *you* are, but the fact is that I am neither your servant nor your child, and I do not think it proper that you should treat me as such."

"Come, come, ladies," Gavin interposed. "Perhaps we should all step back and begin again before we fatally disrupt our partnership. I daresay it is my fault as much as anyone's. 'Lady Kinsale,' I am certain that my aunt meant you no disrespect, but if we *are* to go on, I believe she has every reason to expect frankness."

"Just as we do, sir," said Tibby, speaking up for the first time. "My mistress has made you no promises, nor has she been given any by you. I think it is only right that we all put our cards on the table and begin fresh. Don't you agree, Lady Morphy?"

The older woman looked faintly astonished at being so addressed by a mere maidservant, but her innate humour and common sense prevailed. "The girl is right, of course. I beg your pardon, Lady Kinsale. I am sure I did not mean to overstep the bounds of good taste when I asked about the billet-doux. It is only that both Gavin and myself are certain that you are the ideal partner for us in this enterprise and we tremble at the thought that a rival suitor may throw our plans all about."

"Another suitor? Do you mean Mr. Wycombe?"

"The fact is, your ladyship," said Gavin, following his aunt's lead in lending the title to Susanna in private as well as public conversation, "that if you should take up with Patrick all our plans would go quite awry."

But Susanna was not mollified quite yet. "Oh," she countered silkily, "I had thought all your concern was for Mr. Wycombe and his welfare. Is that not what you were saying to me last evening on the terrace?"

The young man had the grace to look chagrined. "Perhaps *I* should be made privy to that conversation," Lady Morphy interjected. "What nonsense have you been talking now, Gavin?"

A dull thumping on the door of the room signalled the arrival of the slavey with the breakfast tray, a high-piled arrangement almost as big as the tiny girl herself. Tibby immediately hurried to help her.

"My word," Lady Morphy chuckled, "there is surely enough here to feed a regiment."

"Only the usual amount, madam," said the servant, bobbing a curtsey so that the little bow on her cap danced. "It is just that I tried to bring it all at once. I shall come back presently with more water for the tea."

The savoury smells filled the air as Tibby lifted one cover after another. Eggs, ham, potatoes, scones and muffins drenched in butter. "She did bring up rather a lot, miss. I expect Mrs. Maundy wanted to be sure you had enough to entertain your guests."

"Then you will have no reason to run to the kitchen with yours," Susanna decided. "You will be able to carry on the discussion with the rest of us just as a partner should do." She rose and began to fill the plates, handing them around just as the slavey returned with the extra kettle of water. Tibby's laden fork paused halfway to her mouth as the little girl entered, and the child's eyes widened as she saw that Tibby was sitting on equal terms with the others. She said nothing, but her lips pressed together disapprovingly. There were, she believed, levels of society and it was a bad business to move out of your own. Such things merely led to trouble in the long run. Tibby, reading her expression, blushed furiously and made a vow to try to explain it away when they were alone in the kitchen. When the girl had gone, Lady Morphy cleared her throat and began an elaboration of her plan.

"You see, my dear, the sordid truth is that I am always short of money and so is Gavin. It is not that my dear brother does not give me an allowance, for he does—and very generous it might be, too, for anyone else. But for a lady educated into a high position it is . . . how shall I say . . . barely adequate."

"And the duke will not increase it?" asked Susanna naively. Her ladyship had the grace to look a trifle embarrassed, but it was Gavin who made the explanation.

"My aunt has terrible fortune with the cards, you see. It is quite an amazing run of bad luck which has been plaguing her for some time. I believe she feels that if she could only recoup her losses, she would be able to turn her back on the tables forever."

Susanna understood completely. She thought it quite unlikely that Lady Morphy could ever take such a drastic step. "And you, Mr. Marshall? Has your luck at the tables ben so disastrous as well?"

He shook his head. "Frankly, no. If it were not for my own luck in the play of the hand, I should live very poorly indeed. I have never been properly educated—one never is, at the better schools—and I am quite far down on the list of my uncle's charities. There are, you see, two cousins in line before me."

"And you would like to move upward, I take it?"

"As far up as possible." He had, really, a rather nice laugh, Susanna reflected, and a healthy lack of illusion about himself.

"But even if I should marry the duke," she said, "I do not understand how that could benefit either of you. I shall have no control over his money."

Lady Morphy lifted a finger. "Ah, but that is where you are wrong," she admonished.

As if to create a small moment of suspense, she poured herself another cup of tea before she settled down for the explanation. "In the case of each of his wives, you see, William John has had the foresight to make a handsome— very handsome, eh, Gavin?—settlement of money and property upon his bride before the ceremony."

"*Very* handsome," Gavin agreed.

"Now why this should be, I do not know, but undoubtedly he feels that it makes them more equitable in terms of the marriage. In all the cases thus far, of course, the money has returned to him when they passed on to a better world."

"And you believe he would do the same for me if I persuaded him to marry me?"

"No reason why not," smirked Gavin. "We could all be very well off."

"So you expect that I would share this settlement with you?"

"Wait, wait," cautioned her ladyship. "There is more. He will undoubtedly leave you handsomely provided for in his will—and he is not, after all, the youngest of men, you know. The odds are . . . "

Susanna was horrified. "Do you mean to hang about until he dies, like carrion birds? Do you think I would give myself to a man only to wish him dead?" Her eyes fairly blazed. "I do not think I am so very flattered that you thought I would fit into your scheme, after all!"

"Oh, come," said her ladyship with a nervous little laugh, "what an unnatural creature you must think me to wish my brother dead. How can you say such things?"

"What else should I say?" Susanna demanded. "I do not think I am clever enough nor deceitful enough for such a scheme as yours, madam. I rather like His Grace and I have no wish to see him dead so that you can pursue your career in a gambling hell!" She rose from the table. "If you will excuse me, I believe I will take the waters today. They are said to be wonderfully calming to the nerves."

"Please, Miss Archer . . . Lady Kinsale . . . think again," Gavin all but pleaded. "There is enough gold in my uncle's pocket for all of us, a dozen times over! My aunt means no harm to her brother, though I expect she would have no qualms about fleecing my cousins out of a bit of their inheritances."

"He is right, my dear. Will you not hear me out?" her ladyship's conciliatory words rang oddly from that aristocratic throat.

But Susanna was adamant. "I have heard more than enough. I promise that I shall not stand in your way . . . unless real harm seems about to come to His Grace . . . but I think you should look elsewhere for the means to implement your plans. I wonder that you have not drawn Mrs. Fairfax into your scheme, since she is your professed good friend, madam. I daresay that she and Miss Cecily have few scruples about such things."

"By heaven, I believe you are serious!" Gavin cried. "I had never thought to find such a want of principle in anyone!"

His words completely stopped Susanna in mid-step at the door of the dressing room. "Lack of principle? Because I do not fall into your plot?"

"Why, yes," he said hotly. "We take you up, we give you a background, we polish your manners and introduce you to society . . . and what do we reap for our pains? Merely a temper tantrum stemming from your overdeveloped sense of niceness, which you learned in your country parsonage. Come into the real world, my girl!"

"How dare you!" Susanna cried passionately.

But Gavin merely regarded her with that self-satisfied smile of his. "The duke is no fool, my dear girl. He would understand the situation completely if he knew of it. Certainly he is not the protected country gentleman you seem to believe him. He is a knowledgeable and powerful man who has helped shape the policies of the country, not some whining boy. If you are really thinking of him, consider this. How can he be the loser? We shall have given him a beautiful and charming wife, the possibility of an heir and the eventual continuation of his line! As for you, you will have acquired a husband richer by far than any other suitor you are likely to find . . . and you are so close-fisted that you would deny us a measure of the profit? Oh, fie! How ungrateful!"

Susanna's pretty mouth had fallen open with amazement. She could not believe that this man actually suggested that she fall victim to such a specious argument. But when she turned for understanding to the other two women, there was no doubt that they agreed with him. Tibby, especially, seemed to accept his point completely.

There was a little scratching at the door and, when Tib opened it, the little slavey came in and bobbed to Susanna. "If you please, your ladyship, there is a gentleman below who says he is a duke, and would you be good enough to allow him the time of day."

Even allowing for a certain amount of garbling by the unsophisticated servant, this was a curious request. "Oh, but I am not even dressed!" Susanna cried, and turned instinctively to Lady Morphy. "What should I do?"

That august lady was unperturbed. "I should think the first question to be answered," she said, "is exactly *which* duke it is who has come calling at such an unfashionable hour."

"You may recall," said Gavin in the face of Susanna's unqualified astonishment, "that you have an acquaintance of not one, but two such peers of the realm. "My word, my dear child, what a feather in your cap!"

The aunt and nephew left Susanna and went up the stairs to their own rooms. But as they were separating, Lady Morphy paused at her door to give him a word or two of warning. "Do you know, my dear, I sometimes think you are not as objective in this matter as you should be."

Gavin raised his brows in surprise. "I cannot imagine what you mean."

She patted his cheek. "Nothing at all, I daresay. I expect it is only the overactive imagination of an old woman coming into play, but in case it has more substance than that, may I warn you that too much involvement would be death to our plans."

"Involvement? With Miss Archer, do you mean? Aunt, you must be joking. It is with me a case of business as usual, I do assure you! Business as usual."

"As I thought," she answered, "it is only a woman's fancy."

But she eyed him speculatively as he mounted the stairs to his garret room.

Susanna, on the other hand, not knowing what other course to follow for the moment, sent down word with Tibby that "Lady Kinsale is indisposed, sir, and regrets she cannot go driving this morning." The duke in question was observed to go stomping down the steps in disappointment, his wooden appendage clattering against the stones.

== 13 ==

IT WOULD BE foolish to pretend that no child of a vicar or parson has ever entered the portals of a gambling-hell, and perhaps the Lower Rooms of Cheyne Spa should not be so considered. Certainly, following the edicts laid down by Beau Carlisle, the gaming rooms were extremely sedate and the denizens far better bred than any imps or demons had a right to be. they were ladies and gentlemen all, or with generally legitimate pretensions to that estate. Susanna, entering upon the arm of Gavin Marshall in fulfillment of his promise, thought the place vastly interesting, but upon further consideration rather disappointing.

These rooms were even less grand than the Assembly Rooms on the hilltop, for they were carefully decorated in colours of undemanding hue and with unobtrusive furnishings. This had not been done from motives of economy alone, but because Carlisle (who had kept an infamous faro game running without interruption for nearly a decade) had believed that dispassionate surroundings served the patrons and himself better than those which might be supposed to excite the unstable passions amongst them. The space had been made into a pair of spacious chambers connected by an arched doorway; one room for whist, the other for less sedentary games of chance such as barrow, verté, and E.O. At the rear a smaller, less convenient space had been carved out of some old utility rooms and was set aside for those who wished to indulge in the old-fashioned charm of hazard. Amongst the older patrons, not a few chose it because it had been the rage of their vanished youth.

Gavin inexpressively waggled his fingers at an attendant who hurried to his side.

"Good evening, Mr. Marshall. How can I be of service?"

"You may fetch me Mr. Wilberforce, if you would be so good."

The attendant hesitated. "I am not positive that he is free at the moment, sir, but you may be sure I shall tell him the moment I see him." He looked curiously at Susanna, suspecting her to be who she was—Lady Kinsale, the newest rage of the spa. It was not often that he had an opportunity of seeing such a fascinating creature close to. Lovely women came often to the Lower Rooms, of course, but more often than not the lines of strain or the distortions of greed were written so plainly upon their faces as to lay a blemish upon their beauty.

Gavin negligently slipped a coin into the man's outstretched hand. "I daresay he can be found if you but look carefully, eh? I shall be showing this lady about the large room when he comes to find us."

The servant looked at the amount of the *douceur* and all but tugged at his forelock in his eagerness to please such a generous patron. "I am certain I know where he can be located, Mr. Marshall."

"What did you give him?" asked Susanna curiously. "Was it money?"

Gavin gave a cynical shrug of his handsomely fitted shoulders. "The secret is always money, my girl. It oils the wheels of the world. As always, a tip is better than a title to these people. They can spend it far more easily, though a title often impresses."

"A 'tip?' she asked. "I fear I do not know the expression."

"It comes from the exchange coffee-houses in London," he explained. "A little something on the side 'to insure promptness,' you know."

"To insure promptness? Ah . . . T–I–P, 'tip,' I see! How very amusing. I find I learn things from you all the while, sir."

"You have been a good student," Gavin admitted. "Even I never thought the leopard could change its spots quite so quickly as you have done. One would scarcely think you were the same person as that drab companion languishing away at Wycombe Hall."

"Do you think Mr. Wycombe has ever recognised me?"

He raised a mocking eyebrow. "Still on that trail, are we, even after what I have said?"

"I have certainly taken what you said into close consideration, sir, but in the end, you know, I must make up my own mind."

"I never doubted you would," returned Gavin, grinning not altogether congenially.

They moved into the welter of tables and threaded their way between them. "Why is it you particularly wish me to meet Mr. Wilberforce?" she asked.

"A matter of courtesy to you both. As Master of Ceremonies he can be very useful to one in your position. I doubt that he will appeal to you altogether—he rather grates on me—but he is better than he seems, although a bit more timid than old Beau used to be when he reigned in Cheyne."

She was quite amazed at the intense concentration of the players, which resulted in an electric, rather attenuated atmosphere she found to make her a little edgy. When she said as much to Gavin, he agreed. "And well it should be," he explained. "Fortunes ride upon the turn of a card."

She thought he must be exaggerating until they moved into the hazard room and she saw the bullion piled up in traditional manner, in the centre of the table, as the players cried their bets. It was a dazzling sight. "How much do you suppose is there?" she asked wonderingly.

Gavin's careful eye looked it over, calculated. "Only about three thousand pounds," he estimated. "The evening is still very young." It was likely more than her father, the vicar, had earned in all his life. The girl found she was less exhilarated than filled with a certain irritation at such a casual exchange. A full county of poor could probably have been fed by what was heaped up on this table. Talk of Lazarus and the crumbs!

For the first time she truly appreciated that proverb of which the Reverend Archer had been particularly fond, to judge by his use of it: "The love of money is the root of all evil." Or had he merely been justifying his own lack? Certainly, upon the faces of these players she saw not merely love but a passionate rapaciousness.

This philosophic strain was interrupted by the arrival of a wispy little man bearing in his right hand an impressive staff of office. She was introduced to Mr. Septimus Wilberforce, the Master of Ceremonies who had taken Beau Carlisle's place when he retired. Despite mixed feelings about the Beau, it was not a substitution for which everyone cared. Carlisle had been very much of a dandy, it is true; but this overdressed creature, Susanna decided, was everything that is implied by "fop." His garb was just too much in advance of the newest style and just enough extreme; his hair bore just a trifle too much henna, his lips a shade too much gloss, and the airy gestures with which his speech was accentuated carried out the theme.

"You called for me, Mr. Marshall?" he asked in a manner which contrived to be at once both mincing and haughty. "I fear I was caught up in colloquy with your uncle, the dear duke."

Gavin did not look at Susanna as he said, in a forced fashion, "Quince is here? Capital! Just the man I needed to see, yes." Then he remembered his manners.

"Mr. Wilberforce, may I present to you Lady Kinsale, a new and fair addition to our spa?"

Wilberforce immediately swept into a deep and elaborate bow which could only have been accomplished with the use of the tall staff of authority. "Lady Kinsale? At last! My eyes have been questing for a sight of you since your debut at the Cotillion Ball, when circumstances so cruelly intervened against our meeting. Such a night, eh? It gives one quite a flutter to think how easily honoured traditions can be flouted by . . ." he dropped his voice and barely moved his lips ". . . by the bullies of the world, is it not so? That man Cumberland is quite odious. I only regret that I became indisposed just before that moment when you were affronted, Lady Kinsale. If I had been told of it, I would have *flown* to your side!"

"I am sure you would have done. I am grateful that Mr. Wycombe was there to momentarily usurp your position."

"Yes! Oh, ye-s-s," he agreed, rolling his eyes in a Gallic manner. "It is only to be regretted that he should have been subjected to such retaliation for his gallantry."

"Retaliation?" asked Susanna. "You believe it was that?"

"Oh, I do!" Wilberforce fluttered agitatedly. "Everyone does."

"It proved to be quite minor," said Gavin. "I believe he is quite recovered."

"Oh, *very much* recovered," the Master of Ceremonies fluted. "I have seen him strolling about the rooms this very evening. But to have been set upon at all, is horrendous! And in Cheyne Spa, of all places. Nothing seems safe anymore."

He returned his attention to Susanna. "And has your ladyship some preference of gaming?" he asked archly. "If there is not a particular game in progress, I am certain one could be arranged very quickly."

"Yes," Gavin agreed. "Most of these players will bet on anything at all, given a chance."

But Susanna let this slide past as she confessed, "I fear I know nothing whatsoever about gambling."

She could not have left Wilberforce more thunderstruck. He almost dropped his airs, and asked like a mere mortal, "Nothing at all? How extraordinary!"

"Nothing at all. What do you recommend?" It seemed

she saw Gavin Marshall hiding a smile behind his hand, but he turned slightly away just at that moment so that she could not be certain. Mr. Wilberforce had returned to rolling his eyes about, which indicated that it was one of his basic modes of expression. He pretended to consider her question.

"I suppose then it should be something almost elementary to begin," he said with a pout. "Whist is so very complicated for a beginner that we must leave it aside for the moment. . . . But my, there are so many choices!" And he began to run down a list as though it were a bill of fare. "Barrow, ace of hearts, écu, verté, silver pharaoh, regular faro . . ." and on he went, down to roulette, *rouge et noir*, and macao. Even loo was sometimes indulged in by old ladies out for a fling. "Of course, I suppose the simplest of all, if it is simplicity one seeks, is faro. You have heard of the Beau's famous game, I suppose? The Lower Rooms were built upon it."

Susanna looked inquiringly at Gavin, but he merely shrugged. "I try to put myself in a novice's place, but I cannot. One form of suicide is as potent as another, I expect . . . but, yes, faro is simple as sin. You win or you lose."

One of the attendants approached Gavin and whispered into his ear. The resulting reaction was unstudied and eager. "What, here?" His face broke into a wide grin of anticipation.

"What is it?" Susanna asked curiously.

"An old friend is here whom I have not played for a long while, but I daresay the opportunity will arise again."

"Is he very rich?" she asked craftily, knowing a little of how his mind worked.

"As it happens, he is," Gavin showed no resentment of her perspicacity. "And I expect he will remain so, for he is a deuced good player, is old Neibauer."

"I shall be happy to show Lady Kinsale the principles of the games," offered Wilberforce with a little wriggle. Susanna had a horrid premonition her skin would crawl if the man touched her accidentally. He was so like a species of slug, so soft, so yielding. She wanted him merely to go away, but on the other hand it would be a pity if Gavin Marshall should be foiled in his challenge.

"Oh, please do go and engage your friend," she wheedled. "I am sure I shall find my way about with the aid of Mr. Wilberforce."

"Are you certain?" he asked dubiously. Underneath there was an eagerness she had never seen in him before.

"Quite certain. Run off to play unless you have any parting words of counsel."

"I have the distinct feeling that you will not heed them. Play slowly and for low stakes first, to last. It is equally entertaining and easier on the pursestrings."

"That is very funny," Wilberforce giggled, "for we all know, you see, that Mr. Marshall is what we call 'a plunger' and goes for high stakes as a pit dog goes for the throat."

"Is that true?"

"Do as I say, not as I do, is my second piece of advice," Gavin retorted, and went off eagerly to seek out his long-awaited opponent.

Wilberforce led Susanna directly toward the faro tables, chattering animatedly as they went, but she found his conversation so lacking in point that she soon followed very little of it. It affected her much as might the endless chatter of simians in a zoological garden, or the cacaphony in an aviary, where no individual song is distinguishable from another. She supposed one or two phrases of genuine information might also lurk amongst the burbling of the Master of Ceremonies, but she did not trouble to find them.

As she had promised, she found that faro (or pharaoh, as it was originally named from one of the cards in the deck) was a deceptively easy game. At bottom, it was only the basic sort of wagering on whether a higher or lower card will fall into a particular pile.

"It goes like this, Lady Kinsale," Wilberforce explained

with a greater clarity than she had yet had from him. "Each bettor places his stake on any of the pack's thirteen cards, from king down to ace. And when the wagers have been set amongst the company at the table, the dealer here takes the pack and deals it into equal piles, one on either hand. Simple, it is not?"

"It seems so," Susanna answered, "but I am not certain as to how the winnings are determined."

"Ah," said Wilberforce, as if he were taking in hand a particularly backward child. "On the cards falling onto the pile on the right hand, the dealer *pays* the wagers. But on those of the left hand, he collects. You see?"

It did appear so ridiculously simple, but Susanna had not played for very long before she saw that, logically speaking, short term odds might very well apply, but in the long run it would be impossible to win; for there were certain accepted conventions in favour of the house which altered the bias of the game. Not only did the dealer claim all ties when the same denomination of card appeared on both piles, but also the final trick of each hand was claimed by him, no matter on which stack it fell. She could see why the operation of such a bank could be enormously profitable to the owner of it, but eventually disastrous to the inveterate player. No skill applied, only the inexorable decrees of fate. One could never better oneself by skill or knowledge of the game. Ultimately the unending sameness of it bored her, and she retreated from the table, having won only three guineas more than the sum with which she had begun. Of course, she could have had three guineas *less*, she reflected.

As she moved away she found herself colliding with a person approaching the table in great haste, as though she would be denied a place if she were not present at an appointed moment. Murmuring an apology, Susanna stepped back and saw that the encounter was with the redoubtable Mrs. Fairfax.

"Lady Kinsale," cried Cecily's mother, "I do not believe I

have ever seen you here before? And in still another lovely gown, too. I believe we have never yet seen you in the same dress twice."

There was not so much wonderment in this pronouncement as there was a kind of malicious probing. *Who are you?* she seemed to be asking, *and why do you flaunt yourself so conspicuously?* Susanna could almost hear the questions being mentally screamed at her, and she made a note to ask Lady Morphy, her arbiter, about the propriety of wearing so many costumes. Did it not, perhaps, smack a little of the *nouveau riche*, as the French were beginning to call those who had sprung up in the wake of the new empire? Surely in such a place as this, one must beware of ostentation in such matters.

"Good evening, Mrs. Fairfax," she said in a pleasant tone. "You yourself have dressed with unusual elegance. The colour of your camlet is most becoming. A sort of dark rose, would you call it?"

"How clever you are, your ladyship, to notice. The draper spoke of it in almost the same way, Dusty Rose, he called it." She almost preened, arching her shoulders so that the fabric fell becomingly. "I do not have a full closet of gowns, but I try for quality, you know, both for myself and for Cecily."

"Yes," Susanna said, "quality is everything, is it not?" And she went on her way, leaving Cecily's mother to ponder whether she had or had not been snubbed. There was *something* about her ladyship (and no one worships a title more than she who has none, but feels deserving of it) that jogged at her memory, but she could not, for her life, think what it was.

Susanna moved gracefully about the rooms, curiously overlooking the various games of verté, basset, swabbers, and even fish for those whose childhood was never very far behind. It was while she was contemplating the hazard table that she became conscious of a masculine voice just at her ear.

"They often cheat, you know. If you play, you must always keep a sharp eye on the other players."

The player nearest them, overhearing these words, spun his head round angrily, as if to make some cutting remark; but when he saw who the speaker was, he turned back to the table in silence, though his ears and neck burned a fiery red, as though expressing his stifled cholor.

Susanna was surprised to find the Duke of Cumberland standing at her shoulder. There was nothing to do but remain civil, however she felt about his unsettling nearness. "In what way can they be dishonest, sir? The play seems straightforward enough to me. The dice rattle about in the box and then fall out. Is that not the case?"

"Near enough," Cumberland responded, "and I am certain, of course, that no gentleman of Cheyne Spa would stoop to such dishonest practice. But it is not unheard of, even among gentlemen. There are dice which are loaded on one side with minute quantities of metal—almost undetectable, but enough to affect the balance of the roll and ensure certain combinations coming up. Even with fair dice there are ways of cheating. A 'dribble,' for example, is a slow pouring out which allows the manipulation of the cube by an expert."

"You sound, sir, as if you are not a gambler yourself."

The duke gave her a contained little smile. "Not at all, I have enjoyed the tables many times, sheerly as sport, but I decry it as an obsession."

"You make me see that I shall have to be very alert," said Susanna. "I am now almost afraid to try my hand."

"No, no," he protested, chuckling. "Do not let me lead you into the paths of unexpected righteousness. Some have the spirit for play at the tables and some do not. True gamblers are born to the vice and are never out of its power. I have seen men standing at the table like statues, without moving a muscle of their faces and with nothing to show that they were alive except the tears running down their cheeks. Such things are horrifying."

The duke's words quite surprised the girl, seeming to her to be both sensitive and astute. Now he sighed. "I have seen far too many lives wasted because of it, I suppose. I have seen too many men who might have been greatly advantageous to the nation, but whose lives were ruined by falling victim to this *belle dame sans merci*, as the young poet has it."

What a contradiction he was! She recalled Lady Morphy telling her of the great scandal a few years since, when Cumberland's own valet had attacked his master with a sword as he lay sleeping—the origin of that scar which still puckered his face. And listening to him now discoursing on moral rectitude, she could scarcely believe the dreadful circumstance under which she had last seen him in the moonlit square before the Upper Rooms.

Lady Morphy was approaching them with a worried look, which changed to one of surprise when she saw to whom Susanna was talking. "Forgive me, Your Grace," she said to him, then drew the girl a step or two to the side. "Does your ladyship know where my nephew has got to?"

"Gone to meet an old adversary at cards, I believe. I assured him that I could well look after myself since he seemed eager to engage this Neibauer."

Lady Morphy clapped her hands together in exasperation. "Klaus Neibauer? That old Hanoverian fraud? I expect we shall not see Gavin again until dawn, for once those two are joined, there is no parting them."

Cumberland, who could not help overhearing her, gave a mock frown at such words. "I expect you are aware, your ladyship, that my family tree is firmly rooted in Hanover. Believe me, we take our honour seriously. I am sure we have no frauds." It was said lightly, but with a peculiar emphasis.

Lady Morphy could, when she chose, charm the birds from trees, and she issued His Grace one of those melting looks that Susanna knew well enough to discount—except as camouflage for whatever weapon with which she was about to strike. "And, indeed, sir, if all your countrymen believed the same, what a different world we would be living in."

Since this came perilously close to *lese majesté*, the duke would have been within his rights to take umbrage; but instead he pointedly pretended to see the humour in it, though after a few minutes he excused himself with an ironic bow. "I am sure you ladies have feminine chat to exchange, to which a mere male should not be privy."

They did not immediately see him again, but in a few moments an attendant appeared with a tray upon which two cups of claret punch reposed. "At the instruction of the duke," he said, and the women accepted the refreshment with pleasure.

"I wonder what chicanery that wily creature is up to?" asked her ladyship rhetorically. "He is a little mad, but as subtle as the serpent in Eden when he chooses to be. I do not trust him an inch."

Then she roused herself. "Since we are here, dear Lady Kinsale, let me introduce you to the charms of hazard." But Susanna, having been warned off by such an expert as Cumberland, begged off.

"I doubt that I am very much of a gambler after all, your ladyship."

"What? After practically begging Mr. Marshall and me to bring you here? Preposterous. I think you vastly underrate yourself. You are more of a gambler than you believe, or you would not be in Cheyne Spa in the first place, would you?"

Then, dropping her voice slightly, she asked, "Have you by any chance changed your mind, or reconsidered the notion of an alliance with my brother the duke?"

"No," Susanna answered. "I have quite put it out of my mind. I hope we can remain friends despite all?"

Lady Morphy shook her head in grave displeasure. "I

fear you will prove too dangerous to my plans to be a friend . . . Lady Kinsale. It may be that we will find we are at odds more quickly than you imagine."

When the young woman would have pressed her for a broader explanation, she slipped off into the crowd with a noncommittal smile, leaving Susanna to wonder—not for the first time—whether this visit to the spa had been, after all, such a clever idea as she and Tibby had thought.

═ **14** ═

DESPITE THE NEWS of the capture of a dangerous foreign spy in the night, Mrs. Nightshade had every reason to be happy, and she was. In addition to a healthy contribution to her welfare by Lady Morphy, the continuing stipend of hopefulness from Mrs. Fairfax and a few other trifles from other sources, she had this instant been summoned to another conference with the person whom she had come to regard as her primary patron, His Grace, the Duke of Quince.

He was today, however, not altogether content—and he made no bones about where he placed the burden of blame. "See here, my good woman," he said in a decidedly blustery tone, "I do not know that I am entirely pleased at the way things are going!"

The matchmaker assumed a mask of innocence which had stood her in good stead very many times in the past. "Why, Your Grace, I am very surprised to hear that. I believed I had given you every opportunity to pay court to Miss Fairfax."

"Miss Fairfax? Who the devil is Miss Fairfax when she *is* at home?"

Mrs. Nightshade contrived to look supremely troubled. "But, sir, do you not recall that Miss Cecily Fairfax is the young woman for whose sake you came to Cheyne Spa in the first place?"

The duke bit his thumb and considered. "Oh . . . yes . . . that flaxen-haired ninny with the mother in tow? Forget her, madam. Never trust a miss who brings her mother to the party. It isn't sporting, for one thing. No, she could never be the object of my attention for very long. Not a brain in her head, so far as I could tell."

"But Your Grace scarcely spoke a word to her!" Despite all, professional pride and outraged equity vied for place in Mrs. Nightshade's tones.

"Didn't need much conversation to tell she hadn't a word worth listening to!"

"I had believed Your Grace was concerned with certain other aspects of the young woman. She comes from excellent stock, you know; one of the few women born into the Fairfax family in generations. They have always been known for a decidedly masculine strength of body. And as for the distaff side . . ."

"The distaff side? That was another thing against the girl. I couldn't bear to have the mother always hanging about, and I vow she is the sort of whom one could never rid oneself. It would be a poor enough bargain to saddle oneself with a wife who could only talk but say nothing, but to add such a mother would be quite insupportable!"

"I believe your manor house is quite large, is it not, Your Grace?"

"Large? Yes, it is extensive enough, I suppose."

"Surely, then, the mother could be tucked inconspicuously out of the way, eh?" Her manner, if not her elbow, seemed designed to jog him humourously in the ribs. It needed only a broad wink to overstress her point.

The old reprobate chose to chuckle rather than be outraged. "Get her lost in the corridors, d'ye mean? I daresay that would be a solution, but the game is hardly worth the candle. Nay, I am sorry if you are put out by this, but I require more of a wife than good breeding power and a pretty face. I have a fancy as well for good conversation on long winter evenings."

Mrs. Nightshade's catlike smile licked slyly about her lips, then grew deeper, exposing the shallow dimples in her cheeks and, as her eyes widened in a pretence of amazement, the effect was every bit as charming as she intended.

But the duke's mind was upon other quarry. "What of this woman, Lady Kinsale?" he asked with elaborate nonchalance, as if he were only just this moment considering the creature. The Nightshade smile was discreetly covered by an uplifted hand. *Lady Morphy will be so pleased*, she thought, but she feigned innocence still.

"Lady Kinsale? What of her, Your Grace?"

He was cleverer than that. "Come, come, woman do not think to toy with me! I cannot imagine that such a potentially eligible catch as that young woman seems to be has not already been investigated by you. What do you know of her? Is she the quality she seems? D'ye think I could stand a chance with her?"

The balm of direct flattery seemed to be required. "Surely, Your Grace's position alone would qualify for her deepest consideration?"

He stood up and began to stomp about the floor of the room in which they were sitting, his wooden leg clacking on the wooden floor. "Nay, I think there must be more to it than merely that, and more to her as well!"

Her voice grew more silkily confidential. "Surely you do not believe that a small difference in age could alter . . ."

His Grace looked at the matchmaker in genuine surprise. "Why . . . I daresay you could be right, could you not? I must say that such an objection never crossed my mind. I am twice her age, I expect, or even more, but somehow I cannot believe that such a consideration would enter into it with her any more than this business of the title." He paused and pulled at his lip. "Hmmm, that gives me food for thought, I must say."

She could see, now, that he was not like many of the other mature gentlemen who sometimes required more the services of a procuress than an honest matchmaker. The duke, it appeared, was one of those gentlemen who wish naively to be loved for themselves alone, without considering that their very lineage, age, and position contributed to the very person they had become and could not be separated from it.

"Oh, I did not mean to imply that she could *not* be interested, Duke," said Mrs. Nightshade hastily. There was no use in allowing a handsome settlement (perhaps such settlements from two directions) to slip through her fingers. "I have every reason to believe that she is exactly what she seems."

"I am a little doubtful of that Lieutenant-General of Ireland which her late husband pretended to be," he confessed.

"Certainly I will look into the matter very closely," Mrs. Nightshade promised.

Lady Kinsale's triumphal progress continued with great dispatch. So much so that a fortnight later Mrs. Fairfax and her darling Cecily were attending the public breakfast in St. Gerrans's Gardens when they saw Lady Kinsale enter the grounds upon the arm of an annoyingly familiar gentleman. Mrs. Fairfax grew quite red in the face at the sight of still another conquest on the part of her ladyship.

"There she is, that brazen creature!" Cecily's mama fairly hissed—which was rather a mistake, for it meant that she sprayed crumbs from the oatcake with which she was stuffing her mouth while she waited for her kippers and kedgeree. It was not a pretty sight.

Cecily seemed more melancholy than enraged. "Yes, Mama, I can see her very well. Do you know, I cannot think what there is about her that the gentlemen find so attractive, I am sure, unless it is her wonderful wardrobe."

"I cannot think what there is about her that fairly makes my flesh crawl," retorted Mrs. Fairfax, "but whatever it is, you can be sure I will publish it before the world when I discover it. Women like that are a public menace in places like Cheyne Spa. The only happy thought is that, since she is now to be seen with Mr. Wycombe, it may be that she has been thrown over by the duke."

Cecily sighed. "I do not wish to enter upon that subject again just now, Mama, if you do not mind. I know the old gentleman is rich and would make me very well off, but so is Mr. Wycombe quite monied, I believe, even though he has no title."

The young lady pouted as she saw that Patrick was bending over the seated Lady Kinsale's hand with every indication of ardour. "Look how he fawns over her!"

"Oh, I have no patience with you!" her mother said crossly. "Fancy any ambitious young girl who would rather be the wife of a mere gentleman when she could be a duchess! Preserve me!"

Cecily stretched her neck as much as she could in imitation of Susanna. "I am sure that if I had the magnificent clothes she does, I should be able to attract gentlemen every bit as well, but I expect that requires more money than we shall ever see. Her husband must have left her quite a lot, don't you think, Mama? But I am not altogether certain about her personal taste. That darling hat she is wearing is not right for her sort of face, and the colour of that walking dress is certainly better suited to a blond."

"That is undoubtedly true," said Mrs. Fairfax, biting into another oatcake to pass the time. "Her clothes are quite different in the evening." She thought enviously of the court gown which the woman had worn to the Dress Ball two nights previously. Long of line and high of waist, it had made every other woman there look like a fussy dowd by its classic simplicity—though, in Mrs. Fairfax's opinion, even it could have done with a bit of jewellery. Odd how the creature trotted about in such magnificent gowns, yet depended upon a mere ribbon at the neck or wrist to set them off. Admittedly it was a splendid neck and needed little adornment, but there were limits. Cecily's neck, she admitted as well, tended to be a bit short. Luckily, she was possessed of such a pretty face that most gentlemen tended to overlook her few shortcomings. Or they always *had* done so. Now there was this Kinsale creature standing about and casting a considerable shadow.

But the clothes were good, she had to admit. She wished she herself could afford such things, let alone put them upon the back of Cecily.

Across the way Patrick Wycombe was frankly admitting to himself that he was smitten. It rather alarmed him, for he was not sure how a gentleman who had always been so careful as he had been could find himself in this state, but there it was. To be honest about the matter, he had to admit as well that it had little to do with his past caution, for Lady Kinsale was nothing like any other woman he had ever encountered. She was intelligent, charming, beautiful, and clever enough to dress very well indeed despite, he suspected, very little money. Why else would she be living in that respectable but faintly shabby lodging-house on Upper Orson Street? Such places were all very well for people like Lady Morphy, who had the reputation of gambling away all but her last half crown, but it was an unusual setting for a jewel such as Lady Kinsale. There was more here than met the eye, of that he was sure; but he was prepared to overlook all but the most glaring discrepancies if only she would continue to smile at him as she was smiling at him now over the rim of her teacup.

"What is it, Mr. Wycombe, that makes you so attentive to a poor stranger?" she was asking with an impish twinkle in her eye. "I am sure I shall remain forever in your debt for your intervention between that wicked man and myself. How is your poor head, by the way?"

"You ask that with such tender solicitude, your ladyship, that I quite wish that I could still lay claim to wounds of valour, but alas, I have healed so quickly that I have little to show for the adventure."

Susanna shuddered. "I hardly think it could be called an

adventure, sir, to be set upon by a pair of brutes at the instigation of a notorious bully!"

He looked sharply into her face. "You know who it was, then?"

She nodded, although somewhat tentatively.

"You could swear to it?"

Susanna remembered Lady Morphy's cautionary words upon the subject and reflected that Mr. Wycombe, by his own words, appeared quite recovered from the incident. "Why, I can only assume . . ."

"We all so assume, madam, but it cannot be made public without a witness who would swear upon it in a court of law."

But Susanna's masquerade, she knew, would never withstand such scrutiny. However much her open nature urged her to support his complaint, she knew the time was not ripe for the confessions it would entail. Indeed, it was quite possible that the disclosure of her real identity might bring about more gossip and criticism than would be supportive to his allegations against the Royal Duke—and might do him more harm than good.

A slight frown formed upon Mr. Wycombe's brow as he looked over her shoulder at something beyond. She turned curiously to see what was disturbing him and found it might have arisen from either of two causes. From one direction Mrs. Fairfax, of all people, was descending upon them with a determined look in her eye; also, Susanna saw, a far more sinister arrival was striding through the entrance to the Gardens. His Grace, the Duke of Cumberland and Earl of Armagh, with a female upon either arm, was about to take his breakfast *al fresco*. He glanced their way and hesitated very slightly as if debating whether to approach their table. His expression was inscrutable, but whatever his intention, it was Mrs. Fairfax who reached them first.

"Why, Lady Kinsale, good morning! And Mr. Wycombe! When I looked across and saw you I could hardly believe my eyes."

Patrick rose from his seat. "Why is that, madam?"

Cecily's mama contrived to look both arch and smugly self-satisfied. "Oh, it was merely a jest, you know. I have become so accustomed to seeing her ladyship with the dear duke that I could not credit that you had taken his place!" Her false laugh had a brittle quality which grated on the ears.

"I am certain the dear duke will appreciate your concern, Mrs. Fairfax," Susanna said sweetly. She next tried to hold her tongue, but the words fairly forced themselves out. "And how is your lovely Cecily?" She allowed her eyes to rest on the young woman across the garden. "She seems quite lost, sitting all alone. Would you not care to join us?" She avoided Patrick Wycombe's eyes. "I am sure there is always room for one more."

Mrs. Fairfax was obviously torn between the desire to intrude upon on them for its own sake, and the realisation that to do so when she had so obviously completed her own repast would leave her looking rather foolish. It was then that she saw Cumberland and his ladies for the first time.

"Ah, I see we have with us the other duke as well." She leaned closer and the overpowering scent of patchouli enveloped the breakfasters. "Was it not amusing the other evening, when he mistook that dear little German merchant for a Chartist agitator?"

"Not so amusing for the other gentleman in question," said Patrick Wycombe, "since he was arrested and held in custody until his identity could be verified."

"But nothing really dreadful happened to him, you know. It isn't as if he had been executed by mistake or anything like that."

Even Susanna had to admit that a mistaken execution would have had a rather drastic effect on Gavin Marshall's friend, Mr. Neibauer. "At least he was released quite quickly upon the recognizance of the Duke of Quince," she recalled. "Still, it must have been a dreadful experience."

Mrs. Fairfax agreed. "I should think it would quite spoil his holiday." She glanced surreptitiously at Cumberland's table. "The only good effect was the embarrassment it caused certain parties who had created the disturbance in the beginning, I daresay."

"It is a bad business all around," said Mr. Wycombe. "I understand that poor Neibauer had clearer proofs of an alibi than can frequently be produced, having been at cards with Gavin Marshall all the night long and from almost immediately upon his arrival. Still it must have been a harrowing situation to be sitting there wagering fives and ponies on whist in the dawn-cracking hours of morning, and then have yourself set upon to be dragged off before a constable."

"Well, I daresay there are many whose true identity is not as they would present it to the world, is that not so . . . Lady Kinsale?" The words of Mrs. Fairfax all but spewed out of her mouth as though they had been propelled by some terrible internal pressure. Luckily, Susanna had the presence of mind to remain calm and, in fact, to raise her eyebrows in faint inquiry at the woman's transparently veiled accusation. She glanced quickly at Mr. Wycombe to see what effect the words had had upon him, but he seemed almost oblivious to them. It was evident that the implications were lost upon him.

Susanna countered the situation and killed the line of conversation by the bold stroke of smiling genially across the garden at Cecily—looking bored and listless at the table where her mother had abandoned her—and waving her toward them. Miss Fairfax rose with an alacrity not often found in such pretty young women who, more often than not, pretend that their presence is too rare a commodity to be recklessly scattered upon social waters. However, Mr. Wycombe was sitting at the table with Lady Kinsale, and to Cecily that made all the difference.

As it fell out, Susanna was spared Miss Fairfax's company; for just as the young woman hurried along the path to join them, Susanna caught sight of still another arrival and waved to the gentleman standing in the gateway.

"The dear duke has arrived to fetch me for a drive in his

phaeton and I fear I must leave you all. What a pity, Mrs. Fairfax, that you did not bring dear Cecily over to us at the beginning. We have never really had a good chat. . . . Good-bye, Mr. Wycombe, it was good of you to pass the time of waiting with me. I am sure I am very grateful."

Patrick, too, had risen from the table with her and he now bent over her hand once more. "The duke is a lucky man, your ladyship. How I wish I were fortunate enough to merit the favour he receives from you."

Acknowledging the compliment graciously, she moved toward the arm of the waiting peer. As she passed the table where Cumberland sat with his unknown ladies, he, too, rose from his seat and bowed slightly. She was vividly aware of the intensity of his glance, but she merely inclined her head toward him for a moment and swept on.

"Who was it you were breakfasting with?" asked the old duke. "Young Wycombe, was it?"

"Yes," she agreed, "and Mrs. Fairfax and her daughter. A cup or two of tea, really. Not breakfast at all."

The duke had a light, quick hand on the reins and they were already passing beyond the limits of the town and moving into the countryside. She admired the way he handled the horses. "Pleasant chap, I believe?" he pressed further.

"Very pleasant," she agreed, but her mind was in a whirl. Now that Mrs. Fairfax seemed to be indicating that her secret was out—or, at least, that it was suspect and would be divined presently—she supposed that Cheyne Spa would become closed to her. Adventuresses, after all, were not well regarded in polite society. Well, one could think of this as a trial run. There was still a substantial amount of capital left. Enough, at any rate for her to flee with Tibby to another watering hole—Bath, perhaps, though the competition for attention would be stiffer; or Cheltenham, which was rather more frivolous, though their experience of masqueraders might be greater.

"I sense, my girl, that your mind is not altogether upon the beauties of the countryside."

"No," she agreed frankly, "it is not. I beg your indulgence if I am being inattentive."

"Do you have troubles, then, that I can help you with?"

Susanna shook her head and adjusted her shawl a little to cover the bare arms below her curricle jacket's short sleeves. At last she admitted "Yes, I confess I do have troubles, Your Grace, but I fear they are of my own making and must therefore be of my own solving. I hope you have not thought me rude. I have not meant to be." She turned her head about and gazed upon the countryside brightly, but he was not prepared to give up so easily.

"Not at all, my dear, not at all, but I wish you would take me into your confidence. "It isn't money, is it?" he asked guardedly.

"Oh, no, sir!" Susanna could not help but giggle. "Did you think I had lured you out into the countryside to force you to stand and deliver?"

"I suspect," said the duke, "that you are an extraordinary young woman and I would not be surprised at anything you chose to do."

Susanna gathered this to her as a compliment, but she might have been less sanguine had she heard the words which flew about Cheyne as they drove back into the resort village.

"No nice woman would go riding with a man alone. Where is her maid?"

"She is a widow, after all."

"Unless," said a third—and she quickly put her fan before her mouth as she said the words which soon flew all over the town—"unless Lady Kinsale has made a conquest. Perhaps she will be the next Duchess of Quince?"

And once repeated, the speculation turned into the affirmative. Before evening had fallen, Susanna had been definitely raised to the peerage in the minds of the denizens of Cheyne Spa.

═ 15 ═

"WHAT DO YOU mean, she will see no one? Is she ill?"

"No, my lady," Tibby answered. "Lady Kinsale is quite well, but she has instructed me to say that she wishes to be alone for a little and hopes her dear friends will be understanding of her feelings."

"By whom she means me, I expect. Well, it is to no avail. Understanding, indeed!" The duke's sister gathered herself to push past the little maidservant and see for herself what the trouble might be, but something in Tibby's calm eyes dissuaded her. She had the certain feeling that the wench would actually close the door or stand in her way if she attempted such a thing. Ah well, no woman of quality goes where she is not wanted. Not immediately, at any rate.

"Is she attending the concert with us this evening?"

"I do not know, my lady."

Lady Morphy sniffed loudly in annoyance. "It is all very unusual, I must say. Quite thoughtless, in my view! Remind your mistress, if you will, that it is the virtuoso John Field who is playing. He is a personal friend of my nevvy, and his . . . what-do-you-call-'ems . . . his nocturnes are not to be missed. He will be returning to St. Petersburg until next season—if, indeed, he ever comes back to England— and she is a Philistine if she avoids hearing him!"

"I shall tell her that, madam. She is a Flisteen if she don't go to the concert."

"You are certain she is not ill?"

"More than sure, your ladyship. Lady Kinsale is resting

134

at the moment, but I will give her your message as soon as she awakens." And Lady Morphy had to be content with that, though she was certainly far from satisfied as she trudged back up the stairs to her own chamber. She would set Gavin on the little watchdog. Bless him, he could get 'round any woman in the nation if he chose.

But, my word, what time was it, anyway? Past noon and Gavin had not yet returned from the previous night's carouse? The boy must be brought up short or everything would go by the board. But even as she was sounding out the phrases of a scolding, there was a light tapping on her door.

Gavin looked a little the worse for wear. Respectable enough to go through the streets, you understand, but hollow-eyed and showing the need of a razor to remove the dark stubble which darkened his cheeks. His aunt flared her nostrils, seeking some scent of further dissipation, but there was not the faintest whiff of drink. He had been gambling, presumably since she had left him in the Lower Rooms. When his aunt reported Susanna's incomprehensible behaviour, he was quite philosophic about it.

"Some of your women's mysteries, I daresay. My word, my dear soul, I fail to see why you are so alarmed."

Her ladyship could not but own that her premonition seemed flighty. There had been, she felt, something ominous in Tibby's behaviour and her resolute demeanour under questioning, but probably Gavin was right. She was being silly. "You had better get some rest," she advised him. "I do not want you snoring against my shoulder while Field is playing."

Gavin laughed. "John is an old friend. Would I subject him to such behaviour?"

"You have done as much before," she reminded him. "I recall that in Dresden . . ."

He threw up his hand. "Enough! Do not remind me! I will sleep the afternoon away. Do you think I would be so gross as to doze through the voyaging of a virtuoso? I wonder how old John is? We haven't seen him since Tilsit two years ago when I took him for a hundred pounds. I trust he will be as anxious to regain his money as I am to take more from him."

"Go to your bed, boy, and spare me your fantasies."

Gavin grinned at her a little lopsidedly. "One would think, Aunt, that you had never placed a wager in your life."

"I never got up from the tables at noon!" she retorted. "I have more self-respect than that."

"Hoity-toity. How much money have we left in the purse?"

His aunt looked somewhat chagrined. "Enough for the season if we are careful with it. Neither of us can allow ourselves to be less than sensible at the tables, you know. We must be sensible above all."

"Mrs. Maundy is taken care of?"

"Oh, yes. Food, lodging and care are paid until we leave Cheyne in September, but that is not to say we have anything extra."

Gavin frowned. "Appearances must be kept up, Aunt. There is no one from whom Lady Luck flees quite so quickly as a gambler so down on his luck that he becomes seedy."

"Then you had better be in your bed," she counselled. "You look as if the furies themselves had ridden all night on your shoulders. I hope for all this that you at least broke even?"

"I won a little," he admitted. "Very little, but at any rate I did not lose."

His aunt nodded consolingly. She knew exactly how he felt.

A few moments later on the floor below, Tibby closed the door once more and slipped back into the darkened bedroom.

"Who was it, Tib?" asked her mistress drowsily.

"Mr. Marshall, your ladyship. He looked quite terrible, as if he had not slept for a long while. Would your ladyship care for some tea?"

Susanna made an impatient gesture. "You need not use that silly title when we are alone. I cannot think why you continue to do so. You are Tibby and I am Susanna when there is no one else about. Do you think actors use the names of the characters when they have left the stage? We are playing roles here, nothing more."

Tibby verged on scandalisation. "Oh, I could not do that! If I was to get into the habit of it, you see, I might make a slip at the wrong time—and then where would we be? Lady Kinsale's maidservant calling her by her Christian name? That would be a wonder to set up Cheyne Spa, wouldn't it? No, your ladyship, I'll accept the thought for the deed and go along in the way I've begun, if you don't mind."

She looked closely at the reclining figure. "Are you all right, then? I don't care for you lying here in the dark."

Susanna sat up slowly, displaying little energy for the task. "Well enough. I feel as if I have a megrim coming on."

Tibby reached out a hand and felt Susanna's forehead. It was only a very little warmer than it should be. "I feel quite guilty that I wasn't here when you came back from your drive."

"It is no matter," said Susanna. "You have a right to your own time."

"Something happened, didn't it?" Tibby pressed. "There is something you are not telling me."

"No," Susanna answered. She ran her fingers listlessly through her hair. "Nothing happened, but I have a dreadful feeling that something *will* happen if I do not take steps to ward it off."

She swung her feet around and placed them on the floor, searching for her slippers. "The only trouble is that I cannot predict what it will be or what remedy it will require." She explained to Tibby how Mrs. Fairfax's words had first begun to alarm her and the maidservant sat down uneasily on the side of the bed.

"Do you mean to say, miss, that she all but called you an impostor right there in front of Mr. Wycombe?"

"Not exactly. She only hinted at it. I am certain that she herself does not know what exactly is in her mind, though if she once recognised me, I expect she would publish it to the world in no time at all."

"How did Mr. Wycombe react?"

"I am not sure that he even noticed. It was not that she actually came out with anything, you know. It was only a hint, not an accusation. It was the *way* she said the name . . . 'Lady . . . Kinsale' . . . as though it were burning her mouth, that leaves me with the distinct impression that she is not the fool I perhaps imagined. Something is going on in that ferret-like little head of hers, I am sure."

"What are you suggesting, miss? That we take to our heels and run?"

"I don't know. That remedy has certainly crossed my mind." She looked closely at the maidservant. "Why, Tibby, what an expression you have!" Then it dawned. *"Your* young man! Fred. If we go away, you think it will be all over with him, is that it?"

"I don't really know, miss. He hasn't said anything. I am not even sure how he feels, you know. It hasn't been all that long that we've been walking out, has it? How long have we been here in Cheyne, a month and a half?"

It seemed quite otherwise to Susanna. First had come her schooling by Lady Morphy, and then the slow emergence into the life of the spa, the debut at the Cotillion Ball and the attentions from various gentlemen. Lady Morphy had been quick to drive away most of them, but there had been a few pleasurably idle moments along the way. For a young woman unaccustomed to male attention, even the most trifling notice had been a revelation.

She thought of the major ones, the dear duke and Mr.

Wycombe—Patrick Wycombe especially. It was odd that, in the short time she had been acquainted with him, her vision of his character had quite changed. No longer was it his extreme handsomeness which attracted her, although that had certainly not diminished; but his warm and generous nature had become paramount in her eyes. Due to Gavin and Lady Morphy, she had seen relatively little of Patrick; but what she had come to know, she appreciated. He seemed to be as fine a man within as he was fine-looking without. Unlike his friend Mr. Marshall, she thought, whose every thought seemed centered upon his own advantage.

"What did he want when he was at the door, Tibby?"

"What did who want, miss?"

"Mr. Marshall. What did Mr. Marshall want?"

"Only to enquire about your ladyship's health and to be sure you are merely indisposed, I expect, and not unwell."

"He did? Gavin Marshall actually asked about my health? How very extraordinary." Hearing the confusion in the tone of her mistress, Tibby could not help but smile.

"Yes, miss, he did, and I don't think it was from any motive of business, either. He didn't look too good himself."

"Not too good?" Susanna asked. "What do you mean? Is he ill?"

"Oh, I shouldn't think so. More like a bad night at the tables and a lack of sleep, I'd believe."

Susanna took up the brush and began to stroke her hair. "Another night of bilking some poor victim, I imagine."

Tibby took the brush out of her mistress's hand and began to arrange the lovely strands herself. "He looked rather the other way around, if you was to ask me. More as if he had been drubbed himself."

"Never mind," said Susanna, "it will doubtless do him a deal of good. He is a man with much too high an opinion of himself, in my view, is our Mr. Marshall."

Tibby continued to stroke slowly, languorously. "Oh, I

don't know, Miss Susanna. He's certainly been a help to us, hasn't he? Especially since you decided not to go into their scheme."

"I expect it was for business reasons, Tibby. Please remember that. Scheme or no scheme, I don't think we are any more to Gavin Marshall than a possible way of squeezing out a few more pounds from his uncle. Once they see that such a hope is fruitless, I expect they'll give up on us altogether."

"He didn't mention his uncle, miss, nor say anything about the plans when he asked about your health, and that is a fact. You must not be too hard on the gentleman, you know. Nobody is perfect, but there is some good in all of us."

Susanna was not much taken aback by this spirited defense. She had her own opinions of Mr. Marshall, and they were not as generous as those of the little maidservant. Presently she said, "I think I will remain quietly in the house for a few days, Tibby, but there is no reason why you must do so. I expect your young man would become quite alarmed if he were not to see you. Aren't you glad you have been practising your penmanship and your reading, so that you can keep in touch with him if we have to go away?"

Tibby shook her head sadly at this. " 'Twouldn't do no good, my writing Fred, miss. He can't read no more than I could when you took me in hand. I've promised to teach him if we should stay about Cheyne Spa long enough." But there was something in the way she said it that sparked Susanna's mind, and a new and interesting idea took root. What if all this play-acting had merely been a mistake from the beginning?

"Tib," she said, "we still have the annuity Lady Wycombe settled upon me and the money she left you."

"Yes, Miss Susanna, I expect we haven't spent so very much of it."

Susanna's mouth tightened a little and her jaw became

quite firm. "We could go back to our original plan, couldn't we? Find ourselves a little cottage in the country, you know, and live very quietly."

"Yes, miss, I expect we could do that."

Tibby was turned away from her, and Susanna took the girl by the shoulders and turned her back. "Do you care for him so much?" she asked.

Tibby tossed her head. "Who? Fred, do you mean? Lord, he is just another man, isn't he? There's plenty of men in the world if a girl cares to look. I expect I shall find someone to walk out with as easily in the country as here in the spa."

Susanna rose from the chair before the mirror and went into the little room where the gowns were stored, rummaging among them hurriedly. Tibby followed and stood watching in the door. "Whatever are you doing, miss? I thought you was going to lie low for a few days?"

"I have changed my mind," said Susanna. "I see no earthly reason why I should be intimidated by Mrs. Fairfax or anyone else. What can be done to us, in any case? Will they arrest me for using a nonexistent title? If the celebrated John Field, an Irishman, is playing tonight, I see no reason why Lady Kinsale, a bogus Irishwoman, should not be in attendance, do you?"

"I expect you are quite right, your ladyship, and I am quite glad to hear it, but what are you searching for in the press room?"

Susanna blushed a little. "Well, perhaps I am not as uninfluenced by Mrs. Fairfax as I pretend. I am looking for something that is not totally in the front rank of fashion for once. And, do you know, Tibby, here we are with all these clothes—and I cannot find a single thing to wear?"

=== 16 ===

"Do you mean to say to me, William John, that you actually proposed marriage to Lady Kinsale and the silly creature refused you?"

Lady Morphy was more than astonished. It would be fair to announce that she was quite dumbfounded, but her brother shook his head. "No, I did not say that she had refused me, Clemmie."

"I should think not!" She stopped, considered. "Then what *do* you mean to say?"

The Duke of Quince shrugged eloquently. "I mean to say that she has given me no answer at all. She has asked for time to consider my proposal and I have, naturally, agreed to wait until she has had time to do so."

Lady Morphy's eyes narrowed. "That was very clever of her."

"Clever?" asked the duke. "In what way, clever?" But his sister's look told him a great deal more than he truly cared to know. "Ah, I can guess what you are thinking," he said. "It is true that I am an old man in her eyes, nearly twice her age."

"Twice if one is being generous about it," his sister agreed. "Nearly three times her age would be more accurate, but that is not at all the point. You are a clever and well-regarded peer, one of the first gentlemen of the realm, and with a lineage the monarch himself could well envy. You are, as well, as rich as Croesus and as kind as can be. You are quite the kindest man I know, despite the fact that," here she made a grimace, "you are not the least careful of me where money is concerned."

"Stop, I beg you," he said.

"I will allow it as your only fault. I have, even, a certain affection for your parsimony, objectively considered, since it makes you rather endearingly human."

"There is no doubt," he said, "that I am far from being a saint. I have vices of which you know nothing."

"Pshaw! Vices! No, you are not a saint, my dear brother, you are a fool! And if that empty-headed ninny has the temerity to refuse you, she is another!"

"Despite all?" he asked, eyeing her shrewdly.

"Despite all? What do you mean by that?"

"I mean to say," he allowed tolerantly, "that I suspect you and your protégée had something of a falling out. Amn't I correct? I think you are disturbed because she had the effrontery to reject *your* proposal."

His sister's nostrils flared and she tossed her head impatiently like a shying horse. "The girl is ungrateful."

"I suppose some might not say the same of you, my dear? *I* would not, you understand, since I know the circumstances of your life, but some would think your allowance from me quite munificent, eh?"

She said nothing at this and he went on. "Do you think she is truly ungrateful, Clementina, or merely too scrupled for your schemes?"

She studied him curiously. "What *do* you mean? Has that young woman been suggesting something?" His look seemed to her to be too open and straightforward for a man who was making an accusation. "You term her my protégée, but the creature is nothing to me. I was merely kind to her, that is all. I tutored her a bit in the ways of society— Gavin improved her dancing—and we introduced her around a bit."

"As the widow of the . . . Lieutenant-General of Ireland?"

Even Lady Morphy could not brazen out such a thing

completely, and she took refuge in laughter. "Well, you cannot complain that it did harm, can you?"

"No," he said, "none of that matters to me."

"Then what the devil are you getting at, William John?"

The duke looked at his sister sadly. "Let me ask you straightforwardly: Did you expect monetary advantage from my marriage to Susanna Archer?"

To her credit, even Lady Morphy was taken aback by the revelation that he knew what he was about. "Good Lord, you quite astonish me. How long have you known who she is?"

"Only a day or two."

"Before you made your proposal to her?" she demanded in surprise. "You are a treat."

"Yes, before," the duke said. "I only made the proposal this morning." He narrowed his eyes at her, and it seemed to her to be incredibly boyish, as though he were a ten-year-old playing at adult games. "What will it take to buy your silence?" he asked.

"Pshaw! Who do you think me? I am not too old to be amused by the spectacle of my aging brother participating in a farce, such as this one is quickly becoming. I will hold my tongue free of charge for a little while, if you like. Certainly I should do so until she has given you her answer. Then we shall see what my curbed tongue is worth." She considered. "Am I to hold the knowledge of *your* knowledge from Gavin as well?"

"For the moment from everyone, I think. Can you do it?"

"May I ask what will be in it for me in the future? I do not mean to be greedy, but I should like to examine my prospects."

The duke made an ironic little half-bow. "You shall have my eternal gratitude."

Lady Morphy clicked her tongue derisively. "I had in mind something rather more substantial, but I suppose that for the moment I must be satisfied with what I get, since my game is tumbled." Leaning closer to him, she kissed him upon the cheek.

"It is a gamble for high stakes for a man your age, is it not, my dear William? I admire you for the courage of it. As a gambler myself, I can only say that I hope you take your trick."

Gavin, however, reacted to the news of the proposal (which the duke had agreed might be mentioned, though not the unmasking of Miss Archer's identity) with unprecedented fury.

"That little minx!" he cried, stomping about his aunt's chamber, oblivious to the fact that Susanna was just below, "That demmed, cheating little minx!"

"I suspect," his aunt said with a hint of asperity, "that you are being less than reasonable. I wonder if you are not more distrait than the situation calls for?"

He was scornful at the suggestion. "You, madam, have an overactive imagination. The girl means nothing to me in that way, though, I grant you, she has shaped into a magnificent creature. But my taste, as you very well know, runs after the Lady of Fortune and no other. I have yet to find a flesh-and-blood woman who could excite me one quarter as much as those four pasteboard queens."

"If that is really true, not a mere pose on your part," said Lady Morphy, "then you are even more cold-hearted than I had thought—and more pitiable. I feel very sorry for you."

Gavin hooted with laughter. "For me? You feel sorry for me? Oh, come now, teach granny to suck eggs! You and I are as alike as two peas, which is why we fare so well together. Allow me my cold heart, milady, for it matches your very own!"

But later, when he saw Susanna at the concert, sedately dressed in unadorned half-mourning for her nonexistent husband, he remembered his aunt's supposition with an uneasy feeling in his stomach. Rather than listening to his friend's expert touch upon the keyboard, he found that he was studying Susanna's reaction to the sounds. For a moment or two he almost considered his aunt's words carefully—for as much as thirty or forty seconds, in fact—before discarding them. No, the idea was all too absurd.

Completely absurd.

John Field was at the top of his form and popularity. As a pianist he was one of the most popular in Europe; as a composer he had more or less invented a type of composition called "the nocturne," calm, reflective and engaging, which had brought him even greater popularity and approbation than he had previously enjoyed. Originally a child prodigy in Dublin, he was presently a resident of his beloved St. Petersburg where he had settled in as the most fashionable of teachers, though he still returned on frequent tours of Europe as a virtuoso. Gavin had always found there to be a particularly intimate quality about his friend's playing—the attuned mind entering the interior world of the music became a part of it, lifting and amplifying the spirit at the core.

Gavin, drifting upon the waves of sound, found himself seriously considering certain disturbing aspects of his own life which he had always felt to be alien to his basic nature. He had long since accustomed himself to the recognition of the fact that there were parts of the lives of ordinary men which were denied him. It was not that he missed them, particularly. No, their lack provoked no great emptiness in his world. But it must be faced that they were absent.

The lovely pieces rippled one after the other from Field's fingers: the F Major Nocturne, the Nocturne Pastorale, the Nocturne Characteristique, the Malinconia in D Minor. They created an increasingly effective universe of their own, no less real because of their intrinsic fragility. At the interval Gavin slipped quietly from the hall, the echoing waves of applause diminishing behind him as he strode along the river's edge, seeking to clear his head of the notions that the music and Susanna's presence had engendered.

When Field's performance was at last concluded and the concertgoers began dispersing in a kind of abstracted daze, the Duke of Quince pushed through them to Susanna's side. They exchanged greetings quietly to the accompaniment of pointed and curious stares from all about them.

"May I walk with you?" he asked her humbly, as if uncertain of his welcome.

"Of course, Your Grace. I shall always be privileged to be in your company." They moved slowly toward the outer doors. "Did you enjoy the music?"

"Always," he answered. "Field is a particular favourite of mine. Would you care to go to his dressing-room and let me present him to you?"

She coloured, for the notion seemed somehow indelicate to her, though she could not have said why. Perhaps it was because she was still under the spell of the man's music and the thought of intruding upon him at such a time seemed repugnant. "I thank you for the suggestion," she murmured, "but I should prefer to meet him at another time."

"A glass of wine, then? A bit of refreshment?"

Susanna smiled. "That would be most pleasant." As they moved out of the Assembly Rooms into the square, they suddenly found that they were the focus of a crowd of well-wishers who seemed to be of the opinion that certain promises had been made between them. Everyone wanted to be among the first to offer congratulations—smiling at them ingratiatingly, or a little sheepishly, or with defiantly brilliant teeth-flashing, clustering about Susanna and the duke as if to claim a share of fancied achievement. To the young woman, unaccustomed to such public attention, it appeared that the world of fashionable Cheyne Spa had taken it upon itself to decide her future for her. Amidst this rain of good wishes Susanna was aware of her own vulnerability as never before. They were swept up in the aura of

Lady Kinsale, a woman who had never existed. What would they say, how would they react if they knew the truth?

But, at any rate, in Cheyne Spa the attention span is short and the crowd about them began to thin as people took up their own concerns, leaving their temporary idols standing quite alone in the middle of the square. They did not so much drift off as suddenly vanish with a rapidity that was quite astonishing. Susanna and the duke were one moment being pawed by admirers and the next completely alone. Looking at each other in surprise, they burst into rueful laughter.

"Such is the fleeting smile of success," said the duke and restored the humour to Susanna's eyes. They moved across the square to the corner where two choices presented themselves: they could walk along Gravia Street which led to Upper Orson and Susann's lodging-house, or follow the crowd down the hill to the Lower Rooms.

His Grace raised his eyebrows enquiringly and Susanna felt a rush of affection for this upright gentleman with his fatherly benevolence toward her. She knew she must deceive him in this matter of marriage no longer. She felt that he deserved both an answer to his proposal and the truth about herself.

"Shall we walk about for a bit, sir?" she asked.

They turned along Gay Street. He did not press her, but she knew he must be aware of a certain tension in her manner. At last she drew a deep breath and, peering through the darkness at him, she said falteringly, "There are things I feel I must say to Your Grace . . . and I do not know exactly how or where to begin."

"Will it help you if I say that you need have no fear of telling me anything at all?"

"With respect, sir, I am not certain of that." She squared her shoulders and took another deep breath, long this time and rather trembling. "I fear, Your Grace, that I have not been altogether straightforward with you."

He asked kindly, "Indeed, in what way?"

"I hardly know how to tell you!" she blurted out. "I am not altogether as I seem to you to be!"

"In what way, dear girl?" It startled her to find that his eyes seemed to twinkle even in the half darkness. "Do you, by any chance," he asked, "mean to say something to me about your late husband?"

Susanna gasped. "My husband?"

"Yes. Lord Kinsale? The former Lieutenant-General of Ireland, you know."

"No," said Susanna fiercely decisive, "I do *not* know, sir, for I have never in my life had a husband, peer or commoner. I have never been to Ireland and I am not a rich widow. I am merely poor Susanna Archer, the owner of a pack of handsome costumes which I wish to heaven my late employer had left to someone else!"

"I really doubt that Lady Wycombe had anyone else to whom she could have left them," he observed. "I rather think that Patrick would never have found use for them."

It was a moment or two before the gist of what he said sank into Susanna's head, then she giggled uncomfortably. "You knew all this time? I suppose I have been the laughingstock of Cheyne Spa?"

"Not at all," he answered gruffly. "Only the person who obtained the information—whom I trust, you know—and myself, and, I suppose, those erstwhile partners of yours, my sister and nevvy."

"You knew that as well?" She hung her head. "I am very ashamed."

"No, I believe the shame would lie in never telling me. I don't know how long that could have lasted, however. I am a terrible dub at keeping secrets."

"Do you mean to say that you would have married me—even knowing all that—if I had agreed?"

"I will *still* marry you, if you agree, Susanna Archer. Always supposing that you would accept having a rich old husband instead of a young man who still has the world before him. I have very few surprises left in my store, I fear, but I would do my very utmost to make you happy. Will you not reconsider, Susanna? Will you not give me your hand in matrimony?"

She stood stricken at the implications of his proposal. She—Susanna Archer, not Lady Kinsale—could, if she chose, become the Duchess of Quince with all the riches, position and honour which that title brought with it.

And yet she could not answer him.

"I am sorry, sir, that I still have no reply. You have given me even more things to consider than I had before."

His Grace took her hand in his, lightly caressing the fingers. "I understand, dear one, only too well. I know that there are many considerations. I expect it is not an easy decision to make. But," he added brightly, "enough of this pensiveness! You don't really want to trudge back to Mrs. Maundy's manse, do you? What do you say if we head for the Lower Rooms in search of a bit of excitement?"

They changed their direction and began to descend the hill, released from all constraint now and chattering like magpies. In the short time she had known the duke, Susanna had come to suspect that there was a wealth of wisdom within him which had never been tapped. Certainly a man of his age, acuity, and position should be a storehouse of all sorts of impressions and information, adventures and observations and . . . but here she stopped suddenly. She had not yet made up her mind, and yet she was congratulating herself on her good luck as if she had already come to a decision about marrying him. It was uncommonly strange to think of herself—herself!—as a duchess; but, she realised, she had been doing so for the past five minutes. The Duke of Quince was indubitably an easy man with whom to be.

If the crowd outside the Assembly Rooms had been overly attentive to Susanna and His Grace, the same folk gathered into the gambling rooms were much too wrapt in their own concerns to pay attention to such a mundane estate as matrimony when it stood in the way of gaming. The clinking, the ruffling and reshuffling, the murmured cries of pleasure or despair, and the whirr of the wheels provided a sort of music to which even John Field (already seated, back to the wall, at one of the whist tables) was not immune. One of the men at his table, however, cast back the cards which had been dealt him and arose from the table, approaching Susanna and the duke.

It was Patrick Wycombe and, bowing, he gave them a hearty smile. "I understand, Your Grace and your lady-ship, that fervent congratulations are in order."

"I fear you are a trifle premature," the duke said quietly. "I have made the offer, but the lady has yet to make a decision."

There was no mistaking the unsuccessful attempt of Mr. Wycombe to hide the rush of pleasure to his face. "Then," he said candidly, "there remains hope, however faint, for the rest of us?"

Quince did not find this particularly amusing. "I am unfortunately aware," he said, "that I am merely one among many who are attracted to the lady, and that I am disadvantaged in many respects." He bent over Susanna's hand. "If you will excuse me, my dear, there are some gentlemen across the room whom I must see. You will be all right?"

"Of course," Susanna answered. "Mr. Wycombe will attend me."

The duke regarded them with sad eyes. "Of course," he said.

Patrick hardly waited until His Grace was gone before he began to actively plead his case. "Is it true, Lady Kinsale? You have not accepted his offer?"

She wondered what he would say, how he would react, if she disclosed her secret to him as she had been prepared to do to His Grace. Would he turn away from her in disgust? Dared she risk their budding friendship by telling him?

"Yes, it is true that I have not yet given the duke my answer, Mr. Wycombe, but there are reasons for it which you do not know."

The delight with which he reacted to these words made him almost laugh out loud. "I have heard the one thing I wanted to know, your ladyship, that you are as yet unsure of your marriage to the duke."

She looked up into his handsome face and thought what a fine-looking man he was, and thought, too, what a gentleman he was, titled or not. The woman who married him would be very fortunate indeed.

"You are very kind, sir, and I perceive . . ." She stumbled on the words. There was no more reason to deceive this man more than the other, was there?

"Mr. Wycombe, you are very kind, but there is little you really know about me. I am not at all what I seem to be. I am not . . ."

But before she could blurt out her true identity, a familiarly strident voice cut across her explanation. "Good evening, Mr. Wycombe. Good evening, your . . . ladyship."

"Good evening, Mrs. Fairfax." Patrick cleared his throat as if what he was about to say was completely repugnant to the gentleman he had been taught to be. "The . . . ah . . . the fact is, madam . . ."

Cecily's mother looked from one to the other of them. "My word, have I interrupted a private moment? Upon my honour, you have a plethora of suitors, madam. I quite envy you."

Mr. Wycombe," said Susanna gently, "I believe that Mrs. Fairfax and I have a few words to say to each other. If you will excuse me, sir, I hope that you and I can continue our conversation another time soon?"

He bowed stiffly as if offended that she should prefer some woman's conversation to a proposal from him. "I am at your service at any time, your ladyship." He backed slowly away.

"Such a nice young man, isn't he?" commented Mrs. Fairfax a little wistfully. It was a tone that did not sit well upon her. Susanna could scarcely believe there was much that was vulnerable about Mrs. Fairfax.

Susanna unfurled her fan with the flourish she had absorbed from Lady Morphy. "Shall we stroll, madam? I perceive that we have much to talk of." She found she was enwrapt in a kind of inward exultation, and it seemed to her that she did not, after all, really dislike this meddling woman. But—now that she was about to cease being a threat—in fact, she rather liked her. There was a straightforward vulgarity about her that was immensely amusing, viewed from an objective standpoint. All in all, Susanna was rather glad the situation had fallen out the way it had.

"Oh, yes, my dear girl," said Cecily's mother, "a great deal to talk about." She looked up at Susanna with surprising candour. "I hope you know that I mean to keep your secret? It is never wise to let the men in on things, I always say. I do not mean you harm."

"Ah, do you not?" asked Susanna dulcetly. "I am glad to hear it."

"Not at all," the woman explained. "Since you are going to become the Duchess of Quince, there is nothing more to be said about the gowns, is there?"

"The gowns?"

The older woman chuckled and rapped Susanna with her fan. "Come now, you have achieved wonders of transformation, but I am not such an old fool as that. Clemmie Morphy is my friend, you know, and you are not the first young hopeful she has taken in hand."

"And you have had information from her ladyship that you think will be of interest to me?" asked Susanna rather coolly.

"No, not at all. One thing I will say for Clemmie Morphy, she is not a cheat. I expect that you and she have struck a bargain and I will not interfere. I don't say I don't fancy the idea of my Cecily as a peeress, you know, but she was quite in horror of marrying such an old man. Poor thing, she doesn't understand that a gentleman in his mid-fifties can still be in his prime." She sighed. "I certainly would not have turned him away if he had come to my door." She giggled a little wickedly. "Perhaps not at any hour. But I am too indulgent a mother to force my daughter into a loveless marriage against her will, you know."

"I am certain of it," Susanna said drily. "But what is it you have in mind to discuss with me, if it is not the duke?"

The artfully calculated Fairfax laugh fairly rippled out across the room, and more than one head turned to see who it was who found such amusement here. Triumph was often shouted out in the Lower Rooms as a winner took back his money from the house, or even tragedy when the cards fell the wrong way, or that little ball jumped from the hole into which it seemed to have settled and into another for which it was destined.

"Why, nothing very much," answered Mrs. Fairfax. "Only to be assured that, since you have settled your own future with His Grace, you will not interfere with my settling my daughter's with Mr. Wycombe. She is very fond of him, you know. I am certain you can understand why. He is so very handsome."

"And so very rich," said Susanna as if they were conspirators. But there are things you do not know, Mrs. Fairfax," she continued. "For one thing, I have not yet accepted the dear duke, as you call him, and for another, Mr. Wycombe seems to me to exhibit suprisingly little interest in Miss Cecily, do you think?"

"He could," said Cecily's mother coldly.

"Yes," Susanna agreed, "I expect he could. Especially if you were to take it upon yourself to explain about the gowns, eh?"

Mrs. Fairfax's eyes filled with very genuine-appearing tears. "For the life of me, Miss Archer, I cannot think why you are being such a dog in the manger. You have your duke. It is not as if I were holding you up for money in order to keep my tongue silent about your secret. I do not have to remind you that no one shall ever learn it from me—least of all the duke! Clemmie is my friend, after all."

Susanna spoke very kindly, as if to a backward child. "But you see, my dear lady, there is no secret to keep. I have already explained to His Grace who I am."

"You didn't!"

"I am afraid I did. What is more, I was just about to make the same disclosure to Mr. Wycombe when you interrupted us."

She half expected an explosion, but, to her credit, the other woman showed an expression of utter admiration. "I never! I only wish my Cecily had half your spunk."

Susanna concealed her surprise at this approbation. "Perhaps she has it, but has never been allowed to let it be expressed?"

They were standing beside the roulette table and Susanna laid down a small stake, when from across the room there was a shocked murmur, and then an enraged voice raised in fury.

"May the devil take you, you cheating wretch. If you were a gentleman, I would call you out!"

Susanna saw John Field rising angrily from the table to face the Duke of Cumberland, who was standing, clenched fist raised as if he were about to strike.

"I shall be happy to meet you at any time your seconds choose, sir," said the pianist coldly.

The lip of the Royal Duke curled in a sneer. "I said I would call you out if you were a *gentleman*. As it stands, I do not care even to soil my hands with you! I suggest, however, that you leave your stake on the table to be redeemed by the men you took it from. You will, I am sure, be leaving Cheyne Spa by the dawn coach."

"Nothing like," said a decisive voice which Susanna recognised at once. "I saw the whole thing. Mr. Field did not cheat you in the least, Your Grace. It is hardly to his discredit if he is a better player than those who usually consent to play against you!"

"By God, madam, if you were a man . . ."

"No," said Lady Morphy coldly, "if *you* were a man, sir, you would not use your rank and privilege to bully your opponents when you find you are losing at cards!"

"Twenty-four rouge," said the croupier. "Will you leave your stake, madam?"

Susanna started across the room toward the disturbance.

"Twenty-four *rouge, encore*," said the croupier. "Will you leave your winnings, madam?"

"Yes, yes, leave them," Susanna called back impatiently.

"Twenty-four *rouge, double-encore*."

Gavin Marshall, entering the gaming room, heard an altercation and hurried to his friend's side.

"See here," John Field shouted impatiently at him, flexing his large-framed body and leaning forward as if he were about to take on the duke with his bare hands. "I am perfectly capable of dealing with this ass! I thank you for your backing, but . . ."

"But nothing," retorted Gavin. "This Royal Bulgar may refuse you, but I am one he must face, will-he, nill-he!" He looked Cumberland straight in the eye. "I am certain you will not refuse me, will you, sir?"

The Regent's brother looked coldly down his nose at this interloper. "And who are you?" he sneered. "A piccolo player?"

Gavin Marshall's expression changed from aggressive outrage to a cold hardness that matched the duke's own. "I am the nephew of the Duke of Quince. One of the *old* titles." In the phrase was a wealth of implication. "And I say, my *lord*, that you are an upstart poltroon and a disgrace both to your family and to the nation which supports you."

Cumberland smiled as if this were the greatest compliment in the world. His tone was almost genial as he said, "I shall be happy to accommodate you at any hour you name.

Shall we say dawn? Unless your head cools during the night and you decide the game is not worth the candle." He regarded Gavin with some curiosity. "Do you really wish to risk death for the sake of an Irish musician, and a Russified one at that?"

"There will be no question of risk, for there will be no engagement tomorrow morning or at any other time." Gavin's uncle hobbled quickly into the centre of the gathering crowd.

"Twenty-four *rouge, encore trois.*"

"Gavin, since you have invoked my name and the name of our family in one of your disputes, you will now apologise to His Grace the duke for your adolescent behavior."

"I will not!" Gavin cried in outrage.

The Duke of Quince, drawing the aura of his authority around him like a king's trappings, met his nephew's eyes firmly. "You will, by God, sir!" He needed to make no auxiliary threat; the force of his words was almost a physical presence.

The words never came from Gavin, for Cumberland intervened. "Are you a schoolmaster then, Quince? I expect this doltish relative of yours will feel the stroke of the birch, eh?"

Gavin's uncle allowed his eyes to rest for the first time in this encounter upon Gavin's opponent. "As for Your Grace," he said clearly, "I of course cannot dictate to you; but I swear that if you continue to press this matter I will stand witness before your brother and, if need be, before all of Parliament, that you are in the wrong and that you have provoked a quarrel with a man who cannot fight you for the sole purpose of saving your face."

Cumberland's eyes blazed. "How dare you, sir!"

"I dare, Your Grace, because I am a peer of this realm whose forbears drafted the Magna Carta to obviate the very kind of oppression which you are calling into play!"

"I will have your head in a basket."

Quince smiled imperturbably. "Will you call for the tumbrel, sir? Am I to believe that your sort has taken lessons from our Gallic friends in the matter of head-chopping? Give way in this, Your Grace, for I do not think your position is so strong as to resist such publicity, is it?" His eyes narrowed and Susanna, standing near, could imagine what a forceful combatant he must have been upon the battlefield.

"I swear before heaven, Cumberland, that I will not back down if you force this issue."

The other duke's scarred face was now quite contorted with rage. "Take care, Quince. You go too far."

"Gentlemen, please!" cried slim Mr. Wilberforce, trying to insinuate his body between them. "You will have the watch on our heads!" He clasped his hands before his chest in the classic manner of piteous imploring. "Oh, sirs . . . Your Graces . . . spare me this, I beg you. It means too much. They will have no more of me, if you go on."

"You need not worry, little man," Cumberland sneered. "I cannot call out a cripple."

An ominous hush fell across the room. There was the strangled croak of nervous laughter, the faint sobs of a woman overcome by the tension.

"Twenty-four *rouge, encore quatre*," said the croupier monotonously. "Two hundred and forty pounds to the lady."

The Duke of Quince, descendant of Norman lords, raised his chin proudly and looked the Hanoverian scion contemptuously in the eye. "Happily, sir, the loss of my leg did nothing to impair my aim. My seconds will call upon you within the hour."

The Royal Duke favoured him with a twisted smile. "I feel you would do well to summon the best surgeon in Cheyne as well, sir, for I will neither expect nor give quarter."

"But Your Grace," cried one of his few supporters, "think of your position!"

Without seeming to listen, the Duke of Cumberland

showed them his back and walked away. But the surprises were not yet finished. "Your Grace, my Lord Duke," Gavin Marshall cried out after him, "may I crave a word?" Cumberland paused, waiting, as Gavin approached him humbly.

"I see, after all, sir, that Your Grace was correct, and I pray that there is no need for matters to go along to this extreme. I beseech your pardon, sir, and I beg that the threat of a duel between two such illustrious men be abrogated."

It was a relatively gracious way of putting the situation right and avoiding an enormous scandal, but Cumberland was not a subtle man in any sense of the word. "Threat!" he thundered. "I will pose *you* a threat, you insolent young puppy! When I have done with your invalid uncle I will return for you as well, and lop off both ends of your so illustrious line!"

Twenty-four *rouge, encore.*"

"It is far too late for that, Gavin," said his uncle coldly. "You can only extend gentlemanly courtesies to gentlemen in such cases. The villain will always seize the advantage." He clapped the younger man upon the shoulder. "Though, my lad, I must say that I appreciate the gesture."

Cumberland, straight-backed and self-righteous, made his way toward the doors.

Gavin was disconsolate. "Oh, uncle, what can I do to stop you? It was entirely my fault. Surely there is some way out of this difficulty, is there not? No honourable man would take advantage of . . ."

Quince stopped him with a look. "It is *my* honour we are at the moment discussing, boy. I do not concern myself with the tarnished and tawdry glory of the Hanovers."

The chagrined Gavin could only reply, "Of course, uncle. What a fool I am."

"Not a fool, my lad, only something of a difficulty at times."

John Field, white-faced, approached them, but the duke

waved aside his protestations even more easily than he had those of his nephew. "No, no, I do not doubt you in the least. This is no more your fault than that of any victim foolish enough to sit at the gaming table with a scoundrel who understands nothing but his own will."

Now the duke saw Susanna standing uncertainly at the side with Lady Morphy, and he held out his hands to both of them. "Come, my dears, you must not look so stricken. I am not so bad a shot as all that. I daresay that if we were on the field in hand-to-hand combat, I might be at something of a disadvantage, but the pistol is a great leveller. Duels are fought every day."

"Oh, but Your Grace," Susanna sighed, "men are killed in duels every day as well."

The duke's eyes twinkled at her. "Only if they are both demmed bad shots. Even at the worst I shall have nothing more than a minor wound; Cumberland cannot afford anything worse. This may turn out to be a blessing in disguise for our party, in fact, for the episode may so turn the tide against him that the Regent will have no option but to deal with him in a suitable way."

"I do not know what way that might be," said his sister sourly, "but I have a remedy or two, if Prinny has none."

Quince accepted this as drily as she had given it. "I fear yours to be more extreme than those the Regent might devise, my dear Clemmie. I expect that he will be sent out of the country for a time until the climate about him cools. Luckily there is always a spot for him in Hanover or Celle. It is quite a convenience that his brother Adolphus has been appointed Governor-General there."

"Twenty-four, *encore.*" There was more than a touch of wearied boredom in the croupier's voice.

Mrs. Fairfax, struggling through the crowd, caught excitedly at Susanna's sleeve. "Did you not mean to collect your winnings, Lady Kinsale?"

Susanna had quite forgotten the fifteen pounds she had

dropped on the table at the eruption of the quarrel across the room. "I expect it is long lost by now."

Indeed, as she returned to the roulette table the croupier regarded her quite impassively as the ball clicked from hole to hole. "Twenty-four, *encore dix*, madame. Will you go on or remove your stake?"

Susanna laughed. "I expect I had better remove it while I still can. Which is mine?" She looked at the squares, but gold was piled so higgledy-piggledy that she could not immediately tell which was hers, since so many other wagers seemed to be piled about it.

For the first time the croupier looked faintly surprised. "Which, madame? Why, all! You instructed me to leave the bet on twenty-four, and I did as you told me. Did I do wrong?"

"I expect I was not paying complete attention," Susanna murmured faintly. "There was a bit of excitement across the way."

The croupier was a Parisian who had been employed in the gambling-houses of many countries and he understood that there was no accounting for the vagaries of women in such places. He suspected that this one would have screamed to heaven if she had lost her little stake by default. But, *mon Dieu*, it was no business of his, after all. "Will you take or leave your winnings, madame?" he asked a second time, as imperturbably as before. It was, after all, not his money.

"I will remove it. How much is there exactly?" Susanna was more than a little dazed. There was before her only a glittering pile and she was far from being an expert at judging such things. Gavin was still across the room.

The croupier regarded her with true Gallic disdain. "*Exactly*, madame? You began with fifteen English pounds. Before you there is to the amount of fifteen thousand, three hundred and sixty." He allowed himself the luxury of curling his lip at this silly *Anglaise*. "Quite a *partie*, madame, for being handled with such carelessness. Your Ladyship must be very rich, indeed, to have so little concern for money."

Susanna waved her fingers across the room and called out, "Gavin! Gavin!" He came to her at once. "Would you be good enough to help me transport all this?"

The wheel turned, clicking. "Fifteen, *noir*."

— 17 —

SHE AWOKE WITH the terrible feeling she had overslept. Flinging herself out of bed she stumbled into the night-stand, irrationally searched for a lost slipper without light-ing the candle, and drew Tibby to the door of the dressing room in a panic.

"Lord, miss, what is it? Have the French landed?"

"Put the candle down, Tib, so that I can see. Where are my shoes?"

"In the dressing-room, miss, along with your gowns and your hats and your chemises. What's come over you? It is the middle of the night."

Susanna realised that Tibby might not know all the events of the evening, although she was sure that she herself must have babbled about their good fortune; now she only said, "The duel. There is to be a duel at dawn."

Tibby drew a deep, relieved breath. "Do you mean the duel between the dear duke and the Regent's brother, then? That is not this morning, miss, but tomorrow. There is all sorts of niceties and necessities they must go through, I believe. It takes a bit of effort for men to kill each other."

She looked at Susanna with something like unusually deep respect. "Is it true, Miss Susanna, that you offered all the money you had won to the Regent's brother if he would take back the challenge to the dear duke?"

Susanna, still only half awake, reflected how heartwarm-ing it was that, even to a maidservant, the Duke of Quince was so beloved for his kindness that he should be known as "the dear duke." Certainly, no one would ever say that of the other one, Cumberland.

But no, she had offered no money to the Royal Duke. The principal reason was that he had already left the casino when the discovery came of her strike. In truth, she could remember very little of the rest of the evening, and what she had retained she saw only through a thick haze of unreality. She was certain that, in fact, the remainder best seemed forgotten . . . for within moments of the realisation that she had become independently wealthy from that single and unintentional coup at the roulette table, it seemed that the entire crowd which filled the Lower Rooms had surged about her, congratulating, touching her for luck, plucking at her clothes for attention, offering investments, offering proposals, decent and indecent—and there was even one strange, half-mad gentleman from the Balkans who swore that the money was rightfully his and that he had been made a dupe by this thieving woman, Susanna, who had placed his bet for him. He did not elaborate on the matter nor say why *she* had been obliged to lay out his play, but it mattered very little; for within seconds he had been replaced by others equally bizarre in their claims. It seemed to her that it was a form of hysteria, that the lust for gold had driven them "round the bend," as she had heard a young naval officer comment.

She began to understand that she had, herself, been in a state of shock; and looking back at those moments, she wondered to herself that she had moved so calmly through all the excitement, allowing herself to be iconized with all the appearance of docility. It had happened, of course, that some other part of her mind had come into play when her reasoning faculties failed, directing her actions and leaving her true self in a state of suspended animation.

What she would have done without the assistance of her friends (and she had been astonished to discover how many friends she had suddenly acquired), she had no idea. Mr. Wycombe had very kindly taken charge of the money (which seemed for some reason to pique Mr. Marshall); Lady Morphy and her brother, the duke, had acted as a kind of honour guard, fending off the insistent attentions of those who wished to line their pockets at Susanna's expense; and even Mrs. Fairfax had involved herself by firmly cutting a path to the door—quite ruthlessly thrusting people out of the way—so that the new heiress could make her way out of the casino. All had been made as easy as possible. Mrs. Maundy had thoughtfully sent the little maidservant up with a soothing drink, and Tibby had, with Lady Morphy's aid, bathed Susanna and put her to bed.

But now the shock was wearing off. Other things were coming into shockingly clear focus. The money meant very little to her, beside the fact that a dear friend might be severly injured. She knew that she did not care to marry the duke, but that did not mean she would not like him to live long enough for someone else to marry him.

She became aware that Tibby was regarding her with a mixture of sympathy and alarm. "Are you all right then, miss? You don't feel you are having 'sterics?"

"Hysterics?" Susanna considered, then gave her careful answer. "No, I don't believe I shall have hysterics, Tibby." She glanced out of the window and saw that it was still quite dark outside. "What time is it?"

"Oh, it is still the middle of the night, Miss Susanna. I heard you call out, so I come in." She peered at the clock on the mantelpiece. "Half past four, it is."

Susanna struggled with a sombre gown. "Help me dress. What time is dawn, I wonder?"

"Ah, now, you *are* all of a flutter. What do you want with dawn, I wonder? Won't you go back to bed, Miss Susanna? There won't be no fighting this morning, I tell you. They haven't had time."

A light tapping on the door and a low feminine voice calling softly, "Tibby, Tibby."

The maidservant looked peculiarly from the door to Susanna, Susanna to the door. "Yes, who is it?"

"It is Lady Morphy," Susanna said urgently. "Open the door at once."

Her ladyship was fully dressed, and looked at Susanna with approval. "You are up, I see. It will not take you long to dress? I have already ordered the carriage."

Tibby stared from one face to the other. "Why, what is it, your ladyship?"

"It is the duel, to be sure. They have moved it up to this morning, for the Regent has summoned Cumberland to St. James on urgent business."

Tibby cast a quick inquiry in Susanna's direction. "However did you know that, miss? What made you get up at this hour and begin to dress?"

"Never mind *why* she did it, girl, just help her with it. Our time is precious," Lady Morphy snapped, and Tibby, wonderingly, aided her mistress as best she could. It was not much, for Susanna had been dressing herself for most of her life and, being often at the beck of elderly and querulous women, had learned to do it with alacrity and a minimum of wasted movement.

The three women waited in the lower hall until the hackney coach arrived, then as they slipped out of the house Tibby felt a sprinkle of rain. "Should I run back up for the umbrellas, miss?"

"No. Hurry and come along," Lady Morphy commanded. "There is not much time and I believe we have a considerable distance to travel." She raised her voice to the driver. "We are going to a place called Piper's Field."

"Piper's Field?" asked the driver. "You never said that, madam. I thought you meant the regular place they go, up on the cliffs above the river."

"But you know where this other place is?"

"I'm not sure I could find it in the dark."

"Of course you can, man. I have always been told that hackney men can find any place on God's earth."

"Well, now, that may be, madam, and I thank you for the compliment. But if I don't know, then I don't know, and that's a fact!"

166

"Perhaps you should find another driver?" Susanna suggested softly to her ladyship, but it was not softly enough. The driver sniffed offendedly.

"You may feel free to find another man, if you choose, I am sure."

"This was the only one I could hire," Lady Morphy said tersely to Susanna. "The others all seem to be afraid of the dark." Her shoulders slumped.

"Please, you must try," she called up to the man. "It is a matter of my brother's life!"

"I'll do my best, mum," he at last answered grudgingly. "I know it be out and beyond the pike."

"Then try, dem you for a clod!" her ladyship shouted up at him. The man flinched. He had never been so spoken to by a lady before.

"Very well, madam, very well, I'll try, but it would be a fair pair of fools who would go out to shoot each other on a morning like this."

Entering the shabby vehicle, the women were assailed by the scent of stale bodies and rotting leather, but there was no help for it. Susanna, as well, fell prey to a sudden irrational fear for the duke. He might very well have been the finest shot in his regiment once upon a time, but he was older now. Certainly, she thought, his eye could not be as fine as it once was. What if, despite all she had heard about the much vaunted "code of gentlemen," one of the two men was injured beyond a mere "first blood?" Gentlemen were human, after all, and humans could be badly hurt, even killed. Remembering Tib's question, she wished she *had* been in a position to offer her new fortune to Cumberland in an attempt to avoid such a confrontation.

They rattled unsteadily along, the edges of Cheyne Spa falling away into the darkness as the rain began pelting heavily on the roof. Tibby reached across and drew Susanna's cloak more closely about her shoulders.

"You must keep off the chill, miss, or you'll have your death." Then she stopped, appalled at her own words. Susanna glanced apprehensively at Lady Morphy, but the older woman was lost in thought, staring blindly out the window. It seemed to Susanna that, despite her ladyship's willingness to hoodwink her brother into a convenient marriage, she was desperately concerned about this meeting with Cumberland. The Royal Duke was far more experienced as a duellist, after all, having almost made a second career of it; and there was certainly the distinct possibility that his outraged egotism might drive him to more than the mere formalistic ritual of satisfied honour. From what Susanna had seen of the Regent's brother, she was not sure he was an entirely rational being.

They had jolted uncomfortably for half an hour, the rain drumming dolefully on the roof, when the hackney carriage drew to a halt. Susanna expected that they would move on again at any moment, but time passed and they continued to sit in the same place. At length Lady Morphy thrust her head out and called up to the driver, "Where are we?"

She was greeted by only an uncomfortable silence. "Well?" she then demanded. "Are we near the spot? It is the Piper's Field that we have come to?"

The approaching dawn had lightened the sky just enough to show this last to be unlikely, for they were situated in the centre of what seemed to be a fen, though of what dimension it was difficult to say. Certainly there would hardly be a foot of firm ground, save the highway, for some distance around. The rain continued to fall.

Eventually their driver clambered down from his box and peered inside, scratching his beard. The collar of his cape was drawn up against the rain until one could barely discern his features. but it was evident that he was disgruntled and thoroughly out of sorts. "We must ha' taken a wrong turning somewheres, mam," he said in a tone more truculent than apologetic. "I don't see any use of going on, do you? I can't see my way in this weather and I can't say that I could *find* the spot if I could see it!"

But Lady Morphy would have none of this. "What it is, I daresay, is that you wish to take advantage of the situation for the purpose of extracting more money from me?"

The man shifted uncomfortably. "No, mam, that isn't it at all. The fact is that I fear we are lost, that's the line. What with the night and the dark and the rain, you see . . ."

With a moan of disgust, her ladyship flung open the door of the coach. The driver moved to help her. "Get back!" she commanded, and struggled alone to get down into the road. It was true that the darkness ahead was almost inpenetrable, but she peered despairingly into it, the moisture running down her cheeks. She was like a pathetic, though gallant, old figurehead which has looked upon many seas, but in the faint light of the coach-lantern Susanna could discern the frustration which set her ladyship's jaw so firmly and narrowed her eyes into mere slits of annoyance.

"We must find it, man. It is imperative! I cannot let William John die alone in some boggy field on a morning such as this!" She moved gingerly forward, feeling her way along the harness-lines of the heaving horses, still peering into the darkness, still seeking some clue as to their general whereabouts. Taking a wrong step, she slid in the mud and would have fallen but for the hand of the driver, though she shook him off impatiently. "You would do better to look to your horses than to me!"

Then, miraculously, there came through the darkness the drumming of hooves and a faint jingling of harness. One of their horses neighed loudly and received an answering greeting from somewhere in the darkness. "Halloo!" sounded a horn, and a voice shouted out, " 'Ware, there! Weston coach coming through!"

"Weston? The divvel!" mumbled their driver. "We ain't gone so far wrong after all."

The mail drew up alongside and the two drivers engaged in a muttered colloquy. It seemed amiable enough, but Susanna, leaning from the side of the coach nearest the neighbour, fancied she heard the driver of the mail-coach laugh somewhat contemptuously, though whether it was at the ineptitude of their own driver or the foolishness of three women stranded in the midst of marshland, she could not tell.

Presently the other coach passed on and their driver returned to them. "He says," he reported, "that he just passed another hackney a little way along the road behind, just past the river where it is dry." As if to punctuate this he wiped a rivulet of water from his nose. "By dry, I means in normal times, you see, not in a deluge . . . if you follow me."

"We follow *you* well enough," answered her ladyship, still outside the coach, sopping wet. "Let us, instead, follow the road and be upon our way!"

"Wait," said Tibby. "I heard something." The others cocked their heads carefully.

"I don't hear nothing," said the driver. Then he lifted his finger in an admonitory gesture. "Wait, I tell a lie! I do hear something. Another coach is headed this way, I do believe."

The women waited for a matter of some five or six minutes before this second hackney hove into sight, faintly discernible in the dawnlight and a familiar voice called out to them.

"I say, what are you doing there, if you please?" Then, before an answer could be thrown back, "Is that you, Clemmie? What the devil are you doing out on a morning like this?"

"Looking for your rain-washed corpse, you old fool!" cried her ladyship in something between a laugh and a strangled sob. "What possessed you to come off here all this way without bringing me? I hope you are well, William John?"

The Duke of Quince issued a short stab of laughter. "Aye, well enough, for the most part, I expect! The rascal backed off, you know."

"Backed off? Cumberland?" his sister asked in surprise. "That does not seem likely. And what do you mean by saying, 'for the most part'?"

There was muffled laughter from within the other coach.

"Are you wounded? she continued furiously. "Did that

devil more than pink you? I always have said he is not a gentleman!"

The duke's voice was more than a little chagrined. "No, no, my dear, nothing like that. Get back into your coach, do! You will have your death in this drizzle."

"Will you not come and ride with us, sir, and say what has happened?"

More laughter, even from His Grace it seemed.

"No, my pet, I fear I cannot. The thing is, you see, in trekking across uneven ground I fell . . ." There was further hilarity, though it seemed not to be warranted. "I fell, you see, and broke my leg!"

Her ladyship rushed toward the other carriage. "Broke? Oh, my dear man, are you in terrible pain?"

"Not such pain as I might be, sister," the duke explained, leaning to help her into his coach, and assisted by Gavin Marshall and Patrick Wycombe. "The bones God gave me are all well enough; it is the one provided by the carpenter which became the problem. Caught it in a molehill, you see, and snapped it directly off. They had to carry me back to the coach, and I expect that Cumberland will tell the tale all over London!"

═18═

THE PUMP ROOM of Cheyne Spa was rarely crowded at noon, for the patrons who would forgo a meal to take the waters were few. Gavin, sipping a glass of the noxious liquid dispensed there, wondered why he had allowed himself to be drawn into the place at all. To be the escort of the bogus Lady Kinsale showed no profit so far as he could tell. If they had ever been partners, they certainly were no more, not since she had taken the tables of the Lower Rooms for such a startling sum. He sipped again and made a face. Susanna looked on with sympathy.

"Will you not set it aside, Mr. Marshall, since it displeases you so? We could, instead, stop at the Gardens and take tea, if you like."

He replied sourly, an indication of the mood he had been in for the past few days. "Madam, you may take medicine, you may take a walk, you may even take a liberty with certain persons, but you *drink* tea!

Susanna inclined her head patiently. It did not escape her that since the night of her great coup, followed by the morning of the postponed duel, Gavin Marshall had been both difficult and seemingly inescapable. Everywhere she went, no matter with whom, it seemed likely that sooner or later Gavin would appear. Even when he was not present in the flesh, she found herself haunted by the expectation of his imminent arrival. She liked him well enough and, certainly, she was more than grateful for his attentive tutoring when she had first arrived in Cheyne Spa. But enough was enough.

This morning he seemed determined to pursue the subject of her personal future and had already made several abortive fits and starts in that direction.

"I expect you will take a small house in London—Mayfair, perhaps?—where you can move amongst . . ." He hesitated and sought a word. ". . . amongst society?" Susanna had the distinct notion that he had meant to say "amongst your betters." "I daresay Aunt Clemmie can still be of great help to you there, eh?"

"We have not yet decided what we will do," she answered. "It may be that we will take a small house in the country."

"We?" he asked with a lift of his brows. "Have you, then, found yourself a companion along life's path?"

"You needn't sound so scornful, sir. I meant, of course, Tibby and myself—with perhaps Tibby's new husband, if things should fall that way. Tibby was my partner from the beginning. Did you think I would abandon her once I had achieved my own security?"

Again the sardonic glance and the lift of the eyebrow. "It has been known in the past," he said. "Is that what the winning really meant to you? Security?"

The question took her quite by surprise. "What else could it mean?"

Her interrogator shrugged. "All sorts of things—influence, position, entree into higher society."

"In short," she giggled, "a trap wherein I might still catch me a titled but impoverished husband of an acceptable age?"

"Something like that, I suppose."

"Has it not yet sunk into that incredibly dull head of yours, my friend, that I do not care for all that? With the money I now have, Tibby and I—and perhaps even Fred—can live pleasantly somewhere in the country. I would not trade that for an unloving spouse who was interested only in controlling my small fortune. What would be the good of that?"

"True," he agreed, "but supposing you found someone for whom you could truly care?"

She took on an enigmatic look. "Perhaps I have already done so, sir."

His interest quickened. "Have you, then?" he asked. "Well, of course, the choice has always been yours."

"I expect you are still annoyed that I did not see fit to eagerly marry your uncle when I was still impoverished and grateful enough to share the proceeds with you," she said sharply. "Well, who can say? I may elect to be a duchess yet!"

"Gad, what is that to me?" He put down his glass so firmly that it rang against the marble.

"Good morning, Marshall," said a cheerful voice. "Lady Kinsale, you are more radiant than ever. That particular shade of pink surrounds you like a rose."

Gavin all but snarled when he saw who had joined them. "Good morning, Wycombe. I daresay you must have slept in this morning, for I believe the sun is already well past the yardarm."

"Well, then, a very good afternoon to you, my friend." Patrick turned back to Susanna. "What have you done, madam, to put our dear boy in such a curmudgeonly mood?"

"I had believed he required a tonic, but it seems to have done him no good."

Gavin made a face. "I prefer the illness to the remedy, if you don't mind." He spread his hands in implied apology. "I seem to be in a peculiar state of mind recently. It is like nothing I have ever experienced before. I find I sleep badly and sometimes wake up grinding my teeth. I have no patience with either people or cards, a condition nearly fatal to my profession, and am far more prone to fits of melancholy than to my usual, rather carefree way of looking at things." He shook his head in confusion. "I honestly cannot think what is wrong with me. Perhaps I need a change of air and scene."

Patrick clapped him on the shoulder with an amiable exuberance. "It sounds dangerous, old fellow. There's quite a bit of that sort of thing going around. Yes, I'd say very dangerous."

Gavin absorbed all this with a bit of alarm. "How do you mean it? Dangerous in what way, Patrick? Do you know what is wrong with me?"

"It sounds dreadfully familiar to an old romantic like myself," Wycombe laughed. "If I did not know you better, I'd say you were suffering from the classic symptoms of *febris amoris*. Why, I believe you must be in love, my friend!"

"Pray, do not be absurd," snorted Gavin. But his eyes were thoughtful.

Patrick's attention shifted to their companion. "Perhaps, Lady Kinsale, you might be free to attend a concert of ancient music with me this afternoon?"

"In love!" said Gavin. "That is quite the silliest thing I have heard in years. I have not been in love since I was seventeen and engaged in a passion for a pretty milliner."

"Then it must be high time you re-engaged," said Patrick encouragingly. "I believe there is nothing like love to soothe the troubled spirit, my friend."

Gavin took this cynically. "The most love ever did for me was to give me a run of sleepless nights."

"What do you say, Lady Kinsale, will you join me? They are performing Josquin de Prés."

"The motets?" asked Susanna in delight.

"The motets and some of the secular *chansons*, I believe." Patrick was all admiration. "You quite astonish me, your ladyship. How do you come to know of Josquin?"

"Who the devil is this Josquin?" asked Gavin, who had not been paying as strict attention as he might have done, being caught up in the question of his own real or imagined maladies. "A musician, is he? I daresay John Field knows him. He knows everybody in Europe, I think. Everyone in music, at any rate."

"I think a personal acquaintance is unlikely, sir," Susanna explained, "since the gentleman has been dead for some time. Perhaps you should come to hear him as well? You might find him a kindred spirit."

To Patrick Wycombe she explained, "You may have heard of a musician named Charles Burney, an organist? It was he who rediscovered the Josquin works."

"Dr. Burney was quite well known in King's Lynn and London, I think, but that was a mort of years ago, surely?"

"Yes," she agreed, "it does seem as if ages have passed. He was my papa's best friend, you see. I grew up among the Burneys."

"Would that be Fanny Burney, who was at court and then married a Frenchman of some sort? I believe she is a friend of my aunt's," said Gavin. "I say, you are not unconnected after all, are you?"

"Madame D'Arblay," said Susanna. "She has almost been like a second mother to me."

"You do surprise me, madam," said Patrick. "I had believed all this time that you had simply sprung full-grown, like Athena from the head of Zeus."

Susanna shot a quick glance at Gavin, then replied mysteriously, "There are other things about me which you may also find surprising, Mr. Wycombe."

"I look forward to the discovery of them, your ladyship," he answered gallantly. "I am sure they will all be of the utmost pleasantness."

They parted from Gavin, then, and walked along the river where they had strolled when he first met her in Cheyne Spa. They said nothing at first, and then Susanna asked quite straightforwardly, "Does the name Archer mean anything to you, Mr. Wycombe?"

"No, the only person of that name I ever knew, a dowdy companion of my old aunt, bless her, has passed on to another world. I scarcely think she . . ." He looked at her closely, then chuckled. "Could she have been a relation of yours, Lady Kinsale? I believe I see a faint resemblance somehow. I must say that I always had the feeling that she was a gentlewoman fallen upon hard times in the world. Could she have been a cousin, perhaps? There is a definite resemblance."

"A resemblance only?" She turned away from him and stood looking out over the water. Her chin was lifted and the light breeze was blowing the hair away from about her face. Patrick Wycombe thought he had never seen so handsome a profile on a woman.

"No, your aunt's companion was not a cousin of mine, Mr. Wycombe. I have no relatives but myself."

Presently she asked, "And what has become of the property of your old aunt? Did she not have a house? Or did she, I wonder, live with you upon your bounty?"

"No," he answered, "she was a strange old thing who would not have come to me if I had asked her. She lived to herself until the very end in a fine place which she allowed to quite fall into ruin."

"And what has become of it?" his companion asked idly. "Have you chosen to pull it down?"

"Quite the contrary." Susanna seemed to hear the words coming at her from a long distance, swimming toward her, as it were. She lightly laid her hand upon his arm for support as they walked further along the river path. "I have had workmen there for the last few weeks," Patrick explained. "I at first believed the old place was quite lost to me, but it seems possible to save it after all. On the advice of an architect with whom I am acquainted, I am putting things to rights as far as possible. It is not at all a fashionable place, you know, but quite charming in its own way."

A strange fancy seemed to fill Susanna's mind as he

talked. She saw herself in the restored house, sitting down alone to dinner, dressed in one of Lady Wycombe's extravagant gowns. She shivered at the thought.

"Are you cold, Lady Kinsale? Perhaps we had better move away from the waterside."

"No, not cold," she explained. "What is that old saying, 'A mouse ran over my grave'? I think a mouse just ran up my back. I think the time has come, Mr. Wycombe, to impart some things to you with which you are not acquainted."

"Do you mean to say that Cumberland actually sent you a letter crying off from a future engagement of the duel?" asked Lady Morphy of her brother. "That certainly does not sound like the man with whom I am unfortunately acquainted."

"No, it does not," Quince agreed. "But, to be frank, I have been discovering of late how little I know about the labyrinths of the human heart. The more I learn, the less I know. I expect to be as innocent as a babe by the time I reach my dotage."

He handed her the folded paper and she opened it curiously.

"To His Grace, the 13th Duke of Quince, Earl of Bessborough, Viscount Petrie . . ." she read:

> Sir:
> At the behest of my brother, the Prince Regent, I take my pen in hand to ask your pardon for the unfortunate occurrences at Cheyne Spa which are like to prove disadvantageous to us both.

"Well," she interjected, "it sounds as if the Regent raised his voice a little." Then she read on:

> In my own name, may I humbly request that I be allowed to withdraw a certain hot-headed, thoughtless and discreditable remark insulting to a gentleman whose personal courage has always

been held in the highest esteem by all who are
acquainted with him. Let me then pray that. . . .

"Oh, really," she said, "this is too much and too little! I
do not think I can stomach it!" And she threw the letter
down on the table. "That is a political document, not the
screed of a repentant man!"

"I confess," Quince said, "that I do not know how to take
it, nor how to answer it. On the one hand, it is a handsome
apology. . . ." He rubbed his finger alongside his nose as he
considered. "For all its toad-eating tone, it may be intended
to be sincere."

"No," said his sister, "I instinctively distrust it. Our dear
Cumberland is not the man who appears in that mincing
epistle. There is not a word of sincerity in it. What puzzles
me is why he has written it at all."

"I think he makes it quite clear. The instructions of the
Regent, my dear Clemmie, can hardly be directly flouted,
even by his brother. No, I deign to hope we have heard the
last of this business. Honour is surely satisfied."

But Lady Morphy remained doubtful. "There was a look
in his eye that evening," she recalled worriedly, "a look I
remember seeing spring into his eyes on the night of his
dreadful behaviour at the Cotillion Ball in the Upper
Rooms." She moved about the room aimlessly, lost in
thought, then raised her eyes to her brother. "Do you
suppose, Quince, that it is possible that he has inherited his
father's instability?"

He regarded her doubtfully. "Do you mean to suggest,
my love, what I think you mean?"

"I mean to say, Quince, in plain words, that I wonder if
the Duke of Cumberland is mad."

"Oh, Clemmie, be sensible. I know you cannot stomach
the man and certainly he is a bit of a dog-in-a-doublet, but
to call him mad is rather pulling it long."

Lady Morphy shook her head. "I am not at all sure of
that. Madness takes people in different ways."

There was a quiet rapping on the casing which surrounded the doorway of Mrs. Maundy's parlour in which they sat. Susanna Archer stood there, looking more than a little diffident, and at her shoulder was the Apollo-like Patrick Wycombe. "May we disturb you for a moment or two?" asked the young woman.

"By all means, my dear girl," the duke cried. "Come in, come in! You shall be among the first to see me new leg!" and he extended his handsome new appendage, elegantly turned and carved, "Walnut, you know," he said rather proudly. "Takes a nice finish, don't you think?" He winked broadly at Patrick. "Almost worth the rigours of that night when I broke the other one, what?"

Patrick grinned, which gave him a decidedly more mortal appearance. "Oh quite, sir! Though I shall never forget you hopping about Piper's Field for all the world like Rumpelstiltskin."

Lady Morphy gave them both a fierce look. "That is all very well for the two of you to joke about, but women are not by nature provided with such bravado. I will thank you, Quince, to consider your sister more thoughtfully the next time you go off buccaneering in the night!"

Then she turned her attention back to the two young people, stared hard at them, changing her expression as she made an educated guess as to the nature of their interruption. She might have lavished compassion upon her brother; but the duke, it seemed, had made his own deductions.

"Enough of these tales of midnight adventure," he chuckled. "I have the distinct notion that there is some sort of imminent announcement hovering about the room, eh? Well, what is it, lad? Are you the bearer of glad tidings?"

Patrick looked at him rather quizzically. "How have you guessed that, sir? Is it writ so large across my face?" He exuded an air of confidence, sure of the duke's friendship; but Susanna seemed apprehensive and moved slightly closer to him, a movement not unnoted by either the duke or his sister. It affected the peer compassionately and, when he spoke, his words were jocular, but their intention was altogether sustaining.

"I may be an old duffer, my boy, but my brain has not completely solidified as yet. One look at the two of you standing together there is enough to alert my attention. What have you to say for yourselves, eh? Out with it."

"The truth is Your Grace—and your ladyship—that I have made an offer of marriage to . . . to Miss Archer, here, and she has done me the honour of accepting."

Quince did not so much as blink, and Clementina was vastly proud of him for it. Whether her brother had been truly in affection toward the gel or merely infatuated with her youth was no boot; the wounding would merely be a matter of degree.

"Miss Archer, is it then?" Lady Morphy asked, then smiled and nodded approvingly. "I perceive that that matter has been taken care of and that you have chosen to clear the deck before you set upon the voyage, Susanna. That is very wise and also very straightforward of you. I find it very affecting."

"Yes, very affecting," echoed a masculine voice from the hall. Gavin stood there with a peculiar look upon his face. His next words made it obvious that the news he had just now overheard was previously unguessed by him and not altogether to his taste. "I expect now that the lady is endowered with funds of her own, she need not dissemble and can marry where her heart dictates."

Lady Morphy's nostrils flared in distaste. "That is a cruel and unfortunate remark, Gavin. I hope that Mr. Wycombe and Miss Archer will excuse the offensiveness of it."

"Offensiveness, aunt? I do beg to say that none was intended, none at all. I only meant that all of us here are aware of the background and certainly can do no less than applaud the honesty shown. I could not agree with you, aunt, more fully—it is always best to clear these things up before the final vows are taken." He shot a quick look at his uncle, then clapped Patrick genially on the shoulder. "Best of luck, old chap! May you never have need to look back." Was there an undercurrent in his words?

Susanna waited, but he offered no similar sentiments to her and she held out her hand. "Am I not included in your felicitations, Mr. Marshall?"

Gavin's eyes seemed to take on an additional intensity. "Of course you are, dear lady. I wish you every bit of happiness you deserve. You have won yourself a prime prize, of that I stand surety. Patrick Wycombe has been my friend since I was seven and he was six, and there is no finer fellow in all of England, to my mind." However this was meant to affect Susanna, there was no doubt that his words concerning Patrick were sincere.

"Here, my friend, do not let your extravagance carry you away," Patrick said, blushing with discomfiture. "You will frighten the lady off with such talk of my virtues . . . though, of course, they are many," he added with a laugh which took the seriousness out of their conversation.

"This calls for a celebration," decided the duke. He stumped to the service door. "Wine, wine, Mrs. Maundy!"

The landlady, so summoned, looked down her nose at him with a severe and pained expression. "I beg Your Grace's pardon, but I run a temperate house here. My late husband, of blessed memory, was not one to have laid down a cellar."

The duke eyed her roguishly, "Oh, come, my dear lady, I am sure you are not the sort to deny a touch of conviviality to the announcement of a wedding?"

"A wedding, sir?" She became in an eyelid's flicker a completely different woman altogether. "Lady Kinsale, is it, and Mr. Marshall?" She beamed approvingly upon Gavin. "You are a lucky man, sir, if I am any judge."

"I may yet be as lucky," Gavin agreed, "but her ladyship's choice has not fallen to me. Mr. Wycombe is the lucky one, not I."

Mrs. Maundy was not in the least disconcerted. "Well,

some is luckier than is fair, I expect. Congratulations to you, then, sir, and many good wishes!" Patrick thanked her gravely. Then, casting a sly and conspiratorial look at His Grace, she whispered in a tone loud enough to carry, "Perhaps I may find a bit of something, after all. Even the Bible condones a bit of wine for the sake of the stomach, you know. I confess to conserving it for its medicinal properties."

"Arragh!" the duke roared. "Let us have no doctor's remedies, if you please, madam!" He fumbled in his coat. "If you have nothing fit to drink, I beg you to send out for it."

She simpered at him, though pocketing the tip. "I think your lordship will not be unhappy with what I have on hand." She bustled out and presently returned with a tray on which reposed a crystal decanter and glasses. "But Your Grace must not think I am an intemperate woman."

"Well, we shall see." He poured out a thimbleful, rolled it about on his tongue and beamed at her. "You take me by complete surprise, Mrs. Maundy. This is quite a decent little amontillado! You will not convince me that it is here merely by accident."

The landlady flushed. "Not quite by accident, sir. There was last year a gentleman who presented me with a dozen bottles in gratitude for . . ." She dropped her eyes and blushed. "A foreign gentleman, you see, Your Grace, and most gallant!"

He smiled upon her benignly. "Ah, Madam, we all know how effusive these foreign chaps can be."

At which the lady threw her apron up to conceal her fiery flushes.

The little maidservant, answering the door in the front hall, ushered in still another visitor.

"My dears, have I arrived at an occasion?" It was Mrs. Fairfax (without her daughter) and, when she heard the news, she hesitated only briefly before pinching a bit of Susanna's cheek between her thumb and forefinger.

"Oh, you slyboots! One has to watch you all of the time!" But she accepted the proffered glass and lifted it in a toast with as much seeming good humour as the rest. "I am sure my dear little Cecily would join me in wishing you well . . . Lady Kinsale." She very carefully avoided looking in the slightest toward Patrick as she asked, "And will you be returning, now, to live at Wycombe Hall?"

Patrick Wycombe was about to reply, but Lady Morphy quickly intervened. "Not until it has been completely repaired, Irene. You remember the condition it was in when we visited it." She sipped her sherry appreciatively, then asked, "And where *is* dear Cecily? It seems to me I have not seen her about the town for several days. I hope she is not unwell?"

Mrs. Fairfax trilled out one of her artificial laughs. "Unwell? Cecily? La, the gel is as healthy as a . . . as healthy as one could imagine. She has merely gone up to London to visit a relative. I expect her back this evening or tomorrow at the latest."

"Up to town?" Lady Morphy's eyebrows expressed her surprise. "Alone? My stars, that *is* daring."

"Cecily is certainly not alone, Clemmie. You, of all people, know I would never tolerate such a thing. Our maidservant, Mirabella, has gone with her. She is visiting Lady Narwall, you know, who is her late father's cousin once removed. I thought you knew that, Clementina."

"No, I don't believe I did." Lady Morphy's eyes had opened quite wide, since Lady Narwall's reputation as a leader of a rather advanced set of people was well known. "I am sure that dear little Cecily will make a great many interesting acquaintances through someone like Lady Narwall. They say she is known by everyone."

Although the slyness of her words escaped Mrs. Fairfax, Susanna knew her ladyship well enough to read her opinion of such people. Their eyes met briefly and they smiled, though without for a moment thinking there was anything out of the way in Cecily's visit to her cousin. It might, in fact, prove extraordinarily beneficial, since Cecily could well use a patina of the more superior kind.

"But," said Mrs. Fairfax to the newly engaged couple, "I am sure you deserve every chance of happiness." Susanna suspected that she meant no such thing, really, but she also understood why that should be so. Mrs. Fairfax had set Cecily's cap first for the duke and then for Patrick Wycombe, and had lost out to Susanna on both counts. It could not have been an elevating experience.

The Duke of Quince now rose from his place on the settee and prepared to take his leave. "I expect we shall all meet again at the Cotillion Ball this evening, shall we not?"

He bowed gravely over each of the ladies's hands in his courtly old-fashioned way—and before Susanna he lingered an extra moment, but said nothing, although his eyes seemed to search hers for something they did not find.

What a very dear man he is, she thought with regret. If things had been only slightly different she would have been proud to have been the Duchess of Quince. Mrs. Fairfax and Lady Morphy had risen to bid the duke good-bye, but they were chatting about some inconsequential matter. Susanna was aware that Gavin's attention, though, was settled upon her, and she looked past His Grace's shoulder toward his nephew. She had much reason to be grateful to Gavin, and she was. But why must he always make things so difficult by stirring them and causing so much confusion? Thank goodness Patrick Wycombe was nothing like that.

— 20 —

THE COTILLION BALL promised to be only sparsely at-
tended. As the season trailed to an end, many visitors had
already left for London or to resume the duties of their
country estates. The shooting season would soon be upon
them and there were always things to be made ready. It had
not always been so, of course, and this was a source of great
annoyance to Septimus Wilberforce.

"It is the changing times," he excused himself to his
employers, the Corporation of Cheyne Spa. "In Beau
Carlisle's time," he reminded them, "there was the great
bugaboo of unrest on the continent. Since one could not
travel with safety, many of the travellers stayed to home in
England." He smiled at them winsomely. "I do not in any
way at all disparage the Great Wellington's victory at
Waterloo, you understand, but it did strike a strong blow at
the economy of English watering-places, what?"

The mayor, Mr. Tobias, said nothing in reply to this
extraordinary gloss upon history; but he reflected, not for
the first time, that it was time for a change in the position
that Wilberforce held. He recalled, with regret, that Carlisle had held the post of Master of Ceremonies for so long
and filled it so well that, quite naturally, any successor
would be hard put to overtop the Beau's accomplishments.
But this little pippin-squire would not be the one to do it, of
that he was certain. If the rush to the continent was to be
offset, it would take someone stronger in place than Wilberforce. Luckily, his contract expired at the end of the season

and, even if a new Master had not been engaged, there was no need to throw good money after bad by retaining this one.

Now, one may guess that none of these thoughts were in any degree verbalised to Septimus Wilberforce, but he knew of them. His sort always knows that kind of thing. Perhaps they hear a still, small voice, or perhaps the wide variety of complaint against them acts upon their consciousness; perhaps they are able, in some arcane fashion, to read the minds of people such as Mayor Tobias; but Wilberforce was true to his clan, and the message being broadcast to the careful reader from the impassive face of Mr. Tobias struck him to the heart. He knew full well that his days of glory were not so much numbered as withering away before his eyes. Something must be done, but what? Chances must even be taken, no doubt, if one is to come out ahead in the great game, the game of ambition, the great game of life.

"Will this be your last cotillion, then, miss?" Tibby asked as she assisted Susanna to dress for the evening.

"Well, not forever, I hope," Susanna chuckled. "I daresay when I have become Mrs. Wycombe I shall attend many, many such balls."

"No, miss, I meant here in Cheyne Spa."

"I expect so, Tibby. We shall be leaving for London in less than a fortnight. Shall you like it, do you think?"

"Like London, miss?" The maidservant looked acutely uncomfortable. "You see, that's just it, Miss Susanna."

"What is it?" Susanna searched her friend's face. "Is something wrong, love?"

Tibby's face screwed up miserably. "Oh, miss, I don't know what to do!"

A flash of understanding illuminated Susanna's eyes. "It is your young man, isn't it?" Tibby nodded tearfully. "Has Fred asked you to marry him, is that it?"

"Not exactly asked me, but I don't mind that."

Susanna was rather taken aback. As a vicar's daughter she was not altogether unfamiliar with the free and easy ways of the labouring class, but she had not thought of Tibby in such a light. "Don't you *want* to marry him?" she asked, more in curiosity than disparagement. "You would marry him if he asked you, I expect?"

"Prob'ly I would," the girl admitted, considering. "But it don't signify, for he hasn't."

"But you *are* saying, I think, that you want to stay here with him in Cheyne Spa?"

Tib assented dumbly, her eyes wide with concern for the friendship she had fostered with Susanna over the past months. "Here in Cheyne Spa or wherever. I ain't particular where we go, you see."

"And does he know this?"

"Know what?" Tibby asked nervously. Her round eyes exchanged glances with Susanna's in the looking-glass.

"Is Fred aware that you have this feeling? That you are in love with him?"

Tibby's expression was quite blank. "Love, miss? That is a word for the gentry like yourself. Lord, miss, for me and my folks love is just a word in them books you taught me. I ain't sure, even, that I know quite what it means, you see. All I know is that I just want to be with Fred, married or not."

Simple and straight to the point, it gave Susanna something to think about. She was not so naive as to believe that she knew very much about love herself. Certainly she could not say of a surety that she was "in love" with Mr. Wycombe. She knew very little about him, really. Marriage was perhaps merely a lottery, after all. She could only trust to her judgement of character, and hope. There was a romantic side to her nature that acknowledged that she had been deeply drawn to him since the night he and Gavin had taken dinner with old Lady Wycombe. How very strange it was that her whole life had been turned about by that night that Lady Wycombe passed away. Patrick had paid her no

attention at all, but he had become her betrothed, and
Gavin . . . she supposed one could say that, after these
weeks at Cheyne Spa, Gavin had become her friend. She
was very glad that he was Patrick's friend as well.

When she thought about it, it came to her with a shock
that, with the addition of the Duke of Quince, these were
really the only men she knew!

The quartet of musicians were comfortably settled in the
musician's gallery, and the Upper Rooms were saturated
with the silence that small, incidental sounds only inten-
sify. In a short time, in the opinion of Septimus Wilberforce, all this would change. If he was successful in his
innovation, not only would he save his position as Cheyne
Spa's doyen, but this evening's ball would significantly
alter every cotillion held here in the future. Even Cheyne
must change with the times, after all. If the public wanted a
thing, believed the successor of Beau Carlisle, it was the
way to their hearts to give in to their desires. The Beau had
built his career on the inception of changes in the spa's
social routine, had he not? Well, Wilberforce would do the
same.

Although there had been no public announcement of the
betrothal of "Lady Kinsale" to Mr. Wycombe, it was not
considered out of the way that Patrick arrived amongst the
Duke of Quince's party. He was, after all, Gavin Marshall's
best friend, everybody knew. They did not notice that the
two men had hardly anything to say to each other. Gavin,
in fact, was assiduously attentive to his aunt, seating her
comfortably, running an errand to fetch a forgotten fan,
fetching her claret cup from the supper room, and friendly
in a masculine sense only to his uncle. A close observer
might have been somewhat puzzled by the frequent glances
he cast toward Patrick and Susanna, for they were darting
though intense. And a *very* close observer, Gavin's aunt,
aware of such things as usual, tried her best to divert him
from this preoccupation.

"Have you ever seen such a simpering ape?" she asked,

indicating Wilberforce. "He is everything the Beau was not, and in nothing is he superior. Why, even an amateur could do better. Even *you* would not be such an ass."

Gavin half-bowed. "Thank you, aunt," he answered suavely. "I do my best to please."

She hid her face behind her fan to stifle her smile. "Wretch, do not take on airs. I only meant that anyone with any experience at all could do far better. Who but a fool would substitute gardenia sprays for the white roses we have always had in the floral displays? In the first place they will not last, and in the second, the scent will be quite overpowering when the room has filled."

"Perhaps the chap feels it is time for innovation," murmured Gavin. "Nothing ventured, nothing gained."

"Your most original turn of phrase," said her ladyship tartly, "never ceases to astonish me."

The evening's dancing began with a minuet, although the room was far from filling up. Patrick led out his betrothed and the Duke of Quince his sister. Once upon a time, being the senior in rank among the guests, Quince would have actually opened the ball, but that had been a feature of the previous reign. Now the dancers merely moved out upon the floor in whatever way they would. It was more democratic, but far less elegant, though no one had as yet complained about such a small change in the order of things. They did not understand what was, in the mind of Mr. Wilberforce, yet to come.

The musicians then struck up "The Piper's Fall," the second violinist being able to double on the flute; the dancers skittering delightfully about the floor, moved as smoothly as if they were dancing on water. And now the room was at last beginning to fill, though scarcely to the usual crush; perhaps only five hundred persons so far. A substantial amount of them being merely spectators, the floor could scarcely be called crowded. It was a pity to see that so many of those previously in regular attendance had stayed away.

The duke presently led Susanna out for a stately pavanne

and, after two dances with strangers and a breath of air on the balcony, Patrick again ushered her to the dancing floor, though they did not know what dance would now be called. Septimus Wilberforce thumped heavily on the floor with his weighted staff in prelude to an announcement. He wore a faintly smug face as he stood on a little dais and looked across their heads, pausing for effect.

"The next dance," he called out, "will be a reel," which pleased a number of the older people, since that once-popular dance had unaccountably fallen out of fashion in these days, though one might have expected it more frequently at a weekly cotillion where country dances were the standard.

But Mr. Wilberforce was not yet done with his surprises. "It will be," he added, "a kissing reel!"

The murmur of comment slid easily into a ripple of amusement, for kissing reels were considered mostly a servant's hall innovation and, when they climbed to the level of the gentry, had been confined almost entirely to Yuletide celebrations where the mistletoe boughs offered a modicum of encouragement. No one here seriously objected, however, mistletoe or no. One was allowed to be a little less strict while holidaying.

The gentlemen obligingly took out their snowy handkerchiefs and carefully folded them in a diagonal fashion to cover the eyes of their partners. The ladies, almost all, giggled and protested that the men were mistreating their coiffures, but it was taken in good part. The truth was that there was always the chance of an adventure attendant upon this particular dance. It was, traditionally, rarely your partner whom you ended up being kissed by; for whenever the music stopped, the lady must be bussed by whatever random stranger held her hand in his at that moment. And she must not cheat by lifting her blindfold to see what gentleman it was. That was part of the adventure, to be kissed by a pair of unknown lips. To be sure, the mystery would not last very long; for after the dance was done, spectators could be allowed to advise the dancing lady what her fortune had been without her being thought a poor sort of sport. This, in itself, allowed for a certain freedom from personal responsibility while on the floor. And such a situation could, all in all, be most invigorating.

Patrick seemed to think that Susanna was unnecessarily worried about the outcome. "I shall try my best to be at your side when the music stops," he whispered to her, but Susanna thought that the chances of that coming about would be very slim. In her capacity as companion, she had danced at many servant's balls, and she knew that the caller—Wilberforce on this occasion—was generally careful to ensure that the dancers were not in their original configurations when he called for silence.

"Perhaps you will not even know it is I," chuckled Patrick as he bound the linen square about her head. But Susanna had not kissed so many men that she would be unable to recognise the cool and soothing kisses of this man she had become engaged to. She had had few enough experiences before he sought her hand, but she recalled Patrick's oscular salutations to be both pleasant and slightly stimulating to her romantic sense. She did not quite understand, she acknowledged, all the fuss about such things, but she had found the experience of kissing more than satisfactory.

The little orchestra began to play "Windy Hill," its rapid and smoothly flowing tune carrying the dancers effortlessly along, despite the blindness of the ladies. The first to brush Susanna's lips with his did so with such a fleeting and timid pressure that she scarcely felt it; the second, she knew, sported a moustache, for the bristles of it brushed against her upper lip; the third was somewhat older, she deduced from the leathery quality of his lips, and bore a distinct odor of bay rum. It was at that point that she felt the knot of the blinding kerchief begin to loosen from the exertion of the dancing, but, being constantly passed from partner to partner, she could not lift her hands to draw it tight. It seemed, anyway, likely to hold until the dance's end.

Her present partner was a dancer of superlative skill,

whatever else he might be, and she found that her own natural rhythm so matched his that there was not the slightest hesitation on her part when they crossed hands and he guided her into the promenade.

But, when the music stopped, there was no immediate pressure upon her lips. This, in direct contrast to the haste of her previous partners, rather surprised her. Puzzled, she blindly raised her fingers and found them touching a masculine cheek as he bent to fulfill the requirement of the dance. The salutation was no mere social gratification, however, but the movement of an experienced man who knew exactly what the moment called for. Gently demanding, his lips caressed hers firmly, leaving her mouth alive with sensations it had never before experienced. She was faintly shocked at her own involuntary response as, raising on tiptoe, she again presented her lips to his. It had been done completely without thought, but as she thrust herself upward toward him, the linen blindfold fell away and she found herself looking blankly into the eyes of Gavin Marshall.

Quickly he bent and swept up the handkerchief, folded it deftly and rebound it about her eyes. Now that she could not see, what she most remembered from that moment was not the sardonic curl of his lips, but the quite unfathomable expression in his eyes.

She continued the dance like an automaton. Gavin's action and her response to it had seemed so natural, yet so unexpected; in view of her recent betrothal to Patrick, it seemed, as well, so wrong. She changed partners again and yet another time. She heard Patrick's voice in her ear above the music and recognised his lips upon hers at the next break, but her feeling was something more like gratitude than pleasure. She felt nothing of the exhilaration she had experienced from Gavin's kisses. This realisation and a score of conflicting thoughts flew pell-mell through her mind, leaving her confused and breathless. Had she made a dreadful mistake? Or did kisses and marriages, after all, have nothing to do with each other?

At last the music came to an end, the final kiss being bestowed once again by Patrick, a tribute to the vigilance of the Master of Ceremonies who had, so cleverly, brought the couples back to where they had begun. Susanna easily recognised Patrick's kiss—warm and comforting, without leaving her in the least stirred.

Untying the handkerchief from her head, Patrick led her back to the sidelines. She knew from the look on Lady Morphy's face that the encounter with Gavin had not gone unobserved. The older woman held out her arms in an uncharacteristic gesture of affection, sent Patrick for refreshments, and led Susanna toward the balcony.

"I suspect we all need a change of air," she counselled.

At the doorway, Susanna looked back about the room she was leaving. The Duke of Quince gave her a sympathetic look and bowed gravely, but Gavin was nowhere to be seen.

=== 21 ===

"WELL, MY DEAR," her ladyship said, "that was a very interesting exhibition."

"I suppose I have completely compromised myself," Susanna said morosely. "I cannot say what Mr. Wycombe must think of me."

"It is quite possible," said the older woman, "that Mr. Wycombe saw nothing of it. He was, you may judge, engaged in saluting another lady at the time. I would not worry very much about Patrick, if I were you, but about myself. If I saw what I believe I saw out there, I would think there should be time for reconsideration. Your engagement to Mr. Wycombe has not been announced, after all, and there is still time to retreat from the arrangement."

"Retreat to where? I do not even know where I stand now."

Lady Morphy looked very much as if she would like to take Susanna by the shoulders and shake her until some sense rattled into her head, but she did nothing of the kind. Instead, she spoke equitably and with admirable restraint.

"There is nothing in the law that says you must go through with your agreement to marry Patrick Wycombe, Susanna." She coughed delicately. "I should not be saying this, I know, but . . ."

"What is it, your ladyship?"

"Well, it is this. I know Mr. Wycombe is as handsome as Apollo, and certainly very well fixed . . . Gavin thinks the world of him, of course . . . but don't you find him just the tiniest bit dull?"

"Your ladyship!" Susanna hardly knew whether she was more shocked or amused.

Lady Morphy held up a cautioning hand. "If you love him, of course, that probably will not matter. But if you are merely charting what you think to be a safe course, I beg you to reconsider! You have enough money now to keep you for the rest of your life if you invest it wisely and live in a simple fashion. You have no need to hurry into matrimony with anyone. You are now an independent woman and your life is completely your own."

Susanna thought longingly of the effect of Gavin's lips upon hers, and it may be that something of what she was thinking showed in her eyes, for her ladyship put her arm about the girl's shoulders.

"Do not rely too much upon the reflexes of the body, my girl. What is most pleasurable is often least lasting. Shut a wild bird in a cage and the song sometimes dies away."

"You are speaking of Gavin?" asked Susanna. "Do you think that he cannot be caged? Perhaps he cannot . . . perhaps I do not want to cage him!"

"I am not speaking entirely of Gavin, but of the way life is lived. Tell me, Susanna, if you are prepared to live with either of the extremes those gentlemen represent—the safe and unimaginative life Wycombe offers, or the notoriously unstable future that lies before Gavin?"

"As to Gavin," said Susanna sharply, "he seems to have vanished quickly enough."

Lady Morphy laughed acidly. "That is his way, I fear. One never knows what he will be about next."

"What are you suggesting, madam?"

Lady Morphy did not exactly look disgusted with her protégée, but her expression certainly skirted that response. "I am suggesting, miss, that there is a world outside this one you have so recently come into. There are other men than Patrick Wycombe and Gavin Marshall. You are drawn to each for different reasons, but there is no guarantee of happiness with either. And neither, I think, can offer you the thing you are looking for."

"But . . ." protested Susanna.

"But . . ." repeated her ladyship with a none-too-faint mockery. "Come, girl, you cannot base the course of your life upon a dance and a kiss."

Susanna could not help wondering if, indeed, that were true.

Out of the corner of her eye she saw Patrick returning to them and bearing a glass of claret-cup in either hand; but before she could call out to indicate to him where she and Lady Morphy were waiting, he was waylaid by a severely intimidating Mrs. Fairfax. Whatever it was that she was saying to him was something which quite took him by surprise, for he took a quick step back from her. Susanna saw the shocked look on his face and wondered what bad news the woman could be carrying to him. With Susanna and Lady Morphy watching, he seemed to struggle to control himself, then, as if he sadly needed them, he lifted first one glass to his lips, drained it in two or three gulps, and then the other.

"Good heavens!" Susanna heard Lady Morphy exclaim. "What is that woman up to now?"

Susanna experienced a sinking feeling in the pit of her stomach. Whatever it was, she was certain that it was unpleasant. The two women crossed the balcony toward the others, but before they reached Patrick's side there was a flurry of excitement from within the hall. Through the doorway they heard the rap, rap of Wilberforce's staff against the floor of the dais and his sycophantic voice ring triumphantly out across the crowd.

"In honor of our distinguished visitors, the next dance will be a *valse!*"

His words provoked a moment of shocked silence during which the musicians, without much conviction, struck up a faltering tune as if they expected at any moment to be struck with fire from heaven. No such flames descended, but instead something almost as extraordinary came about, which—as predicted by Mr. Wilberforce, though not in the manner he had anticipated—profoundly affected the passage of convention at Cheyne Spa.

Rolling majestically, the stout and florid Prince Regent of Great Britain moved on to the dancing floor. Prinny carefully took out his enameled snuffbox, extracted a pinch and placed it carefully in one nostril. When he had delicately sneezed into his handkerchief, he waved it energetically in the direction of the Master of Ceremonies. Then he raised his quizzer and stared disbelievingly at the man, allowing his heavy glance to linger on and on until Wilberforce was reduced to a fidgety shuffling.

"Nonsense, my dear chap," said the Prince Regent in a voice which would have frozen all but the warmest blood. "One never *valses* at a cotillion. I thought you knew." Behind him the Duke of Cumberland glowered in annoyance.

Susanna turned back from this amusing spectacle just in time to see Mrs. Fairfax depart from Patrick Wycombe's company with her jaw set firmly and her back ramrod-stiff in righteous indignation. Patrick Wycombe's look was one of exquisite anguish as he made his way toward her. Reaching Susanna's side, he bowed courteously, but his whey-white complexion betrayed his distress.

"Miss Archer, I fear I must, with your indulgence, withdraw my recent proposal of marriage." Before Susanna could reply or exclaim, he explained the reason for this unprecedented action.

"It seems," he said through trembling lips, "that I am about to become a father!"

"I can't believe it, miss!" Tibby marvelled. "Mr. Wycombe and that Miss Cecily? Why, who would have thought it? And him such a gentleman, begging your pardon, miss."

Curiously she stole a look at Susanna's face. "I must say, Miss Susanna, that you seem to be taking it with a mort of calm."

Susanna, herself, was not at all certain *how* she was taking the extraordinary news this morning. She had spent a very nearly sleepless night considering the implications of the situation, but found it impossible to come to any sort of conclusion. It was certainly true that her golden idol had proved to have feet of clay, but she suspected, as well, that Lady Morphy's acid comment upon the situation was quite to the point. It had been made privately as the two women and the duke had come back to Upper Orson Street.

"I have always thought Mr. Wycombe dull," she said, "but until this evening I never understood that he was dim of wit as well." Susanna had loyally protested, but her ladyship stood her ground. "My dear, what else could a gentleman be who allowed Cecily Fairfax, of all people, to have her way with him? The only consolation is that they may possibly have a happy marriage."

She had peered through the dark at Susanna's face and said comfortingly, "Do not be too downcast, my pet. It could, you know, have been infinitely worse."

But the young woman had been wrapt in her own sensations, her own apprehensions of the matter. "How?" she had asked dully. "How in the world could it be worse?"

The reply surprised her to the point of slightly unstable laughter. "You *could* have married him."

All that was nothing to her this morning. Somewhere between three o'clock, when her vexatious mind had calmed enough to allow her to drift off into sleep, and seven o'clock when she again wakened, she had disposed of the discomfiture entirely. She had now no idea where her forward-going path might now lie. Should she, indeed, go on to Cheltenham as Tibby thought? Should she even venture for a time into London? She had been there only once with her father and they had stayed at an hotel catering especially to clergymen and their families, so that it had not seemed so very different from her usual sort of life. Something in her kept suggesting that she even return to Bleet, the place of her father's last vicarage and the place closest in her mind to home.

Now she voiced some of her concern to Tibby. The girl was straightforward and plain-minded as usual. "I should think you'd go on being Lady Kinsale, miss, now that you've had a bit of experience at it. I don't mean here, of course, but they's other places would do as well, some of those places abroad where the rich folk congregate. Italy, even, or Austria. I'd think the position would be ever so difficult to give up, what with all them clothes of Lady Wycombe's."

And in Susanna's mind a surprising notion emerged fully formed. She was astonished that it had not come to her before. So there was a way, after all, of combining her interests and her advantages, of profitably drawing the threads of her life together. The sum she had won at the tables—the income from which would be only enough to keep her in a rose-covered cot—could, she believed, be enlarged by a good deal. Oh, not by a return to the lower rooms; she had no illusions about her skill as a gamestress, but it did seem to her that there was another way.

Tibby set about putting the room to rights, chattering as she did so. "I expect you will be leaving Cheyne Spa soon, will you not, Miss Susanna? Just about everyone seems to be doing so, the season being in decline, so to speak."

"Everyone but you, eh, Tibby? You have a reason for staying on. I wonder what Cheyne is like in the winter?"

"Damp and rather smelly, Fred has said. Not the most pleasant place."

"I am surprised, then, that you wish to say," teased her mistress, but there was no reply to the sally.

After a few moments, Susanna said in a bright tone, "In the next fortnight or so, I hope we shall be able to make a determined effort to box up all Lady Wycombe's gowns. I shall be away from the spa, I expect, and so I shall depend for the most part on you." She sighed. "Quite honestly, I do not know *what* I shall do without you, Tib. Not entirely so far as the clothes are concerned, though you are the one who has always taken care of them and I am sure I shall be quite lost in that direction. I expect I shall never find another partner with whom I suit half so well."

Tibby put away the toilet articles with exaggerated care, looking cornerwise out of her eyes the whole time. "I expect you'll soon find someone, miss, but it *has* been a pleasure, I'm sure."

"I shall not find anyone so easily as all that. You and I have always pulled well together. I know I shall be able to train a new maidservant, but doing so will not replace a friend."

"Should you miss me as much as all that, then . . . really?" Tib asked hesitantly.

"Miss you?" Susanna threw up her hands. "My dear girl, I shall be quite devastated! Were it not for your darling Fred, I should have no hesitation in luring you away from Cheyne Spa. No, no, I should never dream of letting you escape me!"

Tibby spoke quietly. "That is not such a problem as you expect, Miss Susanna."

"Not a problem? How do you make that out? You will be shivering here in dank Cheyne and I shall be . . ." She paused, turning to the little maid, eyebrows rising. "What are you saying, really? Do you mean that you are entertaining second thoughts about remaining?"

Tib, looking quite miserable, sniffed and turned her head away, causing her mistress to swiftly fly to the girl's side, flinging her arms about her. "Tibby, what is it? Has something gone amiss about Fred?" A thought sprang to mind. "You asked him about marriage upon my urging, didn't you? Oh, why can I not keep my thoughts to myself?"

"It don't matter," Tibby murmured.

"Of course it matters if you are unhappy. There, there, I am sure it will all come right."

The girl's shoulders began to shake. "No, it won't. It will never come right with *him!*" She fairly spat out the pronoun. "It isn't just that he won't marry, miss. He can't!"

"But you told me that doesn't matter to you, that you'd follow him to the ends of the earth."

Now, at last Tibby allowed herself the luxury of giving way and beginning to wail. "Oh yes, I know I said that, and I meant it, I did!"

"Then what stops you now?"

The tears stopped and the lass turned a serio-comic face to Susanna. "Now, miss, do you expect me to move in with his wife and his two children, what with another on the way? Oh, miss, don't leave me here all alone. I can pay my way, you know, and I've played a bit since I've been here. Fred did me that much good, he showed me how to wager a bit. Just take me with you. I won't be no trouble, honestly I won't. I'll go just anywhere at all, but I cannot stay here in Cheyne Spa!"

"Why, of course I'll take you with me!" Susanna said amiably, and she began to unveil her plan.

THE TOWN OF Bleet is the market centre for its district. It is
not in the least fashionable and has no pretence to sophisti-
cation, although a largish portion of its inhabitants are rich.
It is peculiar that they should have chosen to settle here, of
all places, but perhaps it was a case of first one and then
another. They were retired manufacturers from the north
for the most part, until now actively occupied with supply-
ing the rest of the country with certain necessities—coal
and iron and cloth. They are folk who have none of the
polish of their financial peers in the south, but are bluff and
good-hearted without the drawbacks of excessive over-
breeding.

Bleet is a pretty place of cleanly designed eighteenth-
century houses, climbing roses, tree-lined lanes and a
melodious brook with a wheel and a churchyard with a lych
gate in the old style. The people roundabout are not
overburdened with an overdeveloped sense of culture of
that bookish kind which nurtures introversion. Oh, quite
the contrary. There is an impressive amount of social
activity instead, mostly centered about balls of various
kinds. There are hunt balls, and birthday balls, and Christ-
mas balls and Lady Day balls and all sorts of things . . . but
always balls, you see. They are never merely dancing-
parties nor, grandly, ridottos, but are always on a large
scale as if the rich, retired manufacturers who live here
actively encourage their wives in conspicuous display. And
who is to say they are not right in adopting such an

attitude? What is the fun of being rich if you cannot parade it a bit?

On the High Street there are silversmiths and jewellers, sellers of fine furnishings for carriages, and a dealer in toys of the most delightful sort. But there is not a library nor a bookshop. There is also a rather recent establishment above whose door is the sign "Robes et Modes," and in the window is a splendid court gown. The inhabitants of Bleet do not realise that this handsome piece of goods, elegant though it is, is already a little passé at St. James's, and would be quite démodé in Paris where fashion once more reigns supreme and change is everything. It does not matter in the least. Here in Bleet the gown is quite in the vanguard and will undoubtedly be purchased by some matron slim enough to wear it, or be altered and adapted until she can do so. At that point another splendid ballgown will replace it in the window.

In the lower left hand corner of the shop-window, just next to the entrance, is a discreet bit of script painted upon the glass. "Lady Kinsale, prop." it says in elegantly formed letters. This is rather an inside joke to the older inhabitants of the town, and even to some of the later arrivals; for there is, properly speaking, no such person as Lady Kinsale and they are well aware of it. But, they admit, it does lend a certain cachet to the enterprise to know that the old vicar's daughter once masqueraded in Cheyne Spa and carried it off.

It was to this shop that on an afternoon in late October a well-dressed gentleman purposefully made his way and opened the door with such force that the bell above it jangled inharmoniously as it swung back and forth. The small-boned, darkish young woman who hurried into the front stopped quite dead in her tracks when she saw who it was had entered.

"Well, Tibby," said the gentleman, "so I have found you at last, eh?"

Tib's mouth had gone slack, but she quickly regained her

self-composure. "Well, Mr. Marshall, is it not? Yes, it has been some time since we met, sir. More than a year, I believe. I hope the world has been keeping you well?"

He nodded, noting the alteration both in her speech and demeanor. "Well enough, thank you." Looking about, he said, "I need not ask the same of you. I can see from the look of the shop that you and her ladyship are prospering."

"Oh, as to that," Tibby said, "Miss Susanna is known to almost everyone. The 'Lady Kinsale' name is only a sort of professional one, you might say. Most of our regulars know the tale of it. We are still selling off Lady Wycombe's wardrobe, you can see. Fabulous sums a few of these ladies are willing to pay to impress each other. It is quite a marvel to me. Of course, they do not know the gowns are what you might call 'second-hand.' " She thought that over and amended it. "Not that they are, really. Lady Wycombe wore scarcely any of them. Some she wore over and over and those we disposed of, but most is . . . *are* all but untouched."

"What *do* the customers call your mistress, then? Does she have still another name?"

Tibby looked at him sharply. "Is she married, are you asking? No, she is still Miss Susanna, and I am Miss Tibitha." Which disposed of her former station and defined her present one. Susanna had always called them each other's partners, and so they were.

"I am sure she will be sorry to have missed you," Tibby said.

He looked at her askance. "Then she is not at home to visitors today?"

"Miss Tibitha" took pity on him. "I am sure she would be happy to see you, sir, but the fact is, she is not at home to anyone, but has gone up to London for the day and not due back until tomorrow. Is there a message I can give her?"

"Only that I am staying at the Pentacle and Goblet. I hope she will allow me an hour's conversation."

"I am sure she will, sir, if you are still about when she

returns." She cocked her head at him like a little brown bird. "How long will you be here, did you say, sir?"

He looked back at her with a level gaze. "As long as is necessary, Miss Tibitha. Your partner and I have business that is still unsettled."

"And whose fault is that, Mr. Gavin?" she asked tartly as if flying to the absent Susanna's defense.

Marshall nodded equably. "Mine, I daresay. It is difficult to play the responsible suitor when you have not one farthing to rub against another."

Tib looked as if she very badly wanted to say something further, but refrained. Some situations, she believed, were better left to sort themselves out with no interference, no matter how sympathetic in nature. She only said, "I will certainly give her your message, sir."

The conversation suddenly languished and Gavin tried to read in her face the reason for it, but could not. Then she asked, quite out of the blue, "And how is your lady aunt faring, and the dear duke?"

Gavin was pleased at this evidence of amity. He felt that he could well afford an ally in the matter he had come to discuss, and he answered the question with great good will. "Her ladyship is very well indeed, having on the last night of play at Cheyne this year won a considerable fortune. Not so much as your friend's extraordinary stroke of luck, but a significant amount. As a result she has, for the moment, sworn off the tables, though I don't expect the vow will last. As for the duke, he is marrying quite soon."

"Someone young and pretty, I expect, like Miss Cecily or Miss Susanna?"

Gavin shook his head. "No. As a matter of fact, she is a lady of middle years and very pleasant. Her name is Mrs. Nightshade. She and His Grace are already a veritable Joan and Darby, so I expect the match will take."

"And you, sir, are you prospering? You certainly look it."

"Oh," Marshall answered, "I have had my ups and downs. Nothing is certain in this world, they say, but death and taxes. I have managed to keep my chin above water. At the moment I am in funds. Tomorrow, who knows?"

He prepared to leave the shop. "At The Pentacle and Goblet, remember."

"Oh yes, sir, I'll remember and I'll surely give her the message."

The truth of it was that Gavin had foolishly hoped that Tibby's tale of Susanna gone off to London had been a mere fiction, designed to throw him off balance and test his feelings. All the time he had been within Robes Et Modes he had half expected Susanna herself to come from behind the curtain separating the front from the back of the shop. What was it he had hoped for in this visit? He hardly knew. It had been difficult enough to track Susanna down with so very little to go on, save the mere mention of her happiness in this vicinity. He did not even know what, really, he would say to her when they met. He had not prepared a speech, he knew he must speak from his heart. Was his life too uncertain to ask her to join it? He had in the past believed so; now he no longer knew. He could only put it to her and let the decision rest in her hand.

He was taking a hearty supper in the taproom, prepared to while away the evening with a tankard, when a stout stranger approached him and spoke to him by name. Gavin half rose from the table.

"I fear, sir, that you have the better of me."

"No, no, don't get up. Perhaps you will allow me to join you?"

"With pleasure." Gavin signalled to the waiter to clear away the remains of his supper and gave his attention to his new acquaintance.

The man who sat down with him at the clumsy oaken table was something of an anomaly. He was respectable enough in looks; bullish, but turned out; the coat well cut and of a fine cloth but, as if by design, unobtrusive. It was his eyes that provided the clue to the man who dwelt within: flat, marble-like, veridical eyes with a depth of power within them. Whoever this man might prove to be, he was someone with whom to reckon. He identified himself straightforwardly.

"Tobias, the name is, sir. I daresay you do not remember me, but I have often seen you in Cheyne Spa."

"Have you?" asked Gavin, amiably enough and with no hint of condescension. God forbid the man should be someone to whom he owed money. "I am very fond of Cheyne Spa."

The man smiled, but the warmth never reached so high as his eyes, which remained as flat and cool as before. "I dare venture that you *should* be fond of it, young sir, for you have taken away a good deal of its profit at one time or another."

Gavin allowed himself a tight grin. "I beg your pardon, Mr. Tobias, but you an't a creditor of mine, by any chance? I thought I had settled all that."

The answering laugh was merely a short bark. "No, no, not in the sense you mean, although I expect I could fairly say you owe me much." He leaned back in his chair and drank with gusto from his tankard, examining Gavin with as much care as a farmer would a bullock at a fair. He twisted his mouth a bit, laid a finger aside his nose absently, then nodded as if to himself, not Gavin.

"Yes," he said, "you owe me much."

"Do I, sir?" This was asked in such a mode of innocent surprise that Tobias's answering chuckle resonated deeply in his barrel chest.

"The name Tobias means nothing to you, then?"

"I regret to say that it does not."

"I have the honour, sir, to be the mayor of Cheyne Spa."

The continuing chain of connections now fell into place, and Gavin greeted them with contained amusement. Now even the man's unconscious aura of importance, of power, was understandable—he was, by far, the most important man in that town. The mayor was head of the corporation,

and in all such towns it was the corporation which adminis-
tered everything that mattered: the shops, the theatres, St.
Gerrans's Gardens, the baths and the several inns, and even
a great many of the very best lodging houses, not forgetting
the Upper and especially the Lower Rooms.

"You knew Wilberforce, I suppose?" asked Tobias.

Gavin shrugged noncommitally. "I am acquainted with
him in his capacity. Not so good as the Beau, but not so bad
as he might be. This was his second season, I think? Early
days for him."

"Quite the contrary. His day is done in Cheyne. We
were not satisfied with his first season, and less with his
second. We have not renewed his contract."

"And you are out scouting, sir? I should not have
thought that Bleet offered a wide picking."

Cheyne's mayor smiled. He could appear almost genial,
Gavin supposed, although the steel was always there beneath the surface. "My old mother is here, come back to her
childhood home to last out her days."

"She does not live with you, then?"

Tobias seemed almost sad. "No, she thinks me a dull
dog, I expect, and perhaps I am." He seemed to peruse the
negative word. "No. I come to visit and then I go away
again, suiting us both admirably. She lives a high life here
amongst her friends, I do assure you."

He ordered more ale. "Fresh drink for fresh talk." Gavin
sensed an accent of something in the wind, but he was
uncertain as to what it was until the man began to enlarge
upon Gavin's own past. It veered dangerously toward the
unacceptably personal.

"Not too rakish a reputation, have you? Oh, no, I've
asked around and about a bit—for, you see, I don't mind
confessing I've had my eye upon you for some months. It is
a mere fortunate circumstance that we meet here."

Gavin inclined his head, wondering what the man was
leading up to. "And what have you discovered?" Con-
founded insolence of the man, checking around about him,

was he? Well, Gavin's debts were most paid and his copybook relatively unblotted.

"You conduct yourself well in public," went on the mayor, "handle yourself well at the tables. You have not too much flash nor not exactly invisible neither.

"And," he added with a flourish, almost as if Gavin himself were unaware of the fact, "your uncle's a *dook!*"

"If you know so much, Mr. Tobias," Gavin interposed, still not sure what the mayor was getting at, "then you must be aware that I have no expectations from that quarter. There are two heirs before me, both hale and healthy."

The stout man nodded with satisfaction. "So I guessed. Makes it all the easier, don't it?"

"I might agree, sir, if I knew of what you were speaking."

Tobias shifted in his seat and leaned closer across the table toward Gavin. "Mr. Marshall, were you at all acquainted with the predecessor of Wilberforce?"

"Beau Carlisle? How could I not be aware of him? He all but created society at Cheyne Spa from what I have been told. Though if you mean a personal acquaintance, I have played a game or two with him, but nothing more intimate."

"He was in many ways a fine man," said Tobias, "an ornament, sir, to Cheyne. Yes, an ornament."

"I expect that he was, but . . ."

Tobias held up a restraining hand. "Wait, wait, I beg you. Let me tell you something of Carlisle." Gavin relaxed himself deliberately, certain that this was to be a long process, though he had nothing else to fill the evening.

As it happened, he was incorrect; the mayor came very quickly to the point. "Carlisle," he said, "was a near genius at managing the spa. He was colourful, he was astute, he was certainly a great hand with the ladies—particularly those ladies of a certain age—and he was a wizard at cards!" He smiled reminiscently. "He won phenomenally over the years. I do not believe for a moment that he was a cheat,

211

you know, for if he had been such a person he would have carried off a great deal more money than he did; but I *do* think he was deuced clever, a very genius, as I say."

Not in the least understanding the drift of all this, Gavin agreed. "I am sure of it, sir. I am certain he was a paragon."

Tobias slapped his hand down on the table with considerable force. "You will be kind enough not to humour me, sir! Let me have my own say in my own fashion! When I have done you can jeer as much as you like, if that pleases you."

Gavin's eyes widened but he recognised the equity of the request and smiled a little, encouraging the mayor to continue.

"Carlisle was not so much of a paragon as all that," Tobias went on. "He had many faults. He was, in fact, a liar in his time, a seducer, a sloven and a drinker! I believe, sir, that you are none of these?"

Gavin now spoke, lazily and with much amusement. "On the contrary, Mayor Tobias, in moderation I am all of these things, as what man of spirit is not? I do not think I am excessive in any one of them, but the seed is certainly present which may one day grow into a flourishing green bay tree. I am a human male, Mr. Tobas, and apt to the ills of the flesh."

None of this succeeded in repeating Mr. Tobias's upset. "A good answer, Marshall, a fair one." He signalled. "Waiter! More ale, if you please!"

Then to Gavin: "What say you to five hundred a year, all found, a cloth allowance and, of course, a percentage of the tables?"

Gavin found he could only say, stupidly, "Five hundred?"

"Oh, very well then, sir, I am no niggard and I dare to believe you will be worth every penny of it." He frowned. "You had better be, bedad, or I shall myself have to answer for it.

"You look surprised, sir? You should not be. No man stands alone. A mayor may indeed be the head of a corporation, you see, but he is not the whole of it. Oh, no, I shall answer if you do not command the situation." He peered out at Gavin from beneath heavy brows, now drawn close together. "Well, man, what do you say?"

The other man looked at him stupidly, his brain whirling. "Am I to believe, sir, that you are, in your official capacity, offering me a position?"

Tobias snorted and quaffed his fresh tankard of ale impatiently. What did you think I was doing, you young ape? Six hundred, percentages and found. Will you have it or no?"

"Plus a cloth allowance," Gavin reminded him, "that was what you said."

"So I did and I stand by it. Well, what is the answer?" He wiped away the foam from his mouth. "The truth is, young fellow, I don't mind telling you, we need a man like you. You have the very qualities, and to spare."

"I shall need time to consider, but let me ask you a question if I may?" At the mayor's nod of assent, he continued. "Why did you so quickly slide in the extra one hundred pounds?"

"Well, my young friend, that is hardly a gift, is it? You have an obvious advantage in a place the like of Cheyne Spa, haven't you? Your uncle is a *dook*. They will put up with anything from a title, you know. Anything."

The innkeeper himself now approached the table and stood beside them, waiting, unwilling to interrupt. At last, Tobias completed a long dissertation on Cheyne Spa, its virtues, the extraordinary effects of its salutory waters, and its civilised visitors—"the Prince Regent, himself, sir, he visits, you know."

"Yes," said Gavin patiently, "I know. I have had occasion to view him there." He turned to the innkeeper. "Something, my friend?"

"There is a lady, sir," he gestured in the direction of the inn parlour, but Gavin saw her standing in the doorway as if she were about to make her way into the taproom.

"Excuse me," he said to Mayor Tobias, "I believe I shall have an answer for you shortly."

He began to cross the distance between himself and Susanna, slowly at first and then more and more quickly. Susanna was smiling and holding out her hand.

Susanna was smiling.

Behind him he heard Tobias calling out a cautionary word. "No light of loves, now. We cannot have that sort of trouble, you know! Not with the Master of Ceremonies of Cheyne Spa!"

"It is no trouble, I do assure you," Gavin threw back over his shoulder. He took Susanna into his arms, held her close to him and then led her back into the inn parlour. "So I have found you at last," he said.

"I rather think I have found you, sir. What was the deep discussion with that solid-looking gentleman?"

Gavin lifted her chin and kissed her upon the lips. "I rather think that gentleman would be very pleased if you married me, madam," he said solemnly.

"And you, sir, how would you feel? I must tell you that that gentleman's wishes hold very little sway with me."

Now he looked into her face seriously. "The real truth is, you see, that it is your wishes which are paramount in this matter."

Susanna was no longer smiling at him, but waiting thoughtfully, her beautiful eyes turned upon him. "Then do you not think you should begin to discover my wishes?"

Gavin led her to the settee and drew her down beside him. "I have searched for you for more than a year, Susanna. I did it because I did not know my own mind and I knew I should never be satisfied until I did. At first I believed that I could offer you nothing, and so I stayed away from you; and then I was afraid that you would believe what I think my aunt believed, that I merely wanted the use of your winnings at Cheyne Spa. Then, at last, I understood that none of that really mattered at all."

He took her face between his hands and kissed her upon the mouth and it was just as it had been in the kissing dance at the Cotillion Ball, the same sweetness, the same swooning sensation. It affected Gavin as well as Susanna, for he came out of the kiss and drew a deep breath, then expelled it in a helpless chuckle.

"No matter what comes, my dear, I do not wish ever to be away from you again. Will you be my wife?"

"How do I know it is not my fortune you are after?" she asked with a smile. It was a jest, but he was happy he had an answer for her. He needed nothing from her; he would have six hundred a year, all found, a cloth allowance and a percentage. "I hope you will not mind, my dear, becoming the first lady of Cheyne Spa?"

Susanna echoed his words of a few moments past. "No matter what comes, my dear," she said tenderly, "I wish never to be apart from you again."

"Ah," Gavin answered, as he drew her again into the circle of his arms. "You will have made Mr. Tobias so happy!"

If you have enjoyed this book and would like to receive details of other Walker Regency romances, please write to:

Regency Editor
Walker and Company
720 Fifth Avenue
New York, N.Y. 10019